The Corsican Widow

Tales of Corsica

Vanessa Couchman

Ocelot Press

Discover Vanessa Couchman online:
http://vanessacouchmanwriter.com

To Corsica

"Corsica is a *département* of France; even so, Corsica is very far from being France." (Alexandre Dumas, *Les Frères Corses*)

CONTENTS

ACKNOWLEDGMENTS

I owe grateful thanks to everyone who read the manuscript in whole or in part and provided helpful and perceptive comments: my wonderful Beta readers Evelyn, Jo, Mandy and Sue, and members of the Parisot Writing Group. Deborah Lawrenson and the Savonnerie Marius Fabre provided helpful information about the Marseille soap industry. I also owe a great deal to the late Dorothy Carrington for her meticulous research and contagious love of Corsica. Without the encouragement of Writers Abroad, I would never have started to write fiction at all, and I am eternally grateful for their continuing friendship and inspiration. Sue Barnard's gentle but firm editing kept me on the straight and narrow. Jane Dixon-Smith has come up with a fantastic cover design, again. Last and foremost, thank you to my husband for his unfailing support, encouragement and belief in me.

PART 1

CHAPTER 1

Felicavo, Corsica: April 1755

The girl's naked feet turned this way and that, the heels black and scored with scratches. The breeze ruffled the hem of her skirt, but the body sagged at the end of the cord like a sack of grain. For a moment, Valeria's heart seemed to stop beating, and then the bile seared her gullet and she sank to her knees in the dust.

"Oh, no. Delfina…"

She raised her head. Below Delfina's darkened face the loose dress failed to conceal the bulge in the girl's belly. Valeria closed her eyes and her chin dropped. A gaggle of village women rustled and muttered and shook their heads, crows gathering to pick over the carcass. A few crossed themselves and turned away. Three men elbowed through and held up the body while one scaled the tree and cut the rope.

"At least she's spared her family the job… What a disgrace… Stupid girl."

Valeria crammed a fist against her mouth to stop the words

that boiled up, turned and ran back along the track towards Felicavo. The breath caught in her chest, but she stumbled on, past the village. She pushed aside the *machja* thorns that tore at her dress, and fell on her hands and knees, gasping. The bile spilled from her mouth.

***

In Margherita's one-roomed cottage, Valeria clasped her hands together on the scarred table top until the knuckles whitened. Delfina's swaying feet crossed her vision every time she closed her eyes. Better to keep them open, but nothing could take away the hollowness inside. She looked across at Margherita, who was chopping herbs.

"They say Delfina had been living rough in the *machja* since February, when her parents threw her out. I can't imagine how she managed all that time. Why didn't she let me know where she was? I would have tried to help her, but I thought she'd gone away."

Margherita's pin-bright eyes, filled with trouble, met Valeria's. She tightened the shawl around her and shook her silvered head. "We all did. You couldn't have done much for her. If she'd come to me earlier, as soon as she knew she was pregnant, well, things might have been different. By the time it came out, it was too late."

Valeria turned her gaze to the fire. Delfina was only eighteen, two years her junior, and should have had many more years in her. "But taking her own life? She must have felt so alone to have done it. How could her parents have driven her out? It seems so cruel."

Margherita shrugged. "Once that fellow of hers had disappeared, it was either that or wait for the elders to set up a hearing. To have her judged in public would have brought even more shame on the family, and she would probably have been banished anyway."

"The women who saw her said that she'd saved her family a job." Valeria's hand formed a fist on the table top. "I wanted to pull their hair out, but I ran away instead."

"I would have felt the same, but it wouldn't have done any good to turn them against you."

They fell silent while the fire burnt low. Valeria twisted her hands and opened her mouth to speak several times.

"What is it?" Margherita said.

"I was going to come and see you anyway, before this happened," Valeria said. "I told you Mother and Pietro had been talking with this Signore Santucci about marrying me."

Margherita nodded.

"Well, it's all arranged now, and he's coming up from Zaronza tomorrow to meet me." She sighed and looked down. "Mother hasn't told me anything, except that his first wife died without children and that he's quite rich. I don't even know what he looks like. I don't have any say in it, of course."

Margherita reached across the table and took her hand. "It might not be as bad as all that."

Valeria returned the pressure of the knotted fingers. "If only I knew what to expect. After what's happened to Delfina, I'm so empty and hopeless. I'd feel much better if only I knew how my life is going to turn out. That's what I wanted to ask you…"

Margherita sat up a little straighter. "Go on."

"Read the bone for me, please. You once said you know how it's done. I need to know the future."

Margherita's face closed up and she turned away.

"People don't practice it here," she said at last. "I haven't read it for years, and I'd be taken for a witch if I did it, even more than I am already. Remember your neighbour's grandmother, who had the wasting sickness? She was beyond my help, but your neighbour was convinced I'd put the Eye in her. No good would come of doing this. Don't ask me,

3

Valeria."

Valeria gripped her friend's hand tighter. "I had such a terrible feeling when I saw Delfina. It was almost as if I saw myself swinging there. Please do this for me, and set my mind at rest."

Margherita was silent for a long moment, and then gave an almost imperceptible nod.

"Very well. If it means so much to you, I'll do it. But only this once, and you're not to tell anyone."

The room was now dusk-sombre. Darkness gathered in the corners and rolled outwards, mingling with the smoke from the fire. The only light came from the flames curling up from the central hearth. The pulse beat in Valeria's neck while Margherita rubbed hard at the sheep's shoulder blade with a cloth, muttering unknown words.

For some minutes nothing happened. Margherita stopped, took a breath and started to polish the bone again. A mirror-like sheen appeared in the middle. Margherita held it up and the firelight shone through. Her eyes grew wider. She turned the object over on the table and passed a hand over her face, which was as white as a ewe's milk cheese. A cold fist tightened around Valeria. A presence floated in the air and skimmed her hair, like a bat's wing. She gasped and brushed at it, but touched empty air. Gooseflesh broke out on her arms.

"What is it, Margherita? What did you see?"

She grabbed at the sheep's bone, but Margherita snatched it away and put it on her knees under the table.

"I didn't see anything. I've lost the knack, that's all. The magic didn't work because I've forgotten how to summon it."

Valeria's heart drummed against her ribs.

"You were afraid, Margherita. Something was here in the room. I felt it. Tell me what you saw. Was it so terrible?"

Margherita's dark eyes reflected the firelight. After a moment, she breathed out and gave an abrupt shake of her head.

"I wasn't afraid, and there was nothing there. It was a passing dizzy spell, that's all. I get them from time to time. I'm very old, don't forget."

She gave a thin smile and glanced down at the bone in her lap.

"Look for yourself, if you don't believe me."

Valeria took the age-smooth shoulder-blade and looked at it. She turned it over and rubbed the surface, but nothing appeared. The bone was a lifeless part of a long-dead animal, without any magic powers. Whatever the presence was, if there had been one at all, it had gone. She was foolish to have been frightened, and yet... She rubbed her arms. Maybe it had been wrong to persuade her friend to read the future.

Margherita took the bone, replaced it in a sack and pushed it under the bed with her foot.

Valeria scanned Margherita's face, but read nothing in her closed expression. "You believe in the bone, don't you? You've never denied that it works, and you said people can't fight against their destiny."

"It doesn't always work. In any case, I've lost the power. I keep telling you, there was nothing there."

Valeria opened her mouth to argue, but the set line of Margherita's lips told her she wouldn't say any more.

Valeria looked out of the window. "Oh no, it's almost dark. I hadn't realised how late it was. Mother will send Pietro for me when she sees I'm still out." She pushed herself up from the table. Maybe if she took a calmer attitude, Margherita would tell her more of what she had seen. "Thank you for trying. I wanted to see what's going to happen to me in the future, but I suppose I have to take what comes."

Margherita lit the lamp, smiled and put a hand on her arm. "That's much the best way."

Valeria smiled back to conceal her disappointment.

Margherita, who knew her better than Mother, always saw through her.

The old woman watched her for a moment as if debating something with herself, and then added, "One piece of advice, though. Don't let bright eyes turn your head. Now, come and see me once you've met this Santucci and tell me all about it. He's a lucky man to be marrying such a lovely girl. You'd better fatten up a little, though. Most men prefer a bit of flesh."

Valeria gathered up her rope of dark hair into a loose knot, and wound the headscarf over it. She kissed Margherita on both cheeks.

"I don't know what I'll do without you when I've left here. Will you come and visit me in Zaronza once I'm married?"

Margherita shook her head. "I'm too old to make that journey over the hills. It's as much as I can do now to gather my herbs close by. My spirit will be with you, you know that." She paused and reached up to put an arm around Valeria's shoulders.

Too full to speak, Valeria left the house and hurried along the alley. When she entered the square, she looked back. Margherita was silhouetted in a rectangle of light from her doorway. The old woman made the sign of the cross. A chill rippled through Valeria. On the other side of the square, the shuttered windows of Delfina's house were like sightless eyes.

Valeria hurried home.

***

The following afternoon, she sat in the kitchen gazing into the fire. She tried to shake off the unease that edged up her spine every time she thought of her visit to Margherita.

Her mother came in. "Come along, Valeria. He's here."
Valeria wiped her hands on a cloth, straightened her dress and tucked a stray tendril of hair under her headscarf. She breathed in, trying to calm the fluttering in her stomach, followed her

mother along the corridor to the main room and paused in the doorway. Her brother Pietro stood beside their visitor, who was seated in front of the fire. On the table next to him a glass of wine glinted ruby in the firelight. With a flicker of alarm, Valeria noticed that her other brother, Antone, wasn't there.

She raised her eyes a fraction, wanting, and yet not wanting, to see. Santucci was stocky, but not fat, and his square hands rested on the arms of the chair. His face was neither ugly nor handsome; a face that was comfortable with itself and the world, with a high brow, black hair greying at the temples, full lips and a firm jaw. He must have been at least forty, twice her age, but he held himself straight and upright. It could have been so much worse.

Santucci shifted in the chair, and his dark eyes swept over her. She returned his gaze, feeling like a sheep at a fair, but didn't look away. Instead, she stood straight and tilted her chin upwards. Her mother frowned at her, and turned to Santucci with a thin smile.

"My daughter, Signore Santucci." She gestured towards Valeria. "We're honoured that you want to marry her. It's a pity my late husband couldn't be here to see this, God rest his soul." She shook her head and crossed herself.

Valeria's heart clutched. Even after all these years, she still felt her father's loss like a physical pain.

"It's you who do me the honour, Signora Peretti," Santucci said, and rose from his chair. "Your family is well-known and respected. I'm pleased to be marrying into it."

This was like a dance. Everyone had to make the right movements and say the right things. Santucci approached Valeria and she looked down again. He was the same height as she was, but his proud manner made him seem taller. Her brother towered over him, but was somehow dwarfed by his presence.

"I'm very pleased to meet you at last. Now, since we're to

7

be married, we must get to know each other."

"Yes, Signore," Valeria said, and the heat rose in her cheeks. This man would soon share a bed with her. She chased away the thought, but her face still burned.

"I can see I've made a good choice."

Valeria stifled a spark of indignation. She wasn't a sheep or a goat to be appraised for its breeding qualities. Mother's eyes glittered. Valeria pressed her palms together.

"Thank you, Signore," Valeria said. Thanks were the last thing on her mind.

She had no idea how to behave. Mother hadn't prepared her for this, and just told her to look modest and speak only if spoken to. Valeria knew so little of men and their ways. When her courses started, she was no longer free to go around on her own. Her brother was always a step behind, and watched for any sign of contact with other young men. She covered her hair with a headscarf and kept her eyes averted. Sometimes, walking to church or taking the pitcher to the village well, she caught youths eyeing her, until a glare from Pietro made them look elsewhere.

Mother broke into her thoughts. "Don't stand there dreaming, Valeria. Go and fetch some refreshments for our guest. He'll be hungry, since he's ridden over from Zaronza."

"I'd like that." Santucci smiled at her. Valeria responded with a half-smile that didn't reach her eyes. Just as she would have to grow used to sharing his bed, she would have to become accustomed to wait on him, as she already did for her brother.

Grateful for the break, she escaped to the kitchen, where she prepared the food. Pausing in the doorway with the dish, she looked back at the room; the flames crackling in the hearth, the table battered and scarred by years of use, the uneven floor, and the mushroom smell of damp that competed with the scent of burning wood. Each of these things carried memories. In a short time she would have to get used to another house, to someone else's memories.

In the main room, Santucci talked with her brother, while Valeria stood and looked on. No one asked her to sit. She clasped her hands together to stop them fidgeting.

Santucci voiced high hopes of the newly-elected General, Pasquale Paoli, and his plans for the republic.

"It's a great relief that my village and yours are no longer under Genoa's control, after so many years. The rest of Cap Corse still has to be liberated, of course, but I think it will lean to Paoli. The main ports remain in Genoese hands, which is an obstacle. Still, if anyone can win Corsica's independence, I believe it's Paoli."

Valeria hoped he was right. From their discussions she understood that the struggle against their Genoese masters should now turn in Corsica's favour.

The conversation continued for a while until Santucci announced he must return to Zaronza.

"I look forward to seeing you again at our betrothal." He pressed Valeria's hand.

She was torn between relief and disappointment when he left. Little time remained to get to know him before their betrothal was sealed. Marrying a stranger was the way here; she couldn't expect anything else.

"Pietro and I are very pleased with this marriage," her mother said, while they watched Santucci ride off down the hillside. She turned to Valeria. "We've worked hard for it. You're lucky he's picked you, when he could have had a girl from a wealthier family. He knows we can't afford much of a dowry, but it matters more that you come from good stock."

Good stock. Like a sheep. Valeria pressed her lips together to stop her saying the words. Instead, she asked the question that had been gnawing away at her.

"What happened to his first wife, Mother?"

9

Her mother shrugged. "She died. That's all you need to know."

Valeria frowned. Mother often kept information from her, but she couldn't see why she had to be so secretive about Santucci's first wife. How and when had she died? With mounting anxiety, Valeria saw again the glow in the centre of the sheep's bone.

Her mother turned to Pietro. "Where's Antone? I had to tell Signore Santucci he was ill. I couldn't say he was no doubt wandering about on the hillsides. He can't just go off and miss an important family occasion. It's insulting to our guest." She raised her arms. "I don't know what to do about that boy."

"I'll deal with him when he comes home, Mother," Pietro said. "He needs some manners knocked into him."

"Don't hurt him, please," Valeria said. Unshed tears stung the backs of her eyes. She knew what Pietro was capable of.

"Don't interfere. You're always standing up for Antone, but he'll bring disgrace on us before long if he isn't punished."

Mother stood at Pietro's shoulder and nodded. That was how it always was, Mother and Pietro ranged against her and Antone.

"I need to get some water from the well, Mother."

"Don't stay outside too long. You mustn't do anything to make Signore Santucci change his mind. His future wife should behave properly."

Valerie fetched the heavy stone pitcher from the kitchen. She set it on top of her head, rearranged her headscarf, and made as if to go to the well. Once she was around the corner, she checked no one was about and put down the jug behind a bush. At the back of the house, a path ran up through the cork oak trees and past the little chapel with its ancient cross of rough stone. Forcing her way through the prickly, aromatic-scented undergrowth, she turned up a sharp incline and peered into a hole in the rocks.

"Antone, are you in there? It's me, Valeria. Come out."

Scuffling and scraping sounds followed and Antone's head and shoulders appeared in the opening. He squeezed through and emerged like a stopper from a bottle onto the path below. Valeria shook her head. He was so predictable.

"I knew you'd be in there. You'd better be careful. If you grow much more, you'll get stuck fast one day."

Her brother said nothing. He sat scowling in the middle of the path, spat on his grazed hands and rubbed the dirt away.

"You can't stay here forever, you know. You'd have had to come home sometime."

"I won't go home. I'll take the *machja* like the bandits and you can bring me food. I'll live in a cave up in the hills and shoot wild boar."

Valeria sighed. "You know that's ridiculous. Anyway, what happens to the bandits? They get denounced or tracked down and killed. Is that what you want?"

Antone shrugged. "I don't care now, anyway. You're going to marry an old man and leave me here, so I might as well be dead." His eyes filled.

Valeria took his hand. "You shouldn't have disappeared when Signore Santucci came. He might have been offended. Mother had to tell him you were ill, and now she and Pietro are furious with you. You should think more before you do things like that."

"But he's going to take you away from me, and then what will I do? Don't you care?"

The anger flared. "Of course I care, Antone, but what choice do I have?" She regretted her rough tone and tried to soften it. "Anyway, I'm not going all that far, only to Zaronza. It's an hour's walk over the hills, and you can often come and visit me, but you have to behave yourself in future or Mother and Pietro won't let you. Now, come home with me. I have to stop by the well first, and I've already been away long enough.

Mother will wonder where I am, and she'll send Pietro out to find me." Her stomach contracted. Pietro would make Antone suffer.

She wiped his grubby cheeks with her thumbs and put her hands on his shoulders. He was still only thirteen, but he was almost as tall as her and broad and muscular. People often thought he was older than his years. He would be even taller than Pietro one day. She hoped he would grow up to be different from Pietro in other ways, but he would have to become tougher if he was going to stand up to Mother and Pietro without her support.

"Come on."

Valeria took his hand and pulled him down the path towards their house. His steps dragged behind her.

CHAPTER 2

"You've been very brave."

Red seeped through the fresh bandages Valeria had applied to Antone's back. Her jaw tightened. Pietro hadn't spared him this time, and when he unbuckled his belt and said he would teach Antone to behave better, Mother just nodded. She stood, thin-lipped, for a moment, and then went out, leaving Valeria to watch while Pietro brought the leather strap down on Antone's bare back several times. At least he hadn't used the buckle end. Valeria closed her eyes and flinched at each stroke. The boy cried out, but didn't weep until he was alone with her afterwards.

"Now run to your sister," Pietro said. He tightened the belt around his waist and wiped his hands.

Antone hiccupped and rubbed his eyes. Valeria smoothed down his hair where it stood up at the back of his neck.

"Try to sleep a little now. The poultice will help to soothe the pain and it will heal in no time."

She looked away. The wounds would be more than skin deep.

It would be very hard to leave Antone behind. He was so different from Pietro, and Mother scolded him for faults real or imagined. Why did Mother appear to hold such a grudge against her and Antone? Perhaps because they were closer to each other than to her. Stern, unbending, unsmiling, her face cast in granite, like the hills themselves, always in widowed black, wherever she went she was flanked by her elder son. Pietro was younger than Valeria, but as the eldest son he was the head of the family. Even so, he bowed to Mother's judgement and carried out her orders. Maybe she thought she was never rich enough in sons, despite bearing two after Valeria. She often hinted that a daughter was a burden, an extra mouth to feed, and to be married off as soon as it was proper to do so. Now her wish would be granted. Valeria would soon escape this house of unspoken hatreds and bottled-up violence that sometimes broke out. She must prepare Antone as well as she could.

When the afternoon slid towards evening, Valeria slipped out of the house. Mother was resting, tired out by the day's events, she said. Pietro had gone out and wouldn't be back before nightfall. Arranging her headscarf, Valeria went to Margherita's cottage on the edge of the village, overlooking the valley. The door was ajar, and the powerful scent of herbs floated on the air.

Valeria stopped on the threshold. Her friend's bent figure leant over a pot, which stood on a tripod over the fire. The cottage had a single room with the fireplace in the middle, but it was crammed with jars and bottles, which glowed jewel-like in the evening sun slanting through the narrow window. Valeria tapped on the door, and Margherita straightened up and turned around. A smile transformed her sunken apple face.

"Ah, it's you. You've met him, then. What was he like?"

Valeria poured out the story of Santucci's visit, including

14

Antone's absence and punishment.

"Santucci doesn't sound too bad to me. You see; I'm sure you don't have anything to worry about."

"Yes, but what about the bone, Margherita? It frightens me to think about it."

Margherita looked at her for a moment, and then took her hand. "You mustn't worry so much. You're going to be the wife of a wealthy man. I can't see anything to fear about that. And forget the bone. I told you I didn't see anything." She waved a dismissive hand. "Now, tell me how you treated Antone's back."

Valeria started to speak, but stopped. Margherita wasn't telling the truth, that was obvious, but her friend wouldn't be drawn any further.

"I applied the herb poultice, like you showed me, and I think the wounds will heal in time. Poor Antone. I'm afraid for him." Her voice quivered.

Margherita frowned and shook her head. "I hope Pietro pays for it one day." She gave the fire a fierce poke with a stick.

***

The kitchen was dark and smoky. Mother stood at the table mixing chestnut flour batter, while Valeria stirred the pot over the fire, the sweat breaking out on her forehead. In a few hours, she would be betrothed.

Mother laid down the spoon and stretched her back. "It's just as well the wedding will be in Zaronza. Your betrothal is costing us enough as it is. Santucci can afford to pay for it all. He has a bigger house than we do, anyway."

"Have you seen it, Mother?"

"A long time ago. It's one of the biggest in Zaronza."

She resumed stirring the batter, her grizzled head bent to the task.

Valeria stood with the ladle dripping onto the floor. She had to find out more.

"Do you think I'll be happy there?"

The breath hissed between Mother's teeth. "All this talk about happiness. Please your husband and give him sons. That's all you need to worry about. Now, that's enough. We've still got plenty to do."

She put the batter aside and wiped her hands on a cloth. At the door, she turned back and held Valeria with her gaze.

"Remember that I won't have dishonour brought on the family. Once you're wed and living in Zaronza you'll behave like the wife of a respected man should. I'll hear about it if you don't."

Valeria's cheeks burned. It was no use expecting Mother to provide any comfort. Why did she always assume that Valeria wouldn't behave correctly? Later, she wiped her damp palms on her dress and breathed in before entering the main room. A small knot of people had gathered around Santucci in front of the fire. The conversation died away, and several guests stood back when Valeria passed among them to take her place at his side. This time her mother had told her what to do. In any case, she had been present at the betrothal of her friend, Ghjulia Carbini, a joyful occasion. Ghjulia had married her cousin and it was all arranged, but they had been close since childhood. She lived with him and his family in the next village, and Valeria seldom saw her. Ghjulia had a child and another on the way. Once Valeria had moved to Zaronza, they might not meet again.

The mood in the room was more sombre than at Ghjulia's betrothal. Fewer people were present: just a handful of villagers in addition to her family, and Santucci, who didn't seem to have any relatives. Among the guests was the neighbour who thought Margherita caused her grandmother's death. Margherita wasn't there, but Valeria expected that. Mother and she had little in common. They circled each other like the moon and the earth, bound together but never meeting.

Pietro was in his usual place near the fire, watching her from beneath heavy brows. Mother sat swathed in brooding black like a bird of ill omen. Her eyes darted here and there before they fixed on Valeria. Antone stood in a corner and scuffed at the floor with his boot, his eyes downcast.

Valeria hesitated, before a gesture from Mother reminded her what she was supposed to do. She approached Santucci, who held out a hand, and they kissed each other on both cheeks. Valeria shook a little. This was the first time she had touched a man outside her family.

"Here, Valeria." Her mother handed her the plate of *fritelli*. Valeria offered the chestnut-flour fritters to Santucci, who took one and ate it, and then she passed it around the guests, who each ate one as well. She took the plate to Antone last. He pursed his mouth and shook his head, but Valeria glared at him and said in a low voice, "If you don't take one, you'll be punished again. Now, don't be so stupid." He hesitated, and then snatched one from the plate and crammed it into his mouth.

Valeria bit into a fritter and tried to swallow it, but it was like sawdust in her mouth. Her back to the company, she slid it back onto the plate, but the neighbour tapped Valeria on the arm.

"Oh, you must eat the whole *fritellu*, otherwise you'll invite bad luck into your home."

To avoid attracting Mother's attention, Valeria picked up the fritter again and managed to force it down. Her mother and brother were talking to Santucci, and did not appear to have noticed the incident.

Now she was betrothed. If only she could feel something other than dread and anxiety.

CHAPTER 3

The sun rose over the mountains to touch the treetops with gold. The pale houses of Felicavo with their slate roofs spread out down the hillside below Valeria's window, the alleys still in deep shadow. The bell in the slender *campanile* chimed six times.

She never tired of this view, which had framed her life with the seasons of the year. By the end of the day she would be a married woman, living another life, with new landscapes seen through a strange window. She wondered how different that life would be, if her husband would treat her well, what his house was like, what it would be like to sleep in his bed. A hollow opened at the thought of leaving the village where she had grown up. She would miss Antone above all, but maybe her mother and Pietro would allow him to visit sometimes.

A light footfall sounded behind her. Mother stood in the doorway, clothed in black even on her daughter's wedding day.

"There you are, dreaming again. You should get ready for your wedding, not spend time looking out of the

18

window."

Mother could never say anything kind or encouraging. Couldn't she remember how a bride-to-be feels on her wedding day?

"I was just looking at the view, Mother, so I can think about it when I'm in my new home."

"You won't have time to think about views when you're married. You'll be much too busy looking after your husband and having his sons. Now, hurry up and get ready. Guidoni will be here with his donkey cart soon."

Valeria's dress lay ready on the bed, a simple white robe in line with tradition. She put it on and tugged at the bodice to straighten it, and then hung a blanket behind the window casement. The makeshift mirror blurred her face, but her strong nose and sharp cheekbones stood out, like Mother's. Sometimes, she wished her features could be more delicate. Her thick, dark hair with a hint of chestnut and her large, almond-shaped eyes were her strongest points. Santucci seemed to be satisfied with her, anyway, and Margherita always said she was beautiful. Mother never offered an opinion.

She covered her hair with a white headscarf decorated with fine red embroidery.

"Valeria, Guidoni's here with the cart," Antone said, looking around the door. "You look lovely, but I do wish you weren't going to be married."

"I am, and we have to make the best of it. Come here." She held out her arms and Antone stepped into her embrace.

"I made this for you," he said, handing her a circlet of woven hazel twigs studded with sprigs of *machja* flowers: cestus, rosemary, and lavender.

"It's beautiful, thank you."

She placed it on her head over the headscarf and turned to admire her reflection in the mirror. "Now we had better go, or Mother and Pietro will be cross." She pushed him in front of her from the room.

Valeria and her mother mounted the cart and sat on the sweet-scented hay Guidoni had arranged in the back. Pietro walked beside it carrying his gun. Antone lagged behind them. Guidoni tapped the donkey's rump with a hazel stick and the beast twitched and set off at a slow pace through Felicavo. The people had turned out to watch Valeria go, and some of them tossed a flower into the cart. Valeria smiled at them, but the smile died on her lips when she saw Margherita standing alone outside her cottage. The old woman's eyes shone. The cart rolled past, and Margherita approached and handed Valeria a bouquet of rosemary and lavender.

"Remember everything I've taught you," she said under her breath and pressed Valeria's hand.

Mother frowned at Margherita, but remained silent. Valeria couldn't say anything, but she raised a hand and held Margherita's gaze until the cart turned the corner and she was lost to view. Valeria blinked back the tears and set her face away from Felicavo and towards the future.

The cart continued down the rough track and made slow progress around the steep bends. Valeria and her mother were jolted together each time a wheel hit a stone or dipped into a rut. The sea in the bay ahead was a deep blue beneath a clear sky. The hills on the other side were the colour of heather, while small clouds sat like boats moored above the mountains of Cap Corse itself. The scent of the late spring *machja* was at its strongest after the night's drizzle, and the rain-washed leaves glistened in the sunlight. Apart from the grinding wheels and the stumbling hooves and feet, the only sounds were small birds that flitted and chirped among the branches. Valeria drank it all in. She didn't know when she would travel this road again.

"It's a fine day to hold a wedding," Guidoni said, "but it'll be hot later on."

"Indeed," Valeria's mother replied, her lips two straight lines. They continued in silence, broken by Guidoni's occasional oaths when the donkey blundered over a stone.

An hour or so later, they reached the bottom of the hill and joined the track that hugged the rocky coastline up to the tip of Cap Corse. The donkey picked up speed on the flat, and the cartwheels threw up puffs of dust, long dry of the night's rain. Pietro and Antone had to stride out to keep up. Zaronza came into view, perched on an outcrop overlooking the sea. Above the village, the old castle raised jagged chunks of ruined masonry to the sky. Again, Valeria's stomach sank when she saw the place where she would live for the rest of her life. Her father had taken her to Zaronza once, when she was a child, but she had little memory of it and had barely left Felicavo after that.

The cart rattled up the hill, and Guidoni brought the donkey to a halt. Dark houses surrounded the village square. Opposite stood the church of Santa Ghjulia where the marriage was to take place. The little chapel was homely and intimate, and Valeria's spirits rose a little, but they sank again when Santucci strode towards them across the square.

"I'm sorry not to have been here to meet you, but I was making the final preparations in the house."

He handed down Valeria's mother from the cart and then Valeria herself. He squeezed her hand. She looked down and her cheeks flamed. Santucci shook hands with her brothers and with Guidoni, who was to stay until the end of the celebrations to take her mother home.

Pietro cleared his throat. "As the eldest son, I must ask your permission for my sister to enter your house."

Valeria winced. Her brother was so rough mannered. She glanced at Mother, whose face gave nothing away. Santucci didn't seem to mind, either. His lips broke into a broad smile.

"I'm honoured to grant permission to your sister. First, we must go before the priest and seal the marriage. Everything's ready inside." He waved his hand at the church opposite. The priest stood in the doorway at the top of the steps.

Valeria took Santucci's outstretched arm. Her legs shook when they climbed the short flight of steps. Mother took Pietro's arm and Antone came after. A group of people straggled behind; Zaronza village folk, Valeria presumed. Santucci didn't seem to have any relatives, or none he thought fit to invite. The church was dark inside, except for some candles dotted about, and smelt musty. She and Santucci knelt in front of the massive marble altar and the priest read the marriage service. Valeria's mind wandered back to her last sight of Margherita and her throat closed up. The priest was addressing her, so she blinked and tried to pay attention. A hollow gaped in place of her stomach, and numbness surrounded her heart. To stop the tears rising, she focused on the altar and pressed her knees hard into the stone.

At last it was over and Santucci kissed her. Now she was a wife. They made their way up the aisle to the church door under the gaze of her family and the assembled villagers. When she walked past Antone, Valeria glanced at him. He bit his lip and looked straight ahead.

They emerged from the church and paused outside the door. At first, Valeria was blinded by the sun after the dim interior. She blinked. A small group of men, fierce and unsmiling, stood apart from the rest of the onlookers. They were dressed in coarse sheepskin jerkins and all wore formless woollen caps, even though the sun beat down. Each man carried a gun slung over his shoulder.

"Who are those men?" Valeria said to Santucci.

"Shepherds. They've come down from the mountains to celebrate our wedding. I expect they've brought a present of cheese for the bride." He pressed her hand and smiled.

Valeria scanned the cluster of shepherds. They all looked similar, rough-haired and bearded, tanned and wizened from exposure to the sun and the wind, except for one who stood a head above the rest. He also wore a beard, but it was of a neater trim than the others'. A scar ran from the corner of his eye towards his mouth. The other thing that marked him out was his eyes; they were deep blue, almost violet. She had never seen eyes of such power before. Troubled, she fixed her regard on the landscape across the bay, but something drew her back and she sought out the tall shepherd again. As soon as she met his gaze, he lowered his eyes and removed his woollen cap. The others did the same.

Taking Santucci's outstretched arm again, Valeria descended the steps of the church and he guided her towards the square and his house beyond. He nodded when he passed the shepherds. Valeria kept her gaze averted, although her heightened senses were aware of the man with the blue eyes. Her breath caught, and she stumbled on an uneven cobblestone.

"Are you feeling ill, Valeria? Is it the heat?" Santucci said. His grip on her arm tightened.

"No. I'm sorry. I'm not used to these shoes. Don't worry, I'm not ill."

Valeria smiled at him, conscious all the time of their audience, and of one in particular. She turned her back on the church and the men.

**

When the sun dipped behind the mountains across the bay and tinged the sea with gold, Valeria said goodbye to her family. Guidoni paced up and down in the background and kicked up the dust.

"We must leave," Mother said. "Guidoni and his donkey are restless, and I want to get home before sunset." She gripped Valeria's arm. "Remember, you must never do anything to harm your husband's or our family's reputation."

She kissed Valeria on both cheeks.

"No, Mother, I shan't forget."

Pietro kissed her, too. Hugging Antone would make him look childish in front of everyone, so she squeezed his arm instead and kissed him like the others. His jaw trembled a little, and he turned away to join the others by the cart.

Valeria swallowed. Now she was alone with Santucci.

The afternoon had passed in a blur. She and Santucci and all the villagers sat at tables under the trees, away from the glare of the sun. The shepherds had slaughtered a sheep and carried it down from the mountain, but they had disappeared after the ceremony and, to Valeria's relief, hadn't stayed for the meal.

The company feasted on lamb and bread, cheese and fruit. Valeria ate very little and tasted nothing of the food. Santucci ate well, but drank a sparing amount of the Patrimonio wine he had bought to celebrate the occasion. Valeria only dipped her lips in it. Pietro, on the other hand, ate and drank as if it were his last meal. Mother, who sat opposite the bride and groom, glowered at her son, but he continued as if he hadn't noticed. Pietro staggered and grabbed at the table when he stood up. Valeria's cheeks burned. It was hard to believe they had the same parents. Her husband continued to smile and talk as if nothing were amiss.

Santucci broke into her thoughts. "Come along, Valeria." He held out his hand.

Her stomach slid away and she was unable to speak for fear her voice would shake. She took his warm, dry hand in hers and he led her towards his house. The door grated on the flagstones when he pushed it open.

"Welcome to my home."

He led her inside.

Valeria had seen the house for a brief moment earlier on, but now she became aware of its size compared with her home in Felicavo, which had housed five before her father's death. Santucci's steps resonated on the floor of the hallway, which was filled with the smell of ash and dusty stone. She looked around at the heavy furniture and the massive staircase. This was her home now.

"I had one of the village women come in to prepare the house for you," Santucci said. "I must admit it needed it. So little has been done since my wife…"

Valeria burned with curiosity about his first wife, but said nothing. Now was not the moment.

"Would you like some more wine, or something else before we go to bed?" Santucci said.

She shook her head and clasped her hands together to stop them trembling.

"In that case, why don't you go up and prepare yourself, and I'll join you in a few minutes? It's the second door on the left." He pointed upstairs.

Valeria grasped the banisters and dragged herself up. If only she could be elsewhere; back at home, in the woods, with Margherita, anywhere but here. She had seen animals mate and accepted it as part of life. When it applied to people, to herself, she had no idea what to expect.

She turned the door handle and went in. The spacious room was furnished with the same heavy furniture. A fire was laid in the grate but not lit on account of the heat. The whitewashed walls were bare, except for a crucifix over the bed. She glanced at the latter, and looked away again, the sweat breaking out on her palms. The bag containing her few belongings was on a table in one corner of the room. She hastened to unpack her clothes, and looked around for somewhere to put them.

Just as she had finished dragging on her nightgown and rearranging her hair, Santucci's heavy tread sounded on the stairs. She didn't know whether she should climb into bed and wait, or sit on the upright chair by the table, so she stood, dry-throated, by the fireplace, and shut her eyes. Let it be over fast.

Santucci closed the door behind him.

CHAPTER 4

L ater, Valeria lay awake and listened to the rush of the waves breaking on the shoreline far below. Santucci lay beside her and she could tell from his breathing that he was not asleep. She shifted a little to ease the soreness, but it was not as bad as she had feared. Santucci was gentle and considerate. He had seemed arrogant and full of himself at first, but she judged him too fast on the basis of their scant acquaintance.

He turned to face her and put a hand on her shoulder.

"It's time I told you a little about myself, Valeria, so you understand. My first wife died of the vomiting sickness, many years ago. She was twenty and I was twenty-three. Although our marriage was arranged, we loved each other, and I was heartbroken. Everything I had worked for seemed empty and meaningless. I longed to die, but the sickness spared me."

He sighed and continued. "To start with, I shut myself away with my grief. Little by little it waned, and I returned to the world, but there was still a great emptiness at the centre of my life." He paused again. "Since I was young and well-off, of course every father in the *piève* wanted to marry off his daughter to me, but I refused them all, and caused offence on several occasions. I felt I would be unfaithful to the memory of my late wife if I remarried.

"The years passed, and I changed my mind as I approached forty. I felt lonely in this big house, which ought to ring with the sounds of children laughing and playing. What good is wealth in the afterlife, since we must leave it behind once we have gone? So I decided to marry again and father the family I should have had all those years ago."

He hesitated and shifted further onto his side. "Since I already had enough money of my own, I wasn't looking to marry into wealth. It mattered more to find a good family, one that is respected and springs from an ancient blood line. This is what brought me to you, Valeria. If I'm honest, at the beginning I saw it only as a means to continue my name after I'm gone."

Valeria lay silent. The flash of indignation that kindled when she first met him flared again. Then, she had the sense that he was assessing her like a horse or a goat, and weighing up her breeding possibilities. Of course, she couldn't expect anything else, but she wished there could have been more room for feelings in these transactions.

"That was my view at the start," Santucci said. "It changed when I saw you, and I realised here was someone with whom I could build a life as well as a family. Now we must go to sleep."

Santucci turned over and his breathing became deeper and regular. Valeria lay awake until the grey light of dawn came up, and sleep overtook her.

***

Not long after their marriage, Santucci said, "Valeria, Benedettu Colonna's coming today. Stay out of sight unless

I call you for any reason. I'll answer the door myself when he arrives."

"Yes, of course, Santucci. Who is he?"

"My shepherd. He was there with the rest of them at our wedding. You remember: the group of men who removed their caps in your honour outside the church."

Valeria wondered which of the men it was. The blue gaze floated in her mind's eye.

"I didn't know you had a shepherd."

Santucci smiled. "Who else do you think looks after my flock? Most of the time, he's up on the mountain with the sheep, but he comes every few weeks to give me the produce and to report on the grazing. He also tells me what's going on around the island. I'm always surprised at how much those shepherds know, given that they live apart from other folk."

Her husband turned back to his papers and Valeria went upstairs to check on the old linen she had found in a cupboard. Some of it might still be usable if washed and mended, but it had been neglected for years. The lavender sprigs someone had placed between the folds crumbled to dust when she shook out the sheets. She was soon engrossed in this task, and her thoughts turned to Antone and Margherita, since she hadn't heard from either of them since the wedding. Heavy footsteps rang in the alley below and stopped outside the door.

Although Santucci had told her to stay out of sight, she crossed to the window and looked down. Standing below was a tall man with a gun slung over one shoulder and a sack over the other. A scar ran from a corner of his eye and disappeared into his beard. Valeria held her breath and craned her neck to see him better. He must have noticed her movement, since he looked up, and his blue eyes swept over the façade of the house. She drew back from the window, and the opening door grated on the stone slabs. When she dared to look again, he was no longer at the door and resonant male voices rose from below, which receded as Santucci took Colonna to the living room.

She carried on with her work, and listened out for any sound. Her pulse beat in her temple as it had done on the day of her wedding. She pressed her palms against her eyes. No, not this. Santucci's good to you and you have nothing to complain about. Colonna is your husband's servant and he's nothing to you. But her thoughts still slid back to the shepherd. He and his life were unknown to her, but that made no difference.

Her pulse raced once again when the living room door opened and her husband called up from the bottom of the staircase.

"Valeria, come down a moment."

"Yes, Santucci, what is it?"

"Make some refreshments for me and Colonna, please, and leave them on the table outside the room. Knock on the door when they are ready."

Valeria hurried to prepare food and wine, and then took the plate and the jug along the corridor and set them on the table. As she did so, the door, which Santucci must have left ajar, swung open a little further. Colonna stood facing her and looked up, while her husband sat with his back turned to her. She had a momentary glimpse of the dark blue eyes before she closed the door, waited a few seconds and tapped on it. She rushed back to the kitchen and wiped her clammy palms against her skirt. Not long afterwards, the shepherd left. She breathed again.

Each time Colonna came, Valeria remained closeted in the kitchen until her husband asked her to provide refreshments. She didn't try to catch a glimpse of Colonna again, but when he was in the house her heart knocked against her ribs and she was short of breath. When Santucci reached for her at night, she found herself wondering how it would be with Colonna: his hands exploring her body, his weight on her, instead of her husband's. She pushed these thoughts away, and hated herself for her weakness.

CHAPTER 5

The wind raged and the trees twisted and groaned as if in pain. A bitter taste was in her mouth and she was falling, falling. A thunderous knocking merged itself with the dream, and she awoke with a start and sat up. The banging continued. Drugged with sleep, it took her a moment to understand that someone was beating the heavy knocker up and down against the door.

"Wake up, Santucci." She shook him. "Someone's at the door."

He was a sound sleeper and she knew he disliked sudden awakenings. Even so, he preferred to answer the door himself in case it was another man, since he wanted her to stay out of sight.

"What?... What's happening? Why did you wake me up?"

The knocking resumed. "Ah...," he said. "What time is it? It must be the middle of the night. What the devil do they want?"

He rolled out of bed, threw on a pair of breeches over his nightshirt and padded barefoot out of the room. The heavy door scraped over the flagstones as usual.

"Antone – what on earth are you doing here?" Santucci exclaimed.

Valeria darted out of bed and hurried to the top of the staircase, still in her nightgown. Below, Santucci held the door wide open, while her brother hesitated on the threshold, head down and soaking wet. He shivered and opened his mouth, but no sound emerged. Ignoring the chill rising from the hallway, Valeria rushed down the stairs. Santucci and Antone stood in a frozen tableau, while the wind whisked squalls of rain through the open door.

She took her brother's arm, led him inside and closed the door after him. He stood forlorn on the flagstones. His hair was plastered flat against his skull, and a pool of water formed around his feet. He shook himself, like a dog emerging from a stream.

Santucci frowned. "What's all this, Antone? Why have you come? Is someone ill?"

Antone flung himself into his sister's arms and she flinched when the damp from his clothes seeped through her nightdress to her skin. His head pressed into her shoulder and she looked at Santucci over the top of it. She raised her eyebrows and shrugged.

"Speak, boy. We can't stand here all night. What's happened?"

Valeria lifted Antone's chin and looked into his eyes. "What's the matter? You look frightened and you're soaking wet. You can tell me, can't you?"

"It's Pietro." His eyes widened and he looked around him.

"What about him? Has something happened to him?"

Antone shook his head. "It's terrible. He says he'll kill me this time, and I believe him. I ran all the way here over the hills in the rain. I had to get away from him." His clothes were covered in mud.

"What is all this nonsense?" Santucci said. "Your own brother's going to kill you? I can't believe it. This is ridiculous."

Valeria sensed her brother was in earnest; he was afraid for his life. While she struggled to untangle her thoughts, she realised how cold she was. Antone shivered even harder.

"Santucci, please can he stay here tonight? He can't go back across the hill in this weather, and I believe him when he says he's afraid. I'll light a fire in the other bedroom and we'll talk about this in the morning, when we have all rested."

"I don't know. This is very confusing. He must have done something pretty disgraceful to annoy Pietro so much."

Valeria took a deep breath. "Please let him stay for one night. He's soaking wet and cold, and if we send him away, I am afraid he'll be ill. I know you wouldn't want that."

The seconds passed while her husband looked first at her and then at Antone. Surely he wouldn't send him back out into a night like this?

"Very well. Just this one night, but I want a good explanation for all this in the morning. In the meantime, we had better get to bed and sleep, if we can. Look at your nightdress, Valeria; it isn't proper. Cover yourself."

She looked down. The outline of her breasts was visible through the damp cloth. Folding her arms over them, she ran upstairs and threw a shawl around her. She returned to the hallway, took Antone's hand, led him upstairs and seated him in an upright chair while she lit the fire and made up the bed. She turned her back while he removed his wet clothes, dried himself off and put on one of Santucci's nightshirts, which hung around him like the sail of a becalmed ship. Once he was in bed, Valeria sat beside him and smoothed his hair away from his temples, but made no attempt to talk or to find out what had happened. Despite Antone's distress, sleep claimed him fast and his breathing deepened. Valeria rose from the bed and looked back at him from the doorway while the firelight played over his immobile features, before regaining her bedroom.

Santucci was already asleep when she slipped into bed beside him, but sleep evaded her. She lay deep in thought until the fingers of dawn crept through a chink in the shutters. Then she fell into a fitful slumber until her husband shifted and stretched beside her.

***

"Now, it's time you told me about Pietro and what happened yesterday," Valeria said the next morning while she served Antone bread and warm goat's milk in the kitchen.

His eyes enlarged like a startled deer's and he looked towards the door.

"Don't worry; Pietro isn't hiding behind the door. Santucci has gone out, but he'll be back later, and he will want to know what this is all about. He wasn't in a good mood when he left."

"He'll come for me, won't he? Or Santucci will take me back there, and Pietro will kill me and Mother will just say he's right."

"Listen, Antone. We won't get anywhere if you don't tell me what you did to annoy Pietro so much. If I know what it is, then perhaps we can decide what to do."

Antone's breath hissed through his teeth. "I did something very stupid, I know, but I don't think it was bad enough for Pietro to get so angry and say he'd kill me." He shivered.

"What was this stupid thing?"

"I took his gun."

Valeria gasped. "His gun? What on earth did you do it

for? You know how attached Pietro is to his gun. It's his most precious possession. Whatever got into you?"

Antone shrugged. "I just wanted to borrow it for a while and see how it felt to carry one."

"You don't still have these ridiculous ideas about running off into the *machja* and becoming a bandit, do you?"

"No... at least, I don't think so, but now I wish I could. I'll have a gun of my own one day and I wanted to see how it worked." He paused. "But it wasn't only taking it that made Pietro so angry. How was I to know the gun was still loaded?"

Valeria's hand went to her mouth. "Oh, no. You'd better not tell me you shot someone or something."

"Well, not someone, but... I didn't know it was loaded. How could I? He shouldn't have left it like that. I pointed it at the goat and pulled the trigger."

"Whose goat was it, Antone?"

"Signore Leca's."

Valeria shut her eyes. How stupid could he be? "I can't believe it. It had to be one of Leca's goats, didn't it? No wonder Pietro was angry. You know our family has never got on with them. It goes back a long way. Shooting one of their goats is like declaring war. Vendettas start for less. You might as well have gone to Signore Leca's house and shot him yourself. I don't know, Antone. You never used to do this sort of thing. What's the matter with you?" Her face flared as the anger mounted.

Antone looked down. A wave of sympathy washed over Valeria. This gangly boy who was getting too big for his clothes was growing up, and now she was no longer there he had no one to watch over him or to make sure he was well behaved. Father was dead, Mother wasn't interested, while Pietro just punished Antone when he did something wrong.

36

How could he know what to do?

She sighed. "Well, it's done now and it's obvious this was an accident. Maybe it will teach you never to borrow things without asking, and never to point a gun at anything. I'll speak with Santucci when he comes home and try to get him to arrange this with Pietro and Signore Leca. In the meantime, you can help me to move the furniture so I can clean underneath it."

She tried to bury herself in the work, but a picture of Pietro beating Antone kept crossing her vision.

When Santucci returned several hours later, he was in a better mood, so Valeria explained what Antone had done and tried to play down the situation.

Santucci tutted. "I can see why Pietro's cross with the boy."

"I agree Antone has been very stupid. He knows it too, and is sorry. I talked to him for a long time, and he won't do anything like this again, but I'm afraid Pietro will be too harsh with him. He has a terrible temper when roused, and the fact that the goat belonged to a family with no love for ours makes it so much worse." She paused. "I know this is asking a lot, Santucci, but maybe you could take him back to Felicavo yourself and talk to Pietro and to the Lecas. Perhaps you can stop Pietro giving him too harsh a punishment and help him to come to some arrangement with the Lecas."

"I don't know, Valeria. They may not see my involvement as anything other than meddling, and I don't like to interfere in your family's affairs."

"Please, Santucci. You don't know how it can be up there. It could get out of control, above all with Pietro's temper. If he and Leca start to insult each other, I don't know where it might end. We may not have much time."

"Mm. I still feel uneasy about interfering, but if you

think I can help, well, perhaps I could try… Mind you, the boy has been very stupid, and he will have to submit to some kind of punishment. I can't do anything about that."

Valeria stood at the edge of the square while Santucci's horse laboured up the hill, carrying both its master and Antone, and disappeared into the trees. Her brother had protested, but Valeria insisted he return to Felicavo.

***

Santucci returned as dusk fell. He remained silent when he went upstairs to change out of his mud-spattered clothes. Valeria pushed down the questions. He would tell her what had happened when he was ready.

After he had finished his evening meal, Santucci said, "Well, I think I've managed to arrange this matter between your brother and the Lecas, but it wasn't easy, believe me. I had no idea such hostility existed between them. What's it all about, Valeria?"

She took a deep breath. "It goes back many years. We never speak to the Lecas and they don't speak to us. We avoid each other to the point of sitting on opposite sides of the church. My mother calls Signora Leca an old witch – but not to her face, of course. The story is that a Peretti son was betrothed to a Leca daughter a long time ago, but they were never married because the bride refused at the altar. A brawl followed, and one person was killed and several wounded. Somehow, a truce was agreed between the families, but that's all it has ever been: a truce."

"That explains it. Signore Leca was furious about the goat, and Pietro didn't help matters by refusing to apologise for Antone at first. Leca thought Pietro had put his brother up to it. What a storm about nothing. I had to take Pietro aside and persuade him to apologise to Leca, which he did with very bad grace. I also gave Leca some money to compensate him for the loss of the goat, and Pietro has promised to pay me back when he can."

"What about Antone? Where was he all this time?"

"I made sure he kept out of the way," Santucci replied. "He would have made it worse."

"What happened to him afterwards?" Her head ached with anxiety.

"Pietro led him back to your mother's house, where I daresay he gave him a good beating. I tried to prevail upon him to spare the boy a little, but I don't know if I succeeded. However, I did talk with Antone when we rode to Felicavo. As you can imagine, he was terrified about what would happen, but he agreed in the end that you can't run away from your responsibilities. I hope he sticks to it in the future."

"Thank you, Santucci. I'm so grateful."

"Well, we won't talk about it anymore, but your brother needs to grow up. I won't come between him and Pietro a second time. It's not my place to meddle in your family's business."

Valeria looked down at her hands. Santucci was right. Antone never thought before he did things, and Pietro's beatings didn't seem to make much difference. But maybe this time he had listened to Santucci. In any case, there wasn't much she could do about it.

CHAPTER 6

Zaronza: 1760

"It's good to see you, little brother."

"Not so little any more!" Antone said.

Valeria laughed. "No, that's true. I'm glad you come when you can. I see so few people, and Mother and Pietro don't bother to visit. I suppose that once they got me married off they were happy to leave me to it, as long as I don't damage the family's honour."

Antone looked down at his hands. "I feel sorry for Quillina. I'm sure she can't have wanted to marry Pietro. I think she has a hard time with him."

Valeria sighed. "Wishes don't have anything to do with it. She brought land and some money, and that's what counts. But I don't envy her, with a bad-tempered husband and a gloomy mother-in-law. At least I don't have either of those."

"How is it to live with Santucci?"

"He's very good to me, and we have respect for each other. When I first met him, I'll admit I thought he was arrogant, but in fact he's kind and considerate. He talks to me a lot about Corsica's future and I know he's often anxious, so I do my best to make life easy for him. There's rarely an angry word between us, but, well... many women are less fortunate than I am. I just wish..."

Antone raised his eyebrows.

"I wanted more than anything to give him children, but there's still no sign of one after five years." She waved a hand. "He doesn't blame me; at least, he never says anything, but I sense his regret."

To have children was one of the reasons why Santucci had chosen her, and although it had irritated her at the time of their betrothal, she ached with guilt now. She picked the herbs Margherita gave the village woman who had trouble conceiving, and drank the infusions, but the dark blood always came in the end.

***

Valeria understood from Santucci that the political situation was becoming even more tense and difficult. Pasquale Paoli had succeeded early on in establishing a new government, and was trying to put his plans into action to secure the republic. The Genoese were not his only enemies, and he had had to thwart several conspiracies and defeat a serious rival who almost overcame him.

"Cap Corse is the key," Santucci often said, almost to himself. "If the General can succeed in developing a proper fleet, he'll beat the Genoese at their own game. We have to break the blockade, or Corsica will starve. It's no good continuing to rely on help from Neapolitan and Tuscan merchants. The Genoese hold the major ports, and so Paoli needs the whole of Cap Corse as well as a foothold on the north coast."

Valeria nodded, but remained silent. Women didn't

meddle in politics or give their opinions, and Santucci didn't expect it. In any case, she had no particular love for their Genoese masters, and didn't disagree with Santucci. A niggling doubt made her wonder, though, if this Paoli was fooling himself. Could they really rid the island of the Genoese, who had been their rulers for centuries? Or would it only bring in an even more oppressive period of rule? She feared more troubled times might be in store for Corsica.

One day in early June, Santucci came into the kitchen. He rubbed his hands and grinned.

"Well, Valeria. What do you think of this?" He brandished a paper. "I've just received this letter from Paoli. He tells me he plans to visit Zaronza in a few days' time to see the area for himself. The letter says he's grateful that Zaronza has always been loyal to him and the republic, and he hopes the rest of Cap Corse will follow suit very soon. He has even signed it himself rather than some secretary."

Valeria's arms were up to her elbows in water. She smiled encouragement at her husband. He paced up and down, unable to contain his pride. For Paoli to recognise the importance of Cap Corse in shoring up the republic was what Santucci had worked for.

"After the *consultà* a few weeks ago, I expected him to visit soon. They made some very important decisions about creating a navy, and even a merchant navy. Anyway, I thought you had better know about his visit so you can prepare for it, although I admit his plans still seem a little vague. He doesn't say where he will stay or for how long."

"Which day is he coming?"

"Friday, it says, the day after tomorrow. Of course, he'll need someone to show him around. I understand one of the purposes of his visit is to explore the places with defensive possibilities. Zaronza's position will surely recommend itself to him."

42

"Do you know how many people he's bringing with him?"

"He doesn't say, but I imagine it will be a small group, since he doesn't always like to travel with a large entourage. You'd better make sure we have refreshments prepared. He's a very refined man, and studied abroad before he returned to Corsica."

A twisting worm of apprehension lodged itself in Valeria's spine. This man, Paoli, was the General, the leader of the republic. What sort of food would a man like him eat every day? Would he be happy with their simple fare, or did she have to prepare special dishes? She sat at the table to think it through. If only she could speak to Margherita, who always seemed to know what to do. Mother would scold her without giving any practical advice, and Santucci wouldn't want her to visit Felicavo on her own. After some thought, she decided there was no point in preparing a banquet. If Paoli was as attached to his homeland as everyone said, he would be happy to eat their simple country dishes. Despite the blockade, they had plenty of fish, *brocciù* cheese, eggs, tomatoes and olives.

The news of Paoli's visit had spread fast around the village, and an almost physical cloud of excitement was in the air. The women gossiped about it at the fountain.

"He's a good-looking man, so I hear, but he isn't married," said one gap-toothed woman, shrouded in black. "Perhaps one of our village girls might catch his eye. It would be a coup for Zaronza."

"I've heard he's sworn never to marry," another said. "He's married to the republic."

"Nonsense. A man without a wife is like a shepherd without a staff."

Valeria was filling her jar at the spout, and started at the word 'shepherd'. A momentary vision of Colonna rose up in

43

front of her. She swallowed. Was this all these women talked about: who was marriageable and who wasn't? She turned to them.

"Signore Paoli is here for more important matters. My husband says the future of Cap Corse is in question. I imagine taking a wife is the last thing on the General's mind."

The other women stared at her and she looked away. Valeria had never felt at home among them, and they didn't always welcome it when she spoke her mind.

"Of course, your husband and the elders are receiving a special visit from the General," Signora Rossi, her neighbour, said. "It would be more proper if he met the other men as well, like my husband. I thought the whole idea of this new government was that all men are equal, but it seems they treat the General like a king wherever he goes. He's only allowed to meet the notables." She sniffed.

"I can't answer for what the General will do or who he'll want to meet," Valeria replied. "He's a busy man with a country to run and enemies to fight, after all. I daresay if he knew how much petty squabbling went on behind his back he wouldn't come at all."

She turned on her heel, picked up her jar and stalked back to the house. The women remained silent until she had reached the door, and then started to murmur, talking about her, no doubt. Valeria often felt her neighbour's eyes on her. Signora Rossi was friendly enough to her on the surface, but Valeria sensed that hostility lurked beneath the façade and had almost broken through by the fountain. Perhaps she had been unwise to say what she really felt.

Valeria prepared the house to receive Paoli, but still didn't know what to expect when a small group of horsemen rode into the square early on the Friday morning. Their clothes were dusty from the road, and the horses' flanks sweated as if their riders had pushed them hard. Valeria watched from the window while the men dismounted and watered their mounts at the fountain. Santucci told her, as he always did, to stay out of sight until he called her, and hurried from the house.

Santucci approached the group in the square. Paoli's commanding bearing marked him out as their leader, and Santucci turned to him first without hesitation, bowed a little and extended his hand. A tall, broad man with chiselled features, Paoli nodded in return. Valeria had expected the General to be in his fifties, but this man couldn't have been more than about thirty-five. He radiated energy and looked around him all the time, as if he expected an ambush. Valeria gazed at the wig he wore beneath his broad hat, a fashion unknown to the men of Zaronza and Felicavo. She wondered again if her simple provisions would be good enough, but it was too late to change anything.

Another man stood close to Paoli's shoulder. He resembled him a little but looked older. He was taller and thinner and wore his hair close cropped, almost like a monk. He also looked around him, and Valeria shrank back when his piercing gaze swept the façade of Santucci's house. The man's eyes burned with a strange ardour.

The other village elders joined Santucci and the group and greeted Paoli. Santucci gestured towards his house. Paoli shook his head and pointed past the house towards the hill crowned by the ruined castle. Santucci nodded and signalled for Paoli and his men to follow him. A few snatches of conversation came to Valeria's ears when they passed by the front door, followed by the rolling of loose stones on the rough path. All was silent for a while. Valeria waited in the kitchen. The sound of the men tramping back down the hill jolted her out of her reverie and she listened for the door, but they continued past it. Would all this food go to waste?

An hour passed, and then another. Valeria's empty stomach told her it was time for the midday meal when heels rang on the cobbled alley and stopped outside the house. The door scraped open and the men's boots resonated on the flagstones.

Santucci, his face flushed, looked around the kitchen door. He grimaced. "I'm sorry we've been so long, but the General wanted to have a good look around the village. They're in the living room now. Bring the food and wait outside, and when we're ready for it, I'll call you in." He paused and turned back, grinning. "I think this is turning out to be a very successful visit."

Valeria nodded and hurried to prepare the dishes. She felt a twinge of regret that she could not take part in their discussions.

The living room door was ajar, and the men's conversation was distinct. Paoli's deep tones were mingled with a higher voice, which she took to be the older man who had flanked him by the fountain.

"As you know, Santucci, I'm very keen to develop a fleet to fly the republic's flag. Centuri seems like the ideal place to construct the vessels, since it's on this side of the cape, and the harbour is well protected. However, we'll need fortifications all the way along the coast. It strikes me that Zaronza is in a prime position, since it overlooks the sea and would be easily defensible. I'm minded to order the construction of a watchtower on the site of the ruined castle up there, which would give us a view over the strait towards Saint-Florent and advance warning of troop movements by sea. What do you think?"

"I couldn't agree with you more, General. If the republic is to defeat Genoa, we have to do it at sea as well as on land, and it's of prime importance to break the blockade. Zaronza occupies a natural defensive position, and the mount is an obvious place to site a watchtower. I would be very happy to oversee its construction."

"Excellent. I'm also inclined to build it in the style of the Genoese towers around the coast. I rather like the irony, don't you, Clemente?" A low murmur came in response. Valeria wondered if Clemente was the monk-like figure. "Thank you for your offer, Santucci," Paoli continued. "I hope it won't cause you too much disruption, but I need someone I can trust here. I'll set things in motion as soon as I return to Murato. Before I do, I must visit Isola Rossa. I have plans for that town, too, as a counter-balance to Calvi."

"If only we could take the coastal towns," another man said. "Corsicans are going hungry without grain and other goods."

"It's my greatest hope that we can in the future," Paoli replied, "For the moment, the Genoese defend the ports too well, and it would be folly for us to try, but it seems to me they've all but given up in the interior. Few regions have failed to rally to us except the part of the Balagne around Calenzana. And, as long as we have chestnuts, we'll have bread."

"Speaking of food," Santucci said, "I imagine you must need refreshments. My wife has prepared a meal for you and your men, if you'd do me the honour of taking it here."

"That would be very welcome. We started out before dawn this morning."

Valeria moved away from the door when Santucci's footsteps approached and made sure her headscarf was in place. Santucci nodded at her and held the door open. She entered the room and placed the dishes on the table, conscious of the men's eyes on her.

"My wife, General."

"I'm honoured, Signora," Paoli said, and looked Valeria

47

full in the face. Beneath heavy eyebrows, his shrewd eyes seemed to weigh her up. "Thank you for taking the trouble to prepare food for us."

The heat rose in Valeria's face and she bowed her head a little. "It's the simple food we eat here every day, Signore. I hope you'll be satisfied."

"So much the better. When I was away in Naples, I hankered after good Corsican cooking every day."

Paoli turned towards the table, dismissing her. She stood for a moment, awkward in the men's presence.

"Thank you, Valeria," Santucci said.

The men stayed for a while, and the murmur of conversation reached the kitchen. The scrape of chairs on the floor preceded that of the front door on the flagstones, and the ringing of heels grew fainter as Paoli's group crossed the square. Valeria went to the window. They remounted and rode away in a cloud of dust. Santucci stood and watched them for a moment and then turned back to the house, head down, deep in thought. Their neighbour, Signora Rossi, stood outside her house, looking at Santucci. Her mouth twisted and her eyes narrowed, but she smiled when Santucci drew level with her. She spoke to him and he responded with a nod and a polite wave of the hand.

Valeria went into the main room and cleared the empty plates away. The General and his men hadn't left anything, so they must have enjoyed the food. Her chest expanded with relief.

"A very satisfactory meeting," Santucci said. "The General's a far-sighted man. If anyone can make the republic work, it's him."

"Who was the man with him, the tall one who looked like a monk?"

"Ah, that's his brother, Clemente. He's somewhat older than Paoli, but he saw his brother's qualities and was influential in getting him back from Naples and elected to lead the republic. They say he's a fierce soldier. You're right about his looks. He's very devout, and they say he prays for his enemies' souls before he kills them."

Valeria shuddered. The republic couldn't avoid further bloodshed. The Corsican nationalists had been at war with the Genoese for more than thirty years. Even the General, however skilful a leader he was, couldn't bring it to an end overnight or without further fighting.

CHAPTER 7

Following Paoli's visit, there was a sense in Zaronza that events moved faster, and Valeria felt a ripple of excitement mingled with fear. Other parts of Cap Corse were rallying to the General, Santucci told her, although the main ports around the island were still in Genoese hands.

Paoli sent his own engineer to design the tower, and work began soon afterwards. Every day, the tramp of feet past the house, the ringing of the stonemason's mallet and the calls of the workmen filled the air. Santucci inspected the tower's progress daily and sent reports back to Paoli. Valeria understood the importance of the watchtower for the General's plans, but couldn't help a twist of frustration. When Santucci was out, she used to enjoy climbing the hill and walking about in the castle's ruins. She watched the ever-changing light on the other side of the bay and drank in the sun-baked scent of the *machja* on the slopes behind the village. Now, work on the tower began at sunrise and continued until sunset. She was unable to go up there alone.

At last, the work was complete. Paoli's tower stood

sentinel over Zaronza and dominated the bay. The greenish-grey stonework thrust upwards like a clenched fist in defiance of the Genoese. In the meantime, work had taken place to strengthen the other defences around Zaronza. Paoli didn't visit the village again. Valeria felt a pang of disappointment on Santucci's behalf.

"Well, it's a pity the General hasn't had time to come and see the tower," Santucci said. "However, I've received a very complimentary letter from him. He thanks me for all my work to hasten its completion and for my continued loyalty. He's a great man, Valeria. Corsica needs men like him."

***

A few weeks later, Valeria was stirring soup over the fire when Santucci came into the kitchen.

"Colonna said he would come today, and so…" He broke off and doubled up, groaning.

Valeria rushed to his side and held his arm. "What is it, Santucci? Are you in pain?"

"Here." He clutched his abdomen with his hands. Valeria helped him into a chair and tried to feel his belly, but he pushed her away. "It's nothing, it will pass." He remained bent over and rocked back and forth.

Santucci had complained of indigestion and vague stomach cramps for some time. It was unlike him to be ill, but during the last few months he lost weight and had little appetite, even for his favourite dishes. He said it was no doubt worry about the political situation and how things would turn out in Corsica. His sleep was disturbed, too, and he often awoke sweating in the early hours. Valeria suspected the malady was bodily rather than mental. She drew on the knowledge Margherita had passed on to her and brewed herbal infusions from *machja* plants known for their

51

healing properties. They had a temporary effect, but the cramps always returned.

This time the pain abated a little, but remained.

"I think you should go upstairs and rest for a while. I'll bring you an infusion, which will help the pain and make you sleep."

He nodded. "I can't get word to Colonna in time that I'm unwell." He straightened a little and looked up at her. "You'll have to greet him today, Valeria, this once. I don't like it, but I don't feel well enough."

Her pulse throbbed. She wanted this even less than her husband did. "Do I have to, Santucci? I don't know what you do when he's here, or what you talk about. This is men's business."

"You must receive the produce he brings and pay him his wages, and he will give you his report on the flock. Ask him what news he has."

"News of what?"

"He'll know what you mean. Tell me later what he said, word for word. Now, help me upstairs. I expect this is just another attack of indigestion. It will soon pass."

Valeria helped him to stand, and, clasping his arm, assisted him to climb the stairs. In the bedroom she started to unbutton his shirt, but he stayed her hand and said, "I can manage now. Bring me the infusion and I'm sure it will feel make me much better."

She went down to the kitchen and closed the door behind her. She leaned back against it for a moment, her forehead in her palm, before she roused herself to set water to boil and choose herbs from the bunches hanging from the beams to dry. When she returned to the bedroom, Santucci was in bed with the covers pulled up to his chin. His face was as white as a lamb's fleece. He gave her a weak smile that didn't reach his eyes when she put down the infusion by the bedside.

"Drink it all up, Santucci, and then sleep. I'll come to see how you are later."

She didn't know what time to expect Colonna. No doubt he arrived at an hour to suit him. In the meantime, she tried to occupy herself with mending worn linen, but her palms were slick with sweat and she pricked herself with the needle, leaving spots of crimson on the white cloth. The stitches were lumpy and uneven, and in the end she laid down her work, clasped her clammy hands together, and waited.

After what seemed like hours, footsteps resonated along the alley and stopped close by. Valeria held her breath. The heavy knocker fell once against the door. She swallowed, but was unable to get to her feet. The visitor rapped again, harder this time. Valeria willed herself to stand up, made sure that no strands of hair escaped from her headscarf, and arranged her dress. She opened the door.

For a moment, they looked at each other, and an exchange deeper than words passed between them. Colonna swept off his woollen cap.

"Good morning, Signore Colonna. My husband isn't feeling well today, and regrets he can't talk to you himself. He's asked me to meet you instead. I hope this won't put you out."

"I'm sorry to hear the master's unwell, Signora. I could come back another time if you would prefer it."

"Now you've come all this way, I wouldn't want you to have to come back another day. My husband wouldn't, either. Please come in."

She knew they both mouthed these trite words to conceal what lay beneath. Unable to bear the concentrated beam of his gaze any longer, she turned and led the way to the living room.

Valeria sat down in Santucci's chair and Colonna crossed to the fireplace. Should she ask him to sit down, or should he remain standing? He might take offence if a woman were to treat him like that. Then she remembered the brief glimpse of him through the open door, several years before. He had stood while Santucci sat. That was how it should be. He was her husband's servant, and when she spoke he would hear Santucci speak through her.

The shepherd stood with his legs a little apart, as if he took possession of the hearth. A prickle of indignation at his boldness ran through her. She looked somewhere over his shoulder and asked him to give her the report, which she would pass on to her husband. Valeria listened to his low, mesmerising voice. Her attention wavered, so she sat up straighter and forced herself to concentrate. All was in order with the flock and the produce, Colonna said.

She nodded, not knowing what to do next, while he stood there and waited. Oh yes, the news. "My husband said I should ask you what information you have, and said you would know what that means."

In a few sentences, Colonna described the Genoese troop movements he had seen from the mountains, and passed on the news his fellow shepherds had gathered about what was happening in the coastal towns. Valeria guessed Santucci would send this to Paoli.

"I'll tell my husband what you said. Now I expect you'd like some food before you leave."

She left him standing in the living room and went to the kitchen, where she prepared the usual meal of bread, cheese and wine. Her trembling hands clattered the plates on the table. Another wave of annoyance swept through her when Colonna did not come forward to take the jug and plate from her in the living room. No doubt he regarded this as woman's work, even if she was the master's wife. She banged them on the table, harder than she intended.

"Please, sit and eat."

He inclined his head and took his place at the table. Taking out his knife, he cut into the soft cheese and his even teeth sank into the bread. When she poured him a beaker of wine, their roles were reversed in some odd way; he was the master and she the servant. Her hands trembled and the blood beat in her ear.

He wiped his mouth with the back of his hand and cleaned his knife on a piece of bread.

"Thank you, Signora." Again, he bowed a little. Once more she sensed the pride behind his courteous words.

Valeria showed him out, and when he stepped over the threshold, he pulled on his woollen cap and settled his gun over his shoulder. She shut the door behind him and stood with her forehead pressed against the wood until his ringing footsteps had faded. Grasping the newel post, she lowered herself onto a step and cradled her face in her palms. Next time, she hoped Santucci would be well enough to meet the man himself.

CHAPTER 8

Zaronza: January 1761

Despite Valeria's infusions, Santucci's condition continued to worsen, and she began to fear for him. He still went about his work, but Valeria suspected this was by force of willpower. He complained of stomach cramps, ate very little, and was often unable to keep his food down. The flesh shrank from his bones, and his skin took on a yellowish tinge. At night he turned this way and that, and the dark circles under his eyes betrayed his sleepless hours.

"My movements had a lot of blood in them this morning," he said.

Valeria went cold. This sounded like the wasting sickness that had taken her neighbour's grandmother up in Felicavo. The woman had shrivelled and shrunk in a few months, like Santucci. Her potions were not healing him, although they couldn't harm him. The physician bled Santucci twice, but this had no effect either. Maybe he wouldn't get better at all.

One day he announced he would stay in bed that morning

and see how he felt in the afternoon. Neither healing herbs nor traditional medicine worked, and Santucci sank by the day. Valeria resolved to try another course. Once the sleeping draught had taken effect, she wrapped a shawl around her and took the path into the hills leading to Felicavo. The last time she had set foot there was on the day of her wedding.

The weather could not have been more different. The January day was dark, and a cold drizzle dripped from the lowering skies. Instead of being anchored to the mountain tops, as usual, the clouds had cut their moorings and sunk far down the hillsides. Valeria climbed the hills in a damp mist, and fine droplets lingered on the wool of her shawl. Her feet slid on the rough stones of the mule track. She met no one else on the path. After more than an hour, the footpath sloped downwards and she passed through the grove of cork oaks and by the little chapel with its stone cross. To avoid her former home she took another way that wound behind the village and came out at the bottom, by Margherita's cottage.

She had not seen the old woman since her wedding day, but Antone had said Margherita was still alive. Looking to left and right, she tapped on the door. No scent of herbs or brewing came from the house.

A feeble voice from within said, "Who is it?"

Valeria opened the door and stood on the threshold. Her friend sat by the fire, but no pot bubbled over the flames. Her apple face was even more sunken than the last time Valeria had seen her, several years before.

"Who is it?" Margherita repeated, turning her face to the door.

She must see who I am, Valeria thought, and then the weight of it struck her hard. Margherita could no longer see.

"Oh, Margherita." She approached the old woman.

"I know that voice, but it's one I never expected to hear again."

Valeria knelt and took the knotted and wasted hands between hers. A current passed between them. A whitish-blue film covered Margherita's eyes.

"How long have you been like this, Margherita?"

"Oh, it was coming on before you left Felicavo, but it's been slow to take hold, and I was able to work as usual up until recent days. I had to take care not to fall on the hillsides, though, and now I can't go up there at all. I'm just old, you know." She had said that for as long as Valeria had known her.

A stab of guilt pierced Valeria. "Who looks after you?"

"There are some in Felicavo who are grateful for the little I was able to do for them or their relatives, and they look after their own. Not everyone thinks that way."

"I wish I could have come to visit you long before now, but my husband doesn't like me to travel outside Zaronza. Of course, I must obey him."

"How is life with you, Valeria? Antone gives me news of you from time to time, but you know what young men of his age are like. You have to prise everything out of them. The fact you are here now tells me something is wrong."

"My marriage is good, and my husband has always treated me well, so I'm happy. He doesn't know I'm here, since I left him asleep at home. Margherita, I'm so worried about him."

Margherita's brows drew together when Valeria described his symptoms.

"From what you say I fear it's the wasting sickness, and no remedy I know is proof against it."

"I know it, and believe me I've tried all the cures you taught me. The physician bled him, but it made no difference at all, except to weaken him," Valeria said. "Only

58

one thing might help him now, and that's why I've come to you, since I don't know anyone who practises it. You told me about it many years ago: casting out the Eye."

"If he suffers from the Eye, as you believe, it must be banished, and the illness with it, or he'll die. Only a few receive the gift of signing from others, and I never did. No *signadore* live around here, but I've heard of one in the region of Cisco, although I have never met her. You must be careful what you get mixed up in. Not everyone approves of them."

"How can I find this woman?"

"If you're sure you want to do this, I can send word to her. It would be better for you not to travel to find her yourself. Your place is with your husband, and people would talk."

Valeria took a deep breath. "I can't see any other way. He's sickened and sunk so fast I don't know what else to try. Please send for her and ask her to come to Santucci's house in Zaronza."

"Very well. Now, tell me a little more about yourself. I sense beneath your anxiety for Santucci lies a deeper concern. I may be blind, but I have other ways to see." Margherita's hands tightened on Valeria's, and she drew them away a little.

"No… no. I don't know what you mean," Valeria said, her voice not as firm as she wanted. "There's nothing else, I assure you. What other concerns could I have, living as I do?"

"Are you sure? I must admit there was a time, not long before your marriage, when I worried for your future, but maybe those were the foolish ideas of an old woman. I'm pleased to see your marriage has brought you security and respect. Those aren't always enough."

A cold sweat broke out on Valeria's forehead, and a

vision of Colonna and his blue gaze flashed across her mind's eye. Margherita had always had powers she wouldn't admit to, but how could she know Valeria's deepest thoughts? The incident with the bone, and her extreme reaction, came to mind. At the time, Margherita had shrugged it off, but Valeria never quite believed her explanation that it was only a malaise and that she had lost the ability to read the sheep's shoulder blade. She knew better than to raise the subject now. For the moment, her more pressing worry was to get Santucci better.

"All that concerns me is my husband's health, believe me," Valeria said. "I wish I could stay and talk with you. I've missed you so much. Now, I've been away long enough. I can't imagine what Santucci will think if he wakes up and I'm not there. Antone will bring me news of you and, if I can, I'll try to visit you again when my husband is better."

"I fear I'm not long for this world, my lovely. Sometimes I feel the spirits calling me, and I know my time draws near. I'll be ready when the moment comes. Now, put the sad thoughts from your mind. You've done what you can, and I'll send for the *signadora*."

Valeria kissed Margherita's hands, and then stood and made her way to the door. When Valeria let herself out, she looked back at the old woman, who crossed herself, as she had done all those years before.

***

A few days after her visit to Margherita, a faint tapping awoke Valeria from her thoughts. Santucci was no better. If anything he was worse. He had got up several mornings running, and swallowed some watered-down goat's milk, but returned to bed a short time later. Valeria wasn't sure if anyone was at the door or if it was in her daydream, so she stayed in the kitchen. After a minute or so, the tapping came again, but it sounded like a mouse pattering across the ceiling. She put down the bowl in which she was mixing yet another batch of herbs for an infusion, and went to the door.

A tall, gaunt woman stood in the alley, dressed in black. She carried a basket covered with a cloth. Her coal-black hair was drawn back in a severe chignon, emphasising her curved nose. Her eyes shone with an unusual brightness. She had a noblewoman's demeanour, but she reminded Valeria rather of a bird of prey, like the ospreys that wheeled over the mountains.

"Forgive me, the first time you knocked I thought it was a mouse scratching in the ceiling until I realised someone really was at the door. Can I help you?"

"I prefer to be discreet rather than announce my presence to the whole village. I am here to help you. You called for me."

"Ah, you are the... lady from Cisco."

The woman nodded.

"Please come in, Signora...?"

She stepped over the threshold. "My name doesn't matter. What does is that I see the patient as soon as possible, if he's indeed afflicted with the Eye. Tell me his symptoms."

The *signadora* removed her shawl while Valeria told her.

"It's as I thought. I have seen this malady before. I must warn you: once the Eye has taken hold, it isn't easy to cast it out. Take me to the patient."

A flurry of nerves rippled through Valeria. She hadn't told Santucci about the *signadora's* impending visit, since she was afraid he might refuse to see her. He believed in God, but she knew he was less attached to what he called 'ignorant superstitions'. Even so, he was now so ill that surely he would grasp at any possibility.

She led the way to the bedroom. Santucci was half-sitting up in bed, his face shiny with sweat. He pulled the covers up to his chin and raised his eyebrows at Valeria.

"Santucci, this lady may be able to help you. She knows certain… procedures that can work in cases like yours."

The *signadora* unpacked her basket and laid out a deep plate and an oil lamp on the bedside table.

"Fetch me a taper to light the lamp, and a jug of cold water."

"Oh, but there's already a lamp here."

"I prefer to use my own. You'll see why."

"What's all this?" Santucci said. "What can you do for me that my wife and the physician couldn't?"

"If you're afflicted with the Eye, as I believe, the only way for you to return to health is to cast it out," the woman said. "You do believe in God, I take it?"

Santucci nodded. "How can the Eye have got in? Someone must have put this curse on me, and I'm not aware of any enemies."

The woman raised a finger. "Not always. The Eye can slip in if you feel out of sorts, or if someone has admired or praised you without invoking God in the same breath. This draws the Eye's attention to your good fortune, which it will destroy. It preys on those who are favoured."

Valeria hurried to find the items the *signadora* had asked for. The woman lit the lamp and poured water into the plate. She made the sign of the cross over it three times, and cast nine drops of hot olive oil from the lamp into the water, muttering inaudible words at the same time. She frowned and stirred the water with her finger several times.

"It is the Eye. The drops of oil don't merge together. This shows the Eye is present, and won't be cast out until they do."

Valeria looked into the dish. The oil had spread out in

small globules over the water. She glanced at Santucci, whose eyes widened as if he looked on Death itself.

"How are you going to get rid of it?" he said.

"I must repeat the procedure until it works."

The woman made the sign of the cross and poured the oil into the water again and again. Each time, she breathed out and started afresh. Deep lines appeared on her forehead, and she squeezed her eyes shut when she repeated the incantations and pushed the oil drops with her finger. At last, she exhaled and showed Valeria the plate. In the centre was a compact globule. Valeria closed her eyes and relaxed her clenched fists.

"It's gone, by the grace of God. Now you are free of the Eye. You'll sleep, and after that you will feel better."

Santucci heaved a deep sigh and settled down in the bed. Valeria found it hard to believe this rite could work, but it had saved people whom others had given up for lost. She led the woman down to the hallway, and the *signadora* wrapped the shawl around her shoulders.

"What do I owe you for your help?"

"Nothing. I never accept payment. If you have some ewe's milk cheeses, I'll take one to eat on my way home. Send for me again if you are ever in trouble."

She left the house clutching her basket and disappeared the way she had come. Valeria went upstairs and found Santucci asleep, his breathing regular and even. She stood for a moment and watched him, then went down to the kitchen, where she lowered herself onto a chair by the table, bone tired, too numb to think.

CHAPTER 9

Following the *signadora's* visit, Santucci rallied. He slept for twelve hours after she left, and said he felt refreshed when he woke.

"I've never believed in that superstitious nonsense, but now I think there might be something in it. I feel much better."

Valeria's spirits rose and she prepared a small meal, which Santucci ate with relish. Maybe the *signadora's* spell had worked.

"It's a long time since I enjoyed food so much."

She smiled and put a hand on his arm. "It won't be long before you can enjoy all your favourite dishes again."

For three days, Santucci's recovery continued. He rose in the morning, dressed and went about his business, although he still felt tired and rarely left the house. "It's a miracle," he said.

On the fourth day, Valeria was preparing food in the kitchen when Santucci shouted in the corridor.

"Valeria! Help me!"

She bolted from the kitchen to find Santucci on his knees

on the flagstones clutching his stomach. A dark brown and red stain bloomed over his breeches and spotted onto the stone slabs. The smell made her gag. The Eye. It had come back; or maybe it never left and lurked inside, waiting for the chance to strike again. The *signadora's* magic wasn't strong enough.

"Oh God, help me," he whispered.

Valeria tried to help him to stand, but he was too heavy and toppled onto his side. He gripped his abdomen and whimpered like a child. His shirt was stained from the blood spots on the floor, and still the patch on his breeches spread.

"I'll find someone, Santucci. Don't worry, I'll soon be back." She smoothed his hair away from his eyes, but he gritted his teeth and moaned.

She tugged open the door and ran into the alley. Who could she ask for help? Their elderly neighbours would be no use at all. In the square, filling her jug at the fountain, was her neighbour from the opposite house, Signora Rossi, who had a husband and sons. Valeria was reluctant to ask for her help, since she distrusted the woman, but she had no choice.

"Please, Signora, it's my husband. He's collapsed and I need help to get him to bed. I'm afraid he may be dying." Valeria panted like a cornered animal.

The woman frowned and put down the pitcher. She took Valeria by the shoulders and shook her a little.

"I'll fetch my husband and sons and they'll come and help. Go back to your house and wait for them."

Valeria nodded, unable to speak, and then turned and ran home.

"People are coming to help. You won't have to wait long." Santucci was still and made no sound. Valeria held her breath. She put a hand on his wasted chest and felt his heartbeat, but its rhythm was feeble and uneven. She took his hands between hers and rubbed them to get warmth and life into them.

A short time later, Signore Rossi and his three sons burst through the doorway. They pulled up short when they saw Santucci lying in his own blood, and covered their mouths. It took the four of them to lift him, for his frame was still bulky even if it carried little flesh after months of illness, and they manoeuvred him upstairs with difficulty.

"My wife has gone to see if she can find the physician. He was in the village earlier, but I'm afraid he may have left and ridden onwards. We don't know where he's gone."

Valeria pressed her hands together. "Thank you, Signore, for coming to help so fast. I don't know what to do. My husband's very ill and nothing seems to work."

"Then you must pray. I'll send my wife to you."

All night and the next morning, Valeria and Signora Rossi kept vigil by Santucci's bedside. Valeria opened the window to air the room, but the odour of sickness lingered. Santucci was unconscious, which Valeria felt was a blessing. At least he was out of pain. A strong painkilling infusion of herbs stood ready on the bedside table.

At last, his eyelids flickered and he looked at Valeria. She reached for his hand, which was cold as stone. He opened his mouth but she couldn't hear his words. She leant closer.

"Get the priest," he whispered.

"It's much too soon, Santucci. You'll get better and live for many years."

His brow furrowed. "Get the priest. I know I'm dying."

A chasm opened. He was right, and there was no more she could do for him.

"Very well, I'll do what you say. Do you have any pain now?"

"A little, yes."

"Drink this. It will calm the pains. Signora, could you help me to lift him, please?"

Signora Rossi came to the other side of the bed and, with infinite care, they raised Santucci a little. After he had drunk some of the liquid, he waved it away and they laid him back down. The neighbour lifted the beaker and sniffed it.

"What was it you made him drink? It smells very bitter to me."

"It's a powerful infusion that takes away pain. Now I will go for the priest as he asked. Would you stay with him in the meantime?"

Signora Rossi nodded, took up her place on a chair and folded her hands. Santucci had subsided into unconsciousness again.

Thank God the priest was at home. Santucci had woken again, and his face relaxed when the priest came in bearing the holy oils. It was not too late. Valeria and her neighbour withdrew but stayed outside the door, and the priest's murmurs, mingled with Santucci's barely audible responses, wafted from the room. At last, the priest finished and beckoned them in.

"He has made his confession and received extreme unction. It is a good death and I don't think it will be long now. Courage, my daughter."

Valeria nodded and bent her head when the priest made the sign of the cross over the dying man. She still wore the dress spotted with Santucci's blood, but hadn't the energy to change it and did not want to leave him. Signora Rossi showed the priest out and returned to continue the vigil.

Santucci lingered throughout the day and passed in and out of consciousness, but he no longer recognised her. Valeria held his hand all the time, and her thoughts turned to their life together. When she arrived there on her wedding day, she felt very little except hollowness. She didn't know

Santucci, and had no idea what awaited her in a house and a village that were not her own. Over the years she had developed a strong respect for her husband, and they settled into a kind of companionship. Each knew their role and their place. She appreciated Santucci for the man he was, but love was not there on her side. She could not expect to love a man she hadn't chosen herself, and her wishes in the matter of her husband were irrelevant. The arrangement was a family, not a personal, one.

Unbidden, Colonna's piercing blue eyes came to mind for a moment. What would her life have been like if she had married a man like him? She reproached herself. He was a shepherd, and he was beneath her, even if he bore himself like a nobleman. Even so, it sent a tremor through her knowing she might have to deal with him once Santucci was dead.

A change in Santucci's breathing brought her back from this reverie. It became more laboured and his breath rasped. His ribcage rose and sank, but the gap lengthened between each breath. At last, his chest heaved once, twice, and was still. His head turned sideways and his hand slipped from Valeria's grasp.

"I think he's dead," she said and bowed her head, but no tears would come.

Signora Rossi's face fell and she turned away. She crossed herself and moved to the other side of the room to close the window.

"God rest his soul," she said, her voice quivering, and dashed tears from her eyes.

***

Santucci was buried in the family vault in the cemetery outside Zaronza overlooking the bay. Valeria counted the dark days of her widowhood, and her life stretched before her, cold and barren. She would remain housebound for at least three months, as was the custom, and wear her widow's black for years, maybe for the rest of her life. That was bearable, but the chilly sentence of loneliness wore her down. She had not loved Santucci, but she missed him more than she could ever have believed possible.

Signora Rossi sometimes sat with her and they sewed before the fire, like two old crones. Valeria caught the woman staring at her a few times, and a niggling sense of discomfort lodged itself in her spine. Her neighbour smiled and turned to her mending again, and the moment passed.

Valeria expected little sympathy from most of her family, and received none from her mother.

"It's quite right you should grieve for the appointed period. It's what everyone expects. A woman in your position shouldn't go about alone, even when the three months are up. Many widows would give anything to be as fortunate as you. You have a house, you're comfortable, and above all you're respected. Don't forget I had much less than you when your father died. I can't see what you have to look so miserable about."

Valeria said nothing. Mother would not understand, or would choose not to. Anyway, she benefited from Valeria's position as the widow of a wealthy and respected man. Valeria made sure her relatives wanted for nothing, but despite the loneliness she had no desire to see them, except for Antone. He was the light on her dark horizon. Now a muscular man of nineteen, he was taller than his brother, as she had predicted. Since the episode with the Lecas' goat he had settled down, and Pietro seldom had the opportunity to punish him. At least Antone came to see her as often as he could. He strode over the hills and sometimes brought her a rabbit or a hunk of wild boar he had shot himself.

Now and then he reminisced about his childhood

exploits, and his face twisted when he talked about Pietro's cruelty that was so disproportionate to the offences. More often, they talked of the future – or rather of his future, since she had no right to envisage one for herself.

"You've grown into a strong, handsome man, little brother. Soon it will be time for you to marry and start a family. I bet the village girls vie for your attentions, even if they can't be open about it."

A tide of crimson rose up Antone's cheeks.

"Is there one in particular?" She smiled.

"There might be, but you know what Mother and Pietro are like. They want me to marry an heiress from Cisco. I'm sure I won't have any say in it once Mother starts to talk to them."

Valeria nodded. There was no room for personal emotions in these arrangements. The family always came first.

"What other news do you have from Felicavo or beyond? How's Margherita?"

"Well, she's blind now and stays at home, but apart from that she doesn't change much. Some people help her and bring her food. I take her game from time to time. In fact, she's taught me a thing or two about herbs. She always asks after you. She asked me to pass on her sympathies on Santucci's death."

Valeria had judged it prudent not to tell anyone, not even Antone, about her secret visit to Felicavo and the *signadora's* attempt to heal Santucci. Her efforts had been a failure, and she resolved to turn her back on that type of magic, which some took to be witchcraft. It had done nothing for Santucci except to kindle false hopes. Even so, the incident with Margherita and the sheep's bone came back to her with renewed clarity.

She pushed the thoughts away. "What else is going on? I

70

see so little of people I might as well be in a nunnery. My neighbour speaks only of her family or of the village folk."

"There's talk of another levy of the militia and, if it's true I may be called this time along with Pietro. We hear so many conflicting rumours in Felicavo it's hard to separate what's true from what isn't."

"They can't take both of you, can they?"

Antone shrugged. "I don't see why not. The Paolis need all the fighting men they can get. Anyway, it's time we did something instead of sitting back and letting some foreign country tell us what to do. This is the chance for Corsica to be independent of its masters. They say even the shepherds will come down from the hills to fight."

Her chin jerked upwards. In her grief for Santucci, she had not been able to prevent the image of Colonna from working its way into her thoughts. She drove it away each time, but could never banish it for good. She had not seen the shepherd for months, since before Santucci's death. Some of the herdsmen came down from the mountains, and hovered in the background at the funeral, but Valeria was too sealed off within herself to notice. During her seclusion, she arranged for a neighbour to deal with her shepherd, take the produce from the flock and pay him his wages. There was no reason for her to see him.

"I do hope they won't call you, Antone. You aren't trained soldiers and the Genoese are. How can you hope to win against them with a few guns?"

"We're fighting for our freedom, which makes us brave. They aren't and they're following orders. It means little to them."

She remained silent, but had a vision of Antone lying broken and bloody on a smoke-shrouded battlefield.

71

CHAPTER 10

Zaronza: January 1762

The months dragged by. Valeria spent her time sewing, talking with the few neighbours who came to see her, and counting the days between Antone's visits. The large, stark house was so empty without Santucci. He had filled it with his personality, even when he was ill. His presence was almost real at times, above all in the living room, his former domain. She preferred to remain in the kitchen rather than light the fire in the other room.

She sat by the hearth and watched the glow of the embers. The vivid colours of the *machja* came to her as she relived the day of her wedding. The brighter moments were shot through with darker memories of Santucci's illness, the *signadora's* ritual and his final hours. She forced herself to ignore the blue eyes that came unbidden to her mind so often. Maybe her loneliness was the punishment for lingering on them, for allowing herself to wonder how life might have been with another man. No man at all was the price to pay. Margherita always claimed she had seen nothing in the sheep's bone, but perhaps she had caught a glimpse of this grey, desolate existence.

"I doubt if you can hear me, Santucci, but it's so lonely here without you. If only I could bring you back and we could live as we did before. Won't I ever know warmth and affection again? I'm twenty-six. Do I have to wear black all my life?"

Following her period of seclusion, she was able to go out again. Even so, her life was reduced to a small space. She rarely ventured beyond the fountain, the square and the church. Going into the *machja* to collect herbs was out of the question. In any case, what need did she have of them now? She retained the knowledge, but not the desire to use it.

The rapping of the door knocker made Valeria jump and exclaim. She didn't expect anyone to call. She tightened her shawl against the January evening's chill and went out into the hallway. The door jammed on the flagstones, as usual. Santucci had never had it seen to, and she didn't have the spirit. When she looked up from wrenching it open, her heart turned over.

"Oh, it's you." She brought a hand to her mouth. "I'm sorry, I didn't expect a visitor. You startled me."

Colonna removed his woollen hat and gave a small bow. "Forgive me, Signora. I didn't mean to alarm you. I went to Respighi as usual with the produce, but no one answered the door, so I decided to come and give it straight to you. I understand your seclusion is long over now, so I assumed it would be alright to do so."

Valeria thought fast. The light was fading, and she didn't know who might have seen the shepherd on his way to her door. A woman's reputation could be tarnished for less. It wouldn't be wise to invite him over the threshold.

"Thank you for bringing me the products, Signore

Colonna."

She held out a hand for the sack, which Colonna swung off his shoulder. Valeria placed it on the flagstones.

"Please wait here while I fetch your wages."

"As you wish, Signora." He nodded, but she noted his stony glare. It was too bad; she wouldn't ask him in. His behaviour was less than respectful to his master's widow. His arrogance was overwhelming, but everyone said the shepherds spent so much time on the mountainsides they lost all notions of good manners. They were their own masters, and behaved like nobles even though they were savages.

Her fingers touched his when she placed the coins in his outstretched palm. She snatched back her hand as if scalded, but recovered herself and glared back at him.

"Please send me word when you next plan to visit, Signore Colonna."

He said nothing, but jammed his hat on his head, turned on his heel and strode off into the gathering darkness. Valeria stood on the threshold for a moment. Signora Rossi was fetching water at the fountain, and turned at Colonna's resounding footsteps. Valeria closed the door with a bang. How dare he behave like that? He had been her husband's shepherd, and now he was hers.

Valeria's fingers tingled where they had brushed against his palm, and she plunged her hand into cold water. Clattering the plate and cutlery about, she prepared a light meal, but it was like chewing raw chestnuts. In one movement, she lifted the jug and threw it with all her strength. It smashed against the wall and the shards chinked on the floor. A trail of water darkened the whitewash.

"No. I won't give in. Not to him."

She rushed upstairs and dragged off her clothes. She turned from side to side, but sleep took a long time to claim her. When at last it did, the dream came again and Valeria awoke with a bitter taste on her tongue.

***

A month passed before Colonna visited again. This time, he sent word beforehand.

"The snow lasted longer than usual this year," he said. "Even on the lower slopes, the pasture is scarce. The ewes haven't given as much milk as usual, so there are fewer cheeses."

He had dark rings beneath his eyes and was thinner than before. Valeria's spine prickled. She couldn't leave him on the threshold, like last time. His arrogance had disappeared.

"You'd better come in. I'll make you something to eat. It's cold for the time of year; the wind is from the north."

The living room or the kitchen? A fire burned in the latter, but it was too homely, too intimate. No, the living room. She would have to light the fire, but it was more suitable to receive him in there.

Once the kindling had caught, she turned to him. He stood in the doorway, his eyes on her. "Please come and sit near the fire. It will soon warm up."

He swept off his woollen hat and strode across the room. His foot brushed against the hem of her skirt, and it was as if a bolt of lightning had shot through her. She shook herself and hurried to the kitchen, where she splashed cold water on her face.

When she returned with food, the room was warmer and the glow of the firelight cut through the gloom. Colonna warmed his hands at the fire and smiled at her. She placed the dish on the table next to him and stood back.

"Please, eat."

"Won't you eat something, too?"

"No, I ate before you arrived."

He nodded and tore off a piece of bread. He wiped the plate with the remaining crust and drained the last of the wine from the cup. He must have been hungry. Again, a stab of guilt pierced her.

"I needed that."

He smiled and his eyes crinkled at the corners. Her stomach contracted, and she turned and busied herself with the empty plate and cup. For a while, neither of them spoke.

"Some time has passed since your husband's death, God rest his soul, but I've never offered you my sympathies. He was a good man and a fair one. I never had cause to complain of him. Some men treat their shepherds far less well than he did."

She swallowed. During his last visit, she made him stand on the doorstep and didn't invite him in, so he had had no chance to say much at all before she dismissed him. Maybe she had misjudged him. Moving a chair closer to the fire, she sat down and looked into it.

"Yes, he was a good man, and he treated me well and with respect. I wish he were still here. Now, I must try to take his place." She looked up. "How long were you my husband's shepherd?"

"About ten years. Before that, I had my own flock, but they caught the black illness and there was no remedy, so they were killed, every one. A man must eat, so I sought employment, but I only knew how to tend the flocks and make cheese. No one wanted a farmhand." He fingered the long scar on his face. "Then I heard Signore Santucci was looking for a shepherd. The previous one decided he was too old and went down south to live with a relative. I took the job; I had no choice."

"And... how is it to live up there in the hills?"

"It's a hard life but a good one, provided you're fit and healthy. The sheepfolds are basic, but you get a roof over

76

your head and the company of the other shepherds."

"What do you do all day?"

He smiled. "We're never idle. There are the flocks to tend, the lambing to keep an eye on, sick sheep to cure, milking to be done in the evening, cheese to make, shearing, and fleeces to cure. In the evenings, we tell each other stories and sing."

"Where do you live in the winter? It must be too cold up there."

"We take the flocks down to the lower pastures. I have a small house in Oresta that belonged to my mother."

"I'm sorry for all the questions. I hope you don't mind, but I'm curious to know how you live." Her cheeks burned. "You don't have a wife...?"

His brow darkened, and the light went out of his eyes. He rubbed the scar again. "No. Few women want a shepherd who's away in the hills for much of the year. I wanted to marry a girl from my village, but someone else got her in the end. She found it more important to have a husband around all the time. I heard he beats her. She chose her bed." He shrugged and looked away.

"I shouldn't have asked. It's none of my business." The day was gloomy, and the sole light in the room was the fire. It cast a glow over his sharp features. She looked back into the fire, and the image of Margherita and the sheep's bone came to her.

"Could you tell me something? Do you believe one can tell someone's future using a sheep's shoulder blade?"

"Oh yes. I've even seen it done once, by an old shepherd who lived in my village, but he came from the Niolu. Few people have the gift, as far as I know, but it seems to work. He did it at the request of a pregnant woman who wanted to know if her baby would be born healthy."

"What happened?"

"As the bone predicted, the child was a boy and he lived, but he was a hunchback."

Valeria drew her shawl tighter around her. The room grew cold, and Margherita's pale face and knitted brow appeared in the flickering fire. She blinked, and the image was gone.

"Is something wrong, Signora? You've gone pale."

"No, it's nothing. It's just your story, that's all. Did the man read the bone often?"

"He stopped after that incident. People said it brought bad luck, and since he came from outside the village, he was afraid he would be shunned. I don't think the bone caused the baby to be born deformed, but it did predict what would happen. You can't fight your destiny."

A shudder ran up Valeria's backbone. Her fortune was to be a wealthy man's widow, nothing more, condemned to live without companionship or love. Whatever Margherita had seen in the bone – if she had seen anything at all – could only have been that. What else could there have been?

Colonna coughed. "I should leave now, Signora. I've already stayed longer than I intended, and dusk will soon fall." He stood up. "Thank you for the food and for your talk. We lack the company of woman up there, and we've become coarse and brutish for it."

"I hope you'll forgive my curiosity," she said. "I get so few chances to talk to anyone other than my neighbours or my younger brother, who visits me when he can get away. I hear so little of what goes on elsewhere."

He inclined his head a little, and her throat closed up. It would be so good to run her hands through his thick, black hair. No, she mustn't think like that. She let him out, and waited behind the heavy door while his tread receded down the alley. Colonna – Benedettu – had the other shepherds for company, but his life was as lonely as hers and he had his own misfortunes. She had been so wrapped up in hers that she couldn't see past them.

Valeria went into the kitchen, where she banked up the fire, and then stood and gazed into it. She was sliding down the slope from attraction into a more complicated emotion.

***

Winter turned to spring, and Valeria found she looked forward to Benedettu's visits, now fortnightly as the ewes gave more milk. Each time, she gave him food and they sat by the fire and talked, but she always made sure he left before dusk. Even so, the nagging unease at what her neighbours might think wouldn't go away.

During a pause in their conversation, Benedettu often touched the scar that stretched down his face.

"You'll think I'm prying again," Valeria said. "But I've been wondering how you got that scar."

He looked up and his face twisted.

"You don't have to tell me if it's a painful memory."

"It is, but I don't mind telling you."

The firelight flickered over his weathered face. He leant forward, hands clasped around his knees.

"When I heard that Lucia, the girl I wanted to marry, was betrothed, I was mad with wounded pride. I confronted her intended – I can't bear to say his name – in the square, but before I could do anything, he pulled out a knife and attacked me."

He pointed to the scar. "This is the result."

Valeria drew in a sharp breath.

"I was going to strike back, but the other men grabbed and held us. I swore I'd kill him one day. I might still do it, but I can wait. My house is on the other side of the village from theirs, and we avoid each other. They're unhappy together. That's a fitting punishment for now."

Valeria swallowed. What a contradiction this man was: in some ways so sensitive, and in others so proud. His village was no different from Felicavo, where ancient feuds simmered for generations. Violence always lurked close to the surface, and when pride was injured it broke through. His bad luck was no fault of his, and it had hardened him, but beneath the shell she glimpsed another man. A knot of sympathy uncoiled. She wanted to hold him and smooth the scar. What would be so wrong in that?

Instead she looked into his eyes. The shadow veiling them lifted, and his expression softened. Her skin tingled.

"I'm sorry. I won't mention it anymore. Now, tell me again about the cheese-making."

CHAPTER 11

The late spring weather was more like August than May. The heat built up for several days before it broke in violent storms that cleared the air before the pattern repeated itself. The air was too still to allow a draught to circulate through the house. Leaving all the shutters and windows open made it even hotter. One day, the temperature was more oppressive than usual, and as evening drew on leaden clouds banked up over the mountains.

Not long after nightfall, the first crash of thunder sounded overhead and echoed around the hills. Heavy drops spattered against the shutters and drummed on the roof in a continuous roar. Bursts of light flashed through the gaps in the slats, and the temperature dropped. She would need to light a fire, but most of the wood was piled outside.

Above the beating of rain and the crack of thunder, a deeper knocking sounded. Maybe a shutter was banging in the wind, but the sound was too regular. Someone was pounding at the door.

"Forgive me, Signora." The rain had flattened Benedettu's hair, and rivulets of water streamed down his face. As usual, his eyes were as disturbing; so different from other men's. "May I come in?"

A strong gust snatched his words away, and a flurry of icy water seeped through her dress to the skin in seconds. He couldn't be left outside in such weather. The wretched door caught as usual on the raised flagstones, but closed at last against the wind. What was he doing there on such a night?

"I'm sorry to disturb you. I was on my way from Pietranera when the storm broke."

"I didn't expect visitors on such a night, I admit. Didn't you have anywhere else to go?"

"There isn't so much as a shepherd's hut to shelter in on the lower slopes. I tried to take refuge behind a wall, but I was soon soaked through, and the wind took my hat. I was afraid for my gun, too."

She touched her hair. He would think her improper without her headscarf, which lay up in the bedroom.

"Don't you know someone else in Zaronza who could have given you shelter?"

"I don't mix much with village folk. They don't always welcome us, and say our flocks damage their lands, but they don't do much to stop them coming in. I couldn't think of anywhere else to go." He shrugged and opened his hands.

They couldn't stand there in the hallway talking for ever, both of them in wet clothes, but the situation was very awkward. A man visiting a widow at night would be taken to mean only one thing. Perhaps no one had seen him arrive. It would be unusual for her neighbours to be out in such weather, but it took more than that to deter prying eyes. Some liked nothing more than to find cause for scandal and dishonour, even when there was none.

"You'd better come into the kitchen and dry off."

He laid down his gun and shrugged out of his wet jerkin. The kitchen was cold and dark, and a chill air rose from the

82

flagstones.

"Since my husband died I don't often use the living room when I'm alone. I prefer to sit in the warmth here when the fire is lit. I have a few logs indoors. The rest are outside in the wood store. We'll have to make do for the moment."

The fire caught at last, and the warmth and glow chased the dark shadows into the corners of the room. Benedettu shivered.

"You'd better change out of those wet clothes, and hang them near the fire. I'll find a shirt and breeches of my husband's for you to put on, and I must change my dress, too. In the meantime, here's a sheet I've been mending. I suggest you dry off and wrap yourself in it."

Her dress had a dark patch on the front where the rain had blown in through the open door. It wasn't a night for a dog to be out, and she couldn't turn him away. He worked for her, after all. But if he hadn't been out in the storm near Zaronza, she wouldn't be in this difficult position. He also had a duty to her, to preserve her honour, if only out of respect for Santucci. The villagers held Santucci in high esteem, which extended to her, even after his death, but it would not take much to destroy that regard. Benedettu made her ache with longing, but she had to snuff out her desire, like a candle.

In the hallway, the flagstones were slippery with damp. The only brightness came from the glow of the fire under the kitchen door and the streaks of lightning through the gaps in the shutters. The beating of the rain on the roof was steadier, and the thunder rolled away into the distance over the cape.

He sat with his back to the kitchen door, swathed in the sheet like a ghost or a body in a shroud. She thought of Santucci on his deathbed.

"I've found you some dry clothes."

Benedettu jumped and started up from the chair. He clutched the sheet around him.

"I didn't hear you come in. I was dozing by the fire. Forgive me. It's been a hard day and the warmth made me sleepy."

"I'm sorry I startled you, but you must put these clothes on before you catch cold. Santucci was shorter than you, and so I'm afraid the breeches won't fit you well, but he was broad in the chest and the shirt should be better. While you do that, I'll go and fetch some more logs, since the storm's dying away."

It was disturbing to know he was naked under the sheet. If she went outside for wood it would put some distance between them. Maybe the cold raindrops would help to calm this burning hunger.

He crossed the room to her, clasping the sheet around him. "Valeria," he said. His touch on her arm was like lightning.

"How do you know my name?" As if it were relevant, but the shock of his fingers shot up her forearm.

"Does it matter? What are names between us, anyway? You know as well as I do that we noticed each other on the day of your wedding and knew one another. I found it hard for a woman like you to have to marry the master, God rest his soul." He crossed himself. "Now I find it even harder that you must shut yourself away like a nun because he's dead. It's not right."

His grip tightened.

"Whether it's right or wrong isn't for us to judge", she said. "It's the custom; what people expect. I'm the widow of a respectable man, and my life and what I can and can't do are fixed by that. I've been foolish enough allowing you to come into my house tonight, and you shouldn't take advantage of it. Who knows what the neighbours think

84

already, if they saw you arrive earlier?"

"I'd never ask you to do anything you didn't want to do, but are you willing to deny yourself warmth and love for the rest of your life? As for the neighbours, I didn't see anyone. They wouldn't venture out in this storm."

This was unbearable. His words were persuasive. Love and warmth would be like sunshine and water to a sick plant, but everything was against this: their place in society, private disapproval and public condemnation. The family's reaction would be harsh, but why should anyone be denied the right to love where they wished? Widows with many more years in them had to bow to what others wanted, show themselves in public as little as possible, and deprive themselves of life. Following her heart carried the risk of punishment; following her head would preserve her family's reputation but maintain this arid life. It was a terrible choice. If Santucci were still alive, none of this would have happened.

The dazzling beam of Benedettu's eyes was stronger than ever, and the pressure of his hand overwhelming. No, loneliness was not a choice. She put her hand over his.

"Come with me."

They mounted the stairs. "In here." It wouldn't be right to be together in the bedroom she had shared with Santucci. That room contained too many memories, and maybe even the spirit of her husband himself.

The spare bedroom was fireless and chilly, but it didn't matter. His hands were rough and calloused from his hard life in the mountains, but they were of a surprising gentleness. Every nerve tingled when he ran his hands over her thighs and his fingers slipped between her legs. She abandoned herself to sensations Santucci had never been able to arouse.

Later, Benedettu's chest rose and fell in time with his

breathing, and he had flung one arm over the side of the bed. The sharp scent of his body filled the room.

Aching from their repeated lovemaking, Valeria lay awake. The cold reality of what she had done seeped in.

"Forgive me, Santucci," she whispered, "I was so lonely, but it's your fault. You died and left me here alone. Did you expect me to stay unloved for the rest of my life?"

They would have to be careful. The risks of discovery were great, and the consequences unthinkable. Brooding on the future wouldn't do any good. The present would have to be enough. When sleep came at last, the nightmare was even more vivid than usual. Under the onslaught of the wind, the trees writhed and creaked, something evil lay in wait out of sight, and then the acrid taste overwhelmed everything else.

***

A fortnight later, Benedettu came during the day. People were about in Zaronza, filling jugs at the fountain or sitting at their thresholds taking the sun. A snatched kiss behind the door was the only comfort. He delivered the produce, took his wages and left after a few minutes. Giving him money was a strange situation: whatever else had happened, they were still employer and servant. Nothing had changed there, above all as far as the outside world was concerned.

"I want you to stay with me, and I wish you could come more often," Valeria said. "But we must be careful. If you change your habits, people will notice. What can we do, Benedettu? What will happen to us?"

"Don't you think I want to see you too? It's hard to keep away, but shepherds are supposed to bide their flocks on the hills in the summer, not visit beautiful widows. We have to be content with what we have. It can never be more than this. We both know that."

Yes, she would have to make do with whatever

happiness she could grasp, now that she had made her choice. There could be no question of their marrying; no one would approve of it, least of all Mother and Pietro, not after she had been married to one of the richer landowners in the area. She and Benedettu had crossed a line, and were condemned to a life of secrets and concealment for as long as they could get away with it.

Even so, they grasped any opportunity to see each other. To meet Benedettu on the hillside outside the village from time to time was difficult, but possible if she took precautions. Now the period of seclusion had ended, she could appear in Zaronza again and venture beyond.

"Where are you going with your basket, Signora?" Signora Rossi always appeared when she heard the front door open and close. She must have lurked behind her own door, watching and waiting. It was time to deal with those flagstones, or have the door planed and re-hung. The woman was a busybody, and even though her lips smiled there was something devious about her hooded eyes.

"I thought I'd go a little way up into the hills behind the village. When I lived in Felicavo before I was married, an elderly woman taught me how to use *machja* herbs in medicine and cooking. Since I have so much time on my hands, I'd like to start again, before I forget what I know. Maybe my remedies could be useful to people in Zaronza."

Signora Rossi pursed her lips. "I don't know anything about using herbs like that, although my grandmother swore by them. The potions you gave your husband when he was so ill didn't seem to bring him back to health. I daresay you know more about all this than I do."

"Some people reach a stage where they are beyond help. I'm afraid it was like that for my husband. He had the wasting sickness, and the infusions I gave him couldn't cure him, but they took away his pain at the end, God rest his

87

soul."

The woman's eyes glinted. "I've heard, Signora, that some people call on sorceresses to cast out the Eye when they believe there's no other course. They also say some of these women are *mazzere*, too. By day they do good, but at night they're dream-hunters, and cause the death of those they see in their dreams."

What had her neighbour heard or seen? The *signadora* was discreet, and no one could have known of her visit. The people of Zaronza were not familiar with her, since she came from Cisco, and so she could have been visiting for any reason.

Valeria shrugged, but struggled to prevent her voice shaking. "I don't know anything about casting out the Eye, although I've heard of cases where it has been done. As for *mazzeri*, people told tales of them in Felicavo, but I don't know any. Please excuse me, I must gather my herbs before dusk falls."

A couple of snatched hours on the hillside, well away from the villagers' terraced vegetable gardens, were all she and Benedettu could hope for. She made sure to fill her basket with herbs. It wouldn't do to return to Zaronza empty-handed. Signora Rossi was filling her jug at the well and speaking to another village woman. They must have talked about Valeria, since their eyes followed her while she crossed the square.

"You gathered a good basketful I see, Signora?"

"Yes. I got everything I wanted." Why couldn't the woman leave her alone? What harm did she do, anyway? People committed far worse crimes every day, if falling in love were a crime in reality. Of course, it was unpardonable if you were a widow and your lover was your social inferior.

***

Food became unappetising; the smell of goat's milk or cheese made Valeria gag. Maybe she was sickening for something. Not the wasting sickness; no, its symptoms were not the same, and she hadn't lost weight. Perhaps it was the summer heat, which bore down on Zaronza and made everyone irritable. Dogs lay and panted in the shade. Women cursed their children for raising the dust. The water from the fountain took on a rusty colour and a metallic taste.

Valeria sat on the fountain's hard stone border. She waited for her turn and willed the nausea to subside.

"It hasn't been so hot since we buried my grandfather," said an old woman enveloped in black. "I've never seen the water this colour before."

"Maybe the Eye has got into it," another said. "We shouldn't drink the water in case it gets into us, too." She put down her pitcher and peered into it.

"That's not how it works, Signora. You don't get the Eye from what you eat or drink, but from someone who casts a spell on you. It's just the drought."

Valeria stood and took her turn, her legs shaking.

"Do you feel ill, Signora? You look very pale."

"I expect it's the heat, and maybe I've eaten something that didn't agree with me. I'm sure it will pass. Standing here in the hot sun won't help."

Why was the jug as heavy as a stone? Why was it so hard to put one foot in front of the other? After that, black dots merged together and there was nothing.

Something flapped in her face and her cheeks were wet. A hard object pressed into her back.

"She's coming round at last. Can you hear me, Signora?"

Bright light, the sun beating down, and a ravaged face close to hers.

"What happened?"

"You fainted away in front of us, Signora Santucci.

You've been unconscious for a minute or so. You looked very pale just before it happened. I'm sorry, we sprinkled water on your face and your dress is wet."

What was happening? She had never fainted in her life, and was always in good health. A siesta would do her good, with the shutters closed, and then she would dose herself with a tisane of Artemisia. It must be a stomach upset. Maybe the lamb she had eaten a couple of days before was bad; it had tasted odd at the time. She had almost thrown it away, but forced herself to eat it.

"I'm quite well now. I'm sorry to have caused you this trouble. I can make my own way back to my house."

"Are you sure, Signora? You're still white, and look as if you've had a shock."

"Yes, please don't worry about me. I'll lie down and I'm sure I will feel much better."

One step, two. She would manage it. Her legs no longer trembled, and the nausea had receded. She nodded at Signora Rossi, who was sweeping the dust from her threshold. The woman smiled back, and the brushing ceased until Valeria had regained her house. Just get inside the door and it will be all right. She forced it shut with her last ounce of strength, turned and slid to the floor, her back against the hard wood.

A day later, she lurched out of bed but didn't reach the washing bowl on the table before the bitter bile splashed onto the floorboards. The lamb must have been even more rancid than it tasted. She wiped her mouth, but dry-retched again into the bowl and then drank a cup of water. The sickness subsided, but a terrible tiredness took her over.

The next day, it happened again.

A cold fist gripped and twisted her gut. Her monthly bleeding had last come more than two months ago. At the time, it didn't seem important, since it had always been irregular. Now, too much time had passed. The lamb wasn't bad, she hadn't eaten anything that disagreed with her, and it wasn't the heat. She was carrying Benedettu's child.

CHAPTER 12

"How could this have happened? We've been so stupid."

Valeria beat her thighs with her fists and sank down on the bed. The sun came up and found its way through the chinks in the shutters, birds called, and leaves rustled in the breeze. Life went on, but for her everything had changed. She had never considered this possibility. When she hadn't been able to give Santucci a child, it must have been because God didn't will it. She was resigned to it, so with Benedettu it had not been a matter of concern. They had been too absorbed in each other, in their mutual loneliness, and this was the price to pay for the desire to live. What was it Margherita had said? "Don't let bright eyes turn your head." It was too late for that now. An image of Delfina hanging from the tree crossed her mind's eye. She had paid the price.

The choices were stark: keep the baby and reveal that she was not the respectable widow everyone thought she was, or do away with it and continue to conceal her relations with Benedettu. She placed a hand on her abdomen. She had so wanted to have children, but not like this, not when she couldn't marry the father. Maybe they could go away together, but where? Wherever they went, someone would find them, and people would be suspicious of a strange couple turning up in a village. Perhaps they could go to the mainland instead, Italy or France, but it would mean leaving Corsica forever, and Benedettu would find it hard to get work elsewhere. She had a little money, but she would have to leave her house and land behind. No, that wasn't the answer. They would end up resenting their exile and hating each other.

The alternative was terrible, but she had to consider it. The ewes knew when they carried a dead or deformed lamb, and grazed on poisonous plants to get rid of it. The same herbs could make a woman lose a baby.

"There's no one I can talk to here. Margherita could help me, but I would have to go to see her in Felicavo."

Benedettu was in the hills, and he could do little about this in any case. Margherita would know what to do.

When Valeria slipped out of the house in the early afternoon, the sun beat down on her. In the shade by the fountain a dog lay and twitched the flies away. Nothing else moved, and all the houses were shuttered. The terraced fields below Zaronza were empty. The villagers were all at home taking a siesta until the heat abated in the evening.

She crossed the square, pulled her headscarf around her head, and took the stony path on the other side leading up into the hills. In the distance, the sea shone like a jewel and merged into one with the sky on the horizon. The *machja* was scorched brown, and the scent of burnt leaves arose when she brushed against the bushes. Soon, her armpits were clammy and sweat trickled down between her breasts. Climbing the hill in this heat was madness, but at least the path wound between trees from time to time, which provided some shade.

At last, she reached the stream marking the mid-point. When the mountain snows melted in the spring, the torrent stormed over the rocks like stampeding horses. Now, it was a mere silvery trickle, but it had never been known to dry out. She flung herself on her knees and cupped her hands under the spring. The cool water spread through her and she gulped until she could drink no more. Wiping her mouth, she staggered upright and groped for the flat stone that lay nearby. She sat with her back against a tree, its rough bark pressing into her back. That was better. Coming out without water had been foolish, but now she could go on after a short rest.

"What a terrible mess. You know nothing about this, Benedettu, and I have to face it on my own." Behind her eyes the tears pricked, but she dashed them away. This was no time to weaken.

After the stream, the path was less steep and rock-strewn, and the trees on this side of the hill gave more shade. Even so, Valeria's knees quivered, and she had to support herself with the branches to avoid falling. She passed beneath the cork oaks and came upon the little chapel, where she made the sign of the cross by the crude stone monument. Maybe Santa Ghjulia would help her, since she favoured the prayers of women. No, Valeria had committed a sin; the saint's ears would be closed to her. Her head bowed, she went on.

She skirted her mother's house in a wide arc, but the shutters were all closed and nothing moved. Felicavo was as still as Zaronza. Not even a cat prowled in the shadows. A few hens sat in the dust under a bush. The heat pressed down, but the afternoon drew on. People would start to move about again once the sun lost its edge.

Margherita's house was shuttered up, too. Valeria stopped and looked around before she tapped on the door.

No one called from within, so she knocked a little harder. Still nothing. Where was Margherita? Or maybe she had lost her hearing as well as her sight.

She pressed the latch and stepped into the gloom. The room was bare. The shelves, which had once groaned with jars and bottles, were empty. No bunches of herbs hung from the beams to dry. Bed, table, chairs – all were gone – and the grate was cold.

She almost called out, but that was ridiculous. No one was here. What was that in the corner? A pale object caught the light from the door. Valeria bent down and touched it. The sheep's bone. She flinched and shrank back, forcing away the memory of Margherita's pallid face. Her pulse throbbed.

A shadow fell across the floor. She started.

"Why, it's Valeria Peretti. The last time I saw you it was the day you left to get married. I heard about your husband, God rest his soul." A woman crossed herself. "I thought I heard someone in here. What are you doing in Felicavo after all this time?"

Margherita's neighbour was a pleasant enough woman, whom Margherita had helped each time she was pregnant when she suffered with terrible morning sickness. The bitterness of the morning's bile rose again.

"Yes, it's a long time since I was last here. I came to see Margherita, but she's not here and the place is empty. What's happened?"

The woman frowned. "You came in this heat? All the way from Zaronza over the hill? You must have gone mad. No one walks in weather like this."

Valeria took a deep breath. "I had heard Margherita was ill, and I wanted to come and see for myself, in case it was the last time." Her cheeks flushed.

"Well, you're right, she was ill, but you were too late.

Margherita died a good fortnight ago. I'm sorry; I know you used to be close, and she always spoke about you like a daughter."

Valeria pressed her fists to her mouth.

"Oh, no. Please tell me this isn't true. I had so wanted to see her. Why didn't someone send word to me – my brother, Antone? He would have told me."

"You'd better not upset yourself in this heat. Come next door and I'll tell you all about it. You could probably do with a drink of water, too."

Valeria nodded. Her limbs were numb and her strength ebbed away. The idea of seeing Margherita had kept her going all the way up from Zaronza. Now she would have to go back, but first she had to find out what had happened.

She drank the beaker of water her neighbour offered, and accepted another. The numbness drained away and a dull ache replaced it.

"Margherita had been ailing for a year or so," the neighbour said. "She lost her sight and couldn't go onto the hillsides for her plants anymore. She put on a lot of weight and got short of breath, too. Some of us in the village helped her. I took in food from time to time, since she'd always been good to me. Anyway, I went round one day with some eggs and she was lying on the bed. I thought she was asleep, but she wouldn't wake up, and when I touched her she was cold. I expect it was her heart." She shrugged. "Nothing to be done. It comes to us all. She was very old, but nobody knew her age. I'm not even sure she did."

Valeria screwed up her eyes to force back the tears. "I can't believe I was too late. If only I could have seen her before she died."

"I'm sorry. You came all this way for nothing, and on a day like this." The woman gave a sympathetic shrug.

"What about Antone? Why didn't he come to tell me?"

"He's not here for the moment. Went off a month or so ago to join the militia, I understand. Nobody else thought to send you word. After all, she wasn't a relative of yours, and it is a long time since you lived here."

Valeria's heart clenched. Everyone she loved was either dead or elsewhere. Despite the heat and her widow's black, she shivered.

"Is she buried in the cemetery?"

The woman hesitated. "Yes, but there wasn't any money and she had no relatives, so they had to put her by the wall with the stillborns."

Valeria frowned. What an indignity, to be buried in a pauper's grave when Margherita had done nothing but help others all her life. She would make sure she had a proper burial place.

"I must visit her grave before I go home. Thank you for the water and for telling me about Margherita. Would you do something else for me?"

The woman raised her eyebrows.

"Please don't tell my family I was here. I don't think they'd like that I came to see Margherita."

"Well, if that's what you want, I won't be the one to tell them, but it strikes me as a bit odd. You come here in this heatwave but don't visit your own people. I don't think they'd be pleased if they knew. Still, you needn't worry. I can't say I have much reason to talk to your mother or Pietro."

Valeria put her hand on the neighbour's arm. "I'm grateful. Now I must go."

The narrow path was dusty and cracked with drought, and the hem of her dress was filthy by the time she reached the cemetery, but the sun was no longer quite so brutal. She had better not linger too long. She picked a few *machja* flowers and bound them with a thread from her skirt:

rosemary and lavender sprigs and a few wild carnations. The only new grave was a raised mound of soil by the rough stone wall. Someone had fashioned a crude cross from a couple of sticks, but it bore no name.

Valeria knelt, the packed soil and stones digging into her knees, and placed the flowers beneath the cross.

"Why did you have to leave me, Margherita? I can't believe you're dead. What am I going to do now?"

The pent-up tears spilled over and wet her cheeks, and the breath caught in her lungs. She lost track of how much time passed, but the sun was much lower in the sky when she stood at last on stiff legs. Valeria turned away from the grave and shook the earth from her skirt.

"Who's that down there?"

A man stood on the path above, a gun slung over his shoulder. The sun cast a circle of blinding light around him, but she knew the voice. Pietro.

He left the path and strode towards her. "I thought it was you. What are you doing here?"

She hadn't seen him since Santucci's funeral, but he hadn't changed. Valeria hid her shaking hands.

"What kind of a greeting is that, when you haven't seen your sister for so long?"

"As if you care. I asked what you're doing here." He looked around. "Are you on your own? How did you get here, anyway?"

"So many questions, Pietro. Give me a chance to answer them. It's still hot and I'm very tired. I'm going to sit over there in the shade."

She sank onto a stone bench beneath a cypress and fanned her face with her hand. Pietro followed and stood over her.

"Well?"

He was the last person she wanted to see, but she had

better be as truthful as she could.

"I heard Margherita had been ill and I came to see her, but when I got here I found she was already dead. Nobody bothered to tell me."

"Why should we? You always used to spend too much time with her, and she was a bad influence."

She knew her brother was only parroting what he heard from their mother. Despite Pietro's bluster, Mother was in charge.

"She taught me many things, Pietro, and I owe her a lot. She was kind to me and she didn't have anybody else."

"She was a witch. You didn't answer my other questions."

Valeria sighed. "Yes, I'm on my own and I walked over the hill to get here. Is that so strange? I'm old enough to know my way."

Pietro snorted. "I'm not worried about whether you know your way or not. I am concerned about you tramping about over the hills alone. It's hardly proper for a widow in your position. What if someone had seen you? Do you want to bring dishonour on us?"

"What's dishonourable about visiting an old friend on her sickbed?"

Pietro put his hands on his hips. "Everything. You know it's not done to walk about alone. Anyway, you think nothing of visiting some old woman, but did you plan to visit us while you were here?"

The heat rose in her cheeks. "There… there wasn't time. I need to start soon if I'm going to get back to Zaronza."

"You're not going anywhere today. You'd better come with me and explain yourself to Mother. It's too late now to go back to Zaronza."

She shut her eyes, and weariness flowed through her like poison. It had been a mistake to come, but earlier in the day it seemed a risk worth taking. She shouldn't have stayed so long at Margherita's grave.

Pietro led the way up the path and into the village. A few people were about, and one or two nodded to her and then went about their business. The news that the Widow Santucci was in Felicavo would soon spread like a *machja* fire. She bowed her head.

"Look who's here, Mother," Pietro said when he flung open the door. She emerged from the kitchen, wiping her hands, a smile on her face. Her mouth dropped into a straight line when Valeria stepped across the threshold.

"What's all this?" she said. "Why are you here?"

"I found her on her knees in the cemetery, crying over Margherita's grave. I thought I'd better bring her back here rather than having her wander about over the countryside."

Her mother nodded. "I'm surprised at you, Valeria. I can't imagine what people are going to think of us when you roam around on your own like this."

Valeria's bones ached and she longed to sit down, but she stood straight. "I didn't mean to annoy you, Mother, but I wanted to pay a quick visit to Margherita when I heard she was ill."

"You paid that old witch more attention than you ever did to your own family. Anyway, she's dead now, God rest her soul." She mouthed the usual formula, but Valeria suspected she would rather wish Margherita eternal damnation. "Now you're here, you'd better stay overnight and Pietro will take you back to Zaronza in the morning. You can help Quillina in the kitchen."

Her sister-in-law sat at the table chopping tomatoes. She looked up and a wan smile crossed her lips. Dark rings encircled her eyes.

"I'm surprised to see you here, Valeria."

After the explanations, Quillina stood up to find a knife.

Her rounded belly protruded.

"When is your baby due, Quillina?"

"In a few weeks. This time it's more difficult than it was with Isolda. I've been very sick and I feel so tired all the time. This heat doesn't help. I hope it will soon break."

"Here, let me do it. You need to sit down." Valeria's back ached and a band tightened across her brow, but she daren't give anything away.

"I'm hoping so much it will be a boy this time. Pietro…" Quillina waved a hand. It didn't take much to imagine Pietro's reaction if the baby were another girl. "I'm sure it's a boy," she continued. "They say you get more sickness with boys, don't they?"

"Do they? I don't know." Valeria turned away. "Now, what else were you going to serve with these tomatoes?"

They talked of other things while they prepared the meal. The silences became longer, and Valeria's own predicament hit her with renewed force when she studied Quillina's swollen abdomen.

Soon, Pietro came in, followed by their mother. He sat at the table and the women served him before sitting by the hearth to take their own meal. The food was like dust in her mouth, but she chewed and swallowed, forcing down each mouthful with a gulp of water.

The women sat silent, which was preferable to her mother's expert questioning. From time to time, her mother frowned at her and Quillina, who could never do anything right: girls never could, in Mother's opinion. Quillina sat with her eyes lowered, and a shiver of sympathy went through Valeria. At least she had never had to endure a disapproving mother-in-law and a husband who mistreated her.

She and Quillina cleared the plates in silence.

Something unseen pursued her and the wind rushed in her ears. The trees twisted their roots to trip her up. She sprawled on the ground, and the bitter taste spread over her tongue before she fell from a great height.

Valeria sat up in a rush, her heart beating against her ribs. This wasn't the room she had shared with Santucci. The window was on the other side, the furniture was darker and more massive and arranged in a different way. This bed was narrow and lumpy. A mushroomy scent from long ago brought it all back. Her pulse and breathing slowed.

She swung her legs out of bed and the nausea gripped her. No, not here. Her hand clapped over her mouth, she made it to the bowl on the table and her stomach emptied. Everyone in the house must have heard, but nothing moved, except the floorboards cracking from the previous day's heat. While the sickness subsided, she gripped the edge of the table hard and willed it not to return.

Her black dress was still dusty, so she shook it and pulled it over her head. It was already tighter around her breasts and pulled under the armpits. How much longer before it would give her away? She scraped clammy fingers through her knotted hair and tied the headscarf around it before peering from the window. The sun was rising over the hills to the east, and the last wisps of cloud broke up. Another day of fiery heat was in prospect.

The stairs and the corridor still held the night's shadow when she crept to the kitchen with the bowl, swilled it and flung the contents from the window. The nausea hadn't yet finished its work, and she retched into the bowl again as the door opened. Her mother stopped, her fingers on the handle, and drew in her breath.

"What's the matter with you?"

Valeria wiped her mouth with her sleeve and a chill settled on her. "I'm sorry, Mother. I haven't felt well for a few days, ever since I ate something that didn't agree with me. My walk yesterday in the heat didn't help."

"Why did you come all the way up here, then, if you were feeling ill? Were you so attached to that woman?" She bustled forward into the room. "I thought I heard someone down here. Let me take a look at you."

Valeria swallowed the bitterness and stood straight. Her mother peered into her face, her breath hot on Valeria's cheeks, and pinched her arms.

"You look pale, but you don't seem to be withering away, so it can't be the wasting sickness. You're too young, in any case. In fact, you seem fuller in the figure than I remember, just like Quilli..." Her eyes widened and travelled over Valeria's body. "If you weren't the widow of a respectable man, I'd say you were expecting. That can't possibly be the case, can it?" Her nostrils flared.

Valeria's legs almost gave way. She gave a hollow laugh. "How could you think that, Mother? I'm Santucci's widow and I live a quiet life in Zaronza. Don't forget, I'm not a young girl anymore, so I'm filling out. I must also admit to a weakness for *brocciù*." Her cheeks were on fire.

Her mother stared at her for a moment, and then she nodded. "Even you wouldn't go so far as to bring that kind of disgrace on us. Remember," Valeria recoiled when her mother's index finger jabbed at her, "everything you do must be above suspicion. You mustn't disgrace our name or your late husband's, God rest his soul. You've done enough by turning up here in this odd way. Don't do anything else to bring yourself to people's attention. Now, Pietro will be up soon."

Her mother turned her back. Valeria's shoulders sagged and she exhaled. Was it becoming so obvious, even before

103

any swelling of the belly? Now it was even more urgent that she find a way out. If Mother noticed something, other sharp eyes in Zaronza would, too. She recalled the fainting incident at the fountain, and hoped the old women had believed her story about the lamb and the heat.

Valeria caught her mother's glance on her a couple of times before she left. Pietro stalked off at a rapid pace and she had to hurry to keep up. She looked back. Her mother was still watching them from the door, but turned away without returning Valeria's wave.

She and her brother continued without speaking during the journey back to Zaronza. "I'll leave you here," he said at the edge of the square.

"Don't you want to come to my house and refresh yourself?"

"No, I'll just drink some water from the fountain over there. I want to get back before it becomes too hot. This has wasted enough of my time today."

Valeria nodded. "As you wish." In any case, she didn't want to spend more time with Pietro than she needed to, even if he was family.

The cool of the hallway was welcome after the strenuous walk. Her back ached and her ankles were hot and swollen. She pulled off her dress and lay on the bed, bathed in sweat. Her hands went to her abdomen, where a living thing was growing but not yet visible. She would think about it again tomorrow. For now, it was too difficult. Sleep banished her jumbled thoughts.

CHAPTER 13

Several days passed after Valeria's visit to Felicavo. She kept to the house and went out only to get water from the fountain. Every morning, she decided to leave any decisions until the following day. She had plenty of time. The days stretched to a week, and still she had decided nothing, done nothing. Wandering from room to room in the gloom of the closed shutters, her mind drifted, and images of Benedettu, Antone and Margherita pursued each other.

Rapping at the door broke into her dreamlike state. The light flooded in and she had to shield her eyes for a moment. Benedettu swept off his hat and his lips spread in a broad grin.

"Good morning, Signora."

Her skin tingled, as always, but she was unable to muster a smile to match his. Without meeting his gaze, she held open the door.

"Come in, Benedettu."

Once inside, he put his arms around her, but she pushed him away and shook her head. He frowned.

"What's the matter? Aren't you pleased to see me after all this time?"

"Of course I am. I've missed you; you know that. But something has happened and I have to tell you about it."

"What? Is someone ill?" He paused. "Have they found out about us?"

"You'd better come into the living room. I don't want to talk here. You never know who might be listening outside and how much they can hear."

She led the way into the darkened room.

"Sit down, Benedettu."

Valeria twisted her hands. This was going to be so difficult. She had no idea how he would take this news. Maybe he would leave her when he knew. It would be easy enough for him to claim he wasn't the father, and how could anyone prove otherwise?

Pacing up and down, she told, not daring to glance at him, afraid of his reaction. At last, the torrent of words dried up. She stood still and looked at him. His hands gripped the arms of the chair, and the light had gone out of his bright eyes. A chill rippled through her. For several moments, he remained as if frozen, and then he stood and came to her, taking her hands in his.

"I would give anything for things not to have turned out this way," he said. "I'm sorry. I – we – should have been more careful, but I felt as if you had put a spell on me. I never thought of this."

"Neither did I, since I was under the same spell. But now it has happened, and we have to decide what to do."

"There's only one thing to be done. You can't keep this baby. If we were able to marry, it would be different, but we both know isn't possible, although I wish it were."

Valeria's eyes stung.

"Couldn't we go away together?"

He shrugged. "Where would we go? You can't come and live in the sheepfolds, certainly not in your condition. There's nowhere else we can go as a couple. People would be suspicious, they would find out. We can't run from this."

She already knew this, and hope leached out of her.

"You must lose the baby, Valeria. It's the only way. There are means of doing it."

A glow of indignation pushed the numbness out of her body, and she snatched her hands away. "It's all right for you. You can go back into the hills and pretend nothing has happened and leave me to do this on my own. You can turn your back and pretend it's not your affair, that it's my problem alone. I wish you had never been caught in that thunderstorm, then none of this would ever have happened."

His eyes flashed. "It's my child, too. Do you really think I don't care? You didn't resist very hard, as I recall."

"No, but you thought nothing of taking advantage of a lonely widow."

"It wasn't like that, but if that's what you think, I won't be the one to disagree with you."

His footsteps rang in the corridor, and the knocker banged against the door when he slammed it behind him. Valeria stood in the middle of the room and her anger trickled away. She had turned Benedettu against her at the moment she needed him most. He didn't show much sympathy for her, but perhaps she hadn't given him a chance. Her emotions were tangled like a nest of snakes.

The knocker rapped again and she ran to open the door, but instead of Benedettu, Signora Rossi stood there. Her shoulders sagged.

"Is everything alright, Signora Santucci? I heard raised voices, so I came outside to see what was happening, and your shepherd almost knocked me off my feet as he left."

The woman had a talent for appearing at the wrong

moment. Valeria swallowed.

"Thank you for your concern, but there's nothing the matter. I don't know what you mean about raised voices. Perhaps they came from the square. As for my shepherd, he was in a hurry, but I apologise for him. Living up in the hills these men become rough and uncouth. I'm sure he meant no harm."

Her neighbour smiled, but it didn't reach her eyes. "Well, if you're sure. A woman living on her own like you can't be too careful. You do look a little flushed."

Valeria's hands flew to her cheeks.

"The heat has been exhausting and I had a stomach upset, but I feel better now, so please don't worry."

She smiled and closed the door. A few moments passed before Signora Rossi's footsteps crossed the alleyway. They would have to be much more careful – if Benedettu's pride allowed him to come back.

***

Whether Benedettu returned or not, she couldn't continue like this. Soon, the baby would begin to show, and although she could conceal it for a while, it would be almost impossible to carry it unnoticed full term. When it was born, what then? She needed the remedy fast, since there would come a point where it would no longer be safe.

Margherita never let it be known in public, but as well as helping pregnant and birthing mothers, she gave other remedies to the village women, above all to those who had already sacrificed their youth to a clutch of children. She called it their helpmate and herself an angel-maker. The herbs Margherita gathered on the hillsides included those which made sheep abort their deformed lambs. Valeria was sure she could find the plants and prepare them, but she would have to remember the doses for the infusions. Too much could cause her own death as well, while too little would have no effect.

When the sun's heat faded, Valeria took the path behind Zaronza and scoured the *machja* until she found what she needed. She wrapped the plants in a cloth and placed them at the bottom of her basket, covering them with rosemary and other herbs in case Signora Rossi was prowling around. She was bound to have noticed her going out. Back in her kitchen, she laid out the leaves and roots to dry.

A few days later, she crushed them to a powder in a mortar, took a beaker and measured the dose into it with infinite pains. Enough. The boiling water turned blood-red when she stirred the powder around.

"God forgive me."

With a shaking hand, she raised the cup to her lips and took a sip. The bitterness made her tongue curl when the liquid slid over it, and she spat it out onto the floor. It tasted the same as in her nightmare. She moaned.

"I can't do this. I can't kill my baby."

She took the beaker and threw out the rest of the infusion, and then flung the remaining powder into the fire, which flared. Staring into the flames, she sat at the table for a long time. This was her baby, hers and Benedettu's, and she couldn't murder it. She would accept whatever punishment they could devise once they found out, but the baby wouldn't die by her hand.

Warmth spread through her body and she stroked her stomach.

***

For two more months, while the summer ran its stifling course, Valeria continued as if everything was normal. Benedettu didn't come back, but he was up in the high pastures and would not come down until summer's end – if he came back at all after their quarrel. She had no means of getting word to him, so he knew nothing of her decision.

Towards the end of August, a knocking at the door woke her from an afternoon doze. She rubbed her eyes, put on her headscarf and straightened her dress, which cut into her midriff. She would have to let it out. A bearded man in a sheepskin jerkin stood on the threshold with a sack slung over his shoulder. He took off his shapeless woollen hat.

"Signora Santucci, forgive me for disturbing you. My colleague Colonna has asked me to bring you these products from your flock." He placed the sack inside the door.

"Thank you, Signore. He normally comes himself."

"He's been called up for the militia and has to leave in a day or so. He asked me to look after the flock while he's away. Since I was going to visit my sick mother in Pietranera anyway, it was easy enough to stop by here."

The blood pounded in her ears and a tight band wound itself around her. She gripped the door post hard and bit the insides of her cheeks.

"Signora?"

"I'm sorry. I've been feeling unwell recently. Please would you tell Ben... Colonna I'm sorry to hear this news, and I hope to see him when he returns. Or before he goes, if he has time?"

The shepherd nodded and kneaded his hat. He coughed. "Excuse me, but would you like me to take his wages to him?"

Valeria pressed her hand to her mouth. "Please forgive me. I forgot. This heat has been so tiring I think it's affected my brain." She barely knew what she was saying, so great was the weight on her chest.

She fetched her cash box, counted out some coins and pressed them into his hand.

"Here's something for you for your trouble. Of course,

I'll pay you for looking after the flock while he's away."

He bowed his head a little.

"Don't forget to give him my message."

He replaced his hat, raised his hand to it and went on his way. Valeria watched until he was out of sight, and then dragged herself to the kitchen with heavy steps. She didn't know if Benedettu was obliged to join the militia or not. While the man stood there, she couldn't think of a message that would tell Benedettu about the baby without giving it away to his fellow shepherds.

She stretched out her arms on the table and laid her head on them.

***

Benedettu didn't come. The other shepherd was still visiting his sick mother in Pietranera whenever he could, and so he was happy enough to take Benedettu's place. Every time the shepherd came, she wrapped herself in a shawl to conceal the swelling. Didn't Benedettu care whether she had done away with the baby or not? She must have been wrong to think he loved her. His pride mattered to him more, and her few harsh words had wounded him.

The days succeeded each other, hot and clammy at the end of August, dry and balmy in September, and warm and mellow until late October. Valeria waited for the moment when the villagers would find out, but was glad she had made her decision.

Antone was still away in the militia himself, so she had no one to confide in. In any case, he would be unable to do anything to help her. Even if she managed to conceal her pregnancy to the end, she would still have to explain the baby. She started to let out her dresses and left the house as little as possible.

She still had to get her water at the fountain, but it

became more difficult as the baby grew. One day in the late afternoon, she hoisted the heavy jar of water and drew the shawl around her with the other hand. A sudden scream from a group of children playing in the corner of the square made her look round, and she caught her foot against a raised cobblestone. The pitcher fell and shattered, and water flooded over the stones. Valeria sprawled headlong and rolled, winded, onto her back. She lay dazed for a few moments while the other women rushed to help her up. By instinct her hands went to her stomach and outlined the curve.

"No, no, it's alright, I'm not hurt."

She tried to conceal her front and get to her feet, flapping about like a landed fish. Too late. The women who were closest drew back and stood as if struck by lightning, and the clucking and exclamations ceased. Some of them gasped. Valeria lay helpless, and icy drops slid down her back.

With some scuffling, the front row parted and a gaunt face appeared. Her neighbour, Signora Rossi.

"My God, she's pregnant," she said. "Look at her. She must be at least five months gone."

The women turned from her neighbour to Valeria, and the wave of hostility was almost physical. A searing heat crept up her cheeks but nothing she could say would undo the situation.

"Well, Signora Santucci," her neighbour continued, hands on hips. "Here's a fine thing. A widow whose husband's been dead and buried almost two years – and she's expecting a baby. How do you explain that away? Was it the Immaculate Conception?"

Suppressed laughter rippled through the group, mingled with tutting and clucking. A few of the older women crossed themselves.

"Or was it something more flesh and blood than that?"

Her neighbour was getting into her stride. Valeria had the sense she was enjoying this, and had waited for an opportunity to trip her up. "Perhaps it was someone tall and blue-eyed, covered in sheep's muck and smelling of ewe's cheese?"

Another wave ran through the crowd, but this time it was more menacing.

"What business is it of yours?" Valeria spat back.

Signora Rossi looked around at her audience. "Oh, it's not only my business; it's everyone's in Zaronza. You come here from Felicavo and parade about thinking you're so superior to the rest of us because you married a wealthy man, but in reality you're nothing more than a whore, and you bring shame on the whole place as well as on your own family." Her eyes glowed.

Valeria flinched. The murmuring grew louder, "Shame... Never heard anything like it... A widow... Should be ashamed of herself..."

Signora Rossi raised her hands, and the muttering abated a little. "Yes, she should be ashamed of herself. She's been carrying on with her shepherd, her servant. I've seen him come to visit and I've heard them arguing. There's no doubt in my mind what they've been up to. She often slinks off into the *machja*, too, no doubt after him. He's a man who's little more than a savage, a man who is well beneath her. She's lowered herself to his level, and now look at the result." She pointed at Valeria's swollen belly. "It's hardly a good example for our children."

A glow of anger replaced the icy drops, and Valeria broke her silence. "He may not be of the same class, but he isn't beneath me. He's a fine and proud man, and I'd marry him if I could. He's worth as much as any of your men."

There were several sharp intakes of breath, and a glob of spit landed on the front of her dress.

"How dare you talk about them in the same breath?" Signora Rossi spat out the words. "As for marrying him, I've never heard such an idea. Now your behaviour has been revealed, the elders must hear of it. They'll have to decide what to do with you and your bastard."

Some of the women nodded, and the muttering started again as Valeria struggled to her feet. No one moved to help her up.

"Tell them. I'm not ashamed of anything I've done, and I would do it all again."

Shaking the length of her body, she turned to leave, the coppery taste of fear in her mouth. They made way for her, stood back, and drew their skirts aside when she passed. Cries of "Whore!" and "Shame!" followed her back to her house, where she slammed the door behind her and fastened the bolt. Again, she saw the vision of Delfina's body swinging in the breeze, and the faces of the Felicavo women, twisted with scorn and disgust.

How many of her neighbours were as innocent as they would have her believe? How many of them had had secret trysts with a lover in the *machja* or an old shepherd's hut before settling down and marrying the man their parents had chosen? How many of those men were the father of their firstborn? The only difference was that they had never been found out and she had.

What would happen to her and the baby now? A black pall of fear descended on her again. She should have persuaded Benedettu to take her with him, instead of waiting for her fate like a lamb awaits the knife. How stupid she'd been. Maybe it wasn't too late if she could just slip away at nightfall. Somebody must take her in. She thought of the *signadora* at Cisco, who might take pity on her. It was a very slim chance.

***

The sun set behind a mass of billowing clouds, throwing blood-red light onto their undersides. The wind, which had been a light breeze for most of the day, turned to the north and moaned and tore at the shutters, flinging them back and forth. Valeria gathered some money, a little food and some clothes, and tossed them into a bag. She fastened a shawl around her shoulders and a cloak over it, and then eased open the door bit by bit to avoid it grating on the floor. Pulling the hood over her head, she tiptoed up the alleyway and scurried across the square. If she could get to the path behind the church without being seen, she could use the trees as cover all the way to Cisco. No one could be out on the path on a night like this.

"There she is," a shrill voice said. The echo rang around the square behind her. "She's trying to get away. Stop her."

Without turning to look back, Valeria plunged forward beside the church, escape her only priority. Heavy footsteps sounded on the cobbles and her heart drummed, keeping time with the steps. The rain beat hard in her face when she entered the track. The wind whipped the trees, and the branches thrashed back and forth like souls in torment. It was muddy underfoot now and she needed both arms to steady herself, so she tossed away the bag and unfastened the cloak, but she was tiring fast. If she could get into the trees and the scrub, maybe they wouldn't find her.

Shouts rang out behind her, coming closer now, like some wild boar hunt. Ragged breaths tore her lungs and the rain streamed into her eyes, so she could barely see ahead of her. Leaves eddied around her and stuck to her face as she ran on. Her foot caught on something hidden in the mud and she flung out her arms to save herself, but she crashed down for the second time that day and hit her brow against a stone.

The blackness of the night deepened and she heard nothing else.

***

Voices murmured in the distance, came closer, and receded again. Valeria opened her eyes and raised a hand to shield them from the light. She touched an egg-shaped swelling on her forehead. A face came close and peered at her.

"So you've woken up at last. That was a very stupid thing to do, trying to get away."

The memory washed over her. She had been running, running away from something evil that wanted to kill her, with the trees twisting above her. The recurring dream. Her guts tightened. This was no dream. She sat up, her temples throbbing. A woman stood over her, and a tall, bony man warmed himself by the fire. They were in her bedroom. She recognised the couple who lived on the other side of the square, near the church.

"What happened?"

"Don't you remember?" the woman said. "You were very foolish and tried to run away. They came after you and you fell down. You hit your head."

Valeria touched her forehead again and pain arced through it. So it was all true. They had found her out, and now she would have to pay. They wouldn't give her the chance to get away again.

"The elders are waiting for you downstairs. Do you think you can stand up?"

She swung her legs over the side of the bed and a wave of nausea hit her, but she waved the woman away. She would do this herself. At least the baby appeared to be all right.

Valeria descended the staircase with halting steps. The woman at her side steered her to the living room. Three

116

dark-hatted men stood there. She knew them all as village men. Santucci had had business dealings of some sort with the middle one, who was tall and slightly bowed. His eyes slid to her middle, which she made no attempt to conceal. The men didn't take off their hats in her presence.

"Signora Santucci, we have received serious accusations of misconduct on your part, and I can see for myself they are true. You're a widow who has not married again, and yet you are with child when your husband has been dead for some time."

"I don't deny it."

"You've managed to conceal your sin until today, when it came to light by accident. Under normal circumstances, you could make this good by marrying the father. This man is your servant, a humble shepherd, whom you can't marry without dishonouring your dead husband's name, your family and yourself. What do you have to say?"

She couldn't deny it or refuse to name Benedettu, since she had admitted as much to the village women earlier. That had been stupid, since she could have left Benedettu out of this, but she couldn't produce anyone else as the supposed father, and it wouldn't be fair to put an innocent man in that position.

"I don't deny it, either. He and I are – were – lovers, but there is nothing unworthy about him and I would marry him if I could. We haven't done any harm to anyone."

The man shook his head as if in disbelief. "These are serious matters to do with family honour as well as public morality. I'm not sure if you realise the gravity of your situation. Trying to run away tonight has done nothing to help your cause. Corsica might be in turmoil, but if we don't uphold morals and traditional justice we're not worthy to govern ourselves. The elders have discussed this, and we have decided to hold a tribunal to hear your case. You will

117

present yourself the day after tomorrow to answer this charge...and others."

She gasped. Delfina had killed herself rather than go through that. "A tribunal? Is it really necessary? Couldn't I go away from here instead?"

"No village would accept you once they knew what you had done. We have to be seen to deal with our own matters in our own way. You'll remain in your house until the time of the tribunal, in the care of Signore and Signora Jacopini. They will stay with you at all times and provide you with food and drink. Don't think of trying to escape again."

The men trooped out, and Signora Jacopini saw them to the door. Valeria toiled up the stairs, her feet like lead, and closed the bedroom door behind her.

CHAPTER 14

When they came for her on the second day, the sun was sliding behind the mountains and the sky was afire with crimson and gold. Such sorrow amidst such beauty. In the time before they came, she sat in the kitchen, and the fire cast its glow over her but she was cold to the bones. If she had the choice again, it would be no different and she would take the same decision, even though the price was high. The baby was stirring; it was a person, and it deserved to live. Thank goodness she hadn't done away with it, but still her child's life was uncertain. There was nothing to be done but await their judgement.

"You must come now. They're waiting," Signore Jacopini said. "My wife and I will take you."

Head bowed, Valeria walked across the square between the man and his wife. The November evening chill rose from the paving stones. She shivered, but not from the cold. They continued a little way down the hill and stopped in front of a large house whose shutters were closed as if it were unoccupied. The door opened and a faint light shone within.

"We've brought her," Signore Jacopini said.

"I'll tell the tribunal. You're to wait here until they call for you."

Two rough, cane-seated chairs stood in the hallway, which the Jacopinis took. Neither of them spoke to her. So the sentence had been passed already. She was presumed guilty, with not even the right to sit down. Some time passed, broken by murmuring in a back room. On occasions, a voice rose above it and then fell silent. The chill from the flagstones crept up her legs and she stretched her back, which ached as if a herd of goats had trampled over it.

A door creaked somewhere, and footsteps rang in the corridor.

"They're ready for her now."

Everyone spoke about her but not to her, as if she were not there or had already passed beyond recognition. The chaperones stood, and the woman took Valeria's arm. Anyone would think she was going to escape. She wouldn't get very far in her condition, and there was no running away from this. If they could get it over fast, she would accept whatever followed. She crossed the threshold, Signora Jacopini's hand still on her.

After the dim hallway, the light blinded her for a moment. The grate was cold and filled with ashes. Across the room, five men sat behind a long table. The oil lamp lit them from below, so their faces floated free as if severed from their necks. The glow exaggerated their features. All were village men, and some had visited the house when Santucci was alive. Papers and a quill lay in front of the one who sat in the middle.

"Approach the table," he said.

Signora Jacopini took a seat in the corner and Valeria stepped forward. No one offered her a chair. A strange detachment settled on her, as if she were looking down at

120

herself, another woman who stood on the bare boards. This was happening to someone else; it couldn't be her.

"Valeria Santucci, born Peretti, you are here to answer serious charges against you. This tribunal will hear your case and then pass judgement on you. Do you understand?"

"Yes."

"You are accused of seducing your servant, the shepherd Colonna, thereby bringing dishonour on your name and on your family. The fruit of your shame is evident."

Seducing? It hadn't happened like that at all. If anything, he had seduced her, although she made her choice and responded to him of her own will. Was the fault all hers because of her social standing or her sex? Only the woman did wrong in such a case, it appeared.

"But I…"

"You may not speak until we question you. Even more serious matters have emerged, but we can't deal with those until the witness is available. He is away from home today and will return tomorrow. For the moment, we will consider this first charge against you."

Who was this witness and what did he see? The president of the tribunal talked of graver matters, but she hadn't done anything she could think of that could be considered more serious. The *signadora*? Consulting one was no crime, even if some disapproved. The charge against her was already weighty enough. The whole thing was a pretence, anyway. They wanted her downfall, and nothing she could do or say would change it. But she would give them her truth, whether they chose to believe it or not.

The president coughed. "Colonna was seen on several occasions leaving your house. When did he visit and how long did he stay?"

"Benedettu… Colonna used to visit my husband, God rest his soul, every few weeks, bring him the produce from

121

the flock, and collect his wages. When Santucci died, I remained housebound, as custom demands, and I asked a neighbour to meet the shepherd and take my place. Some time after my husband's death, I felt it would be acceptable for me to deal with my own servant again. Nobody objected at the time or said it was wrong. He came during the daytime and stayed a few minutes. I gave him food and then he left."

"The evidence we have is that he stayed more than what you call 'a few minutes' on each occasion. At what point did you seduce him?"

Their "evidence" must have come from her neighbour. She was poisonous.

"I didn't seduce him. We felt a growing attachment for each other, and we both consented to what happened between us. I was lonely in that big house after my husband's death, and needed company and affection. I couldn't bear the idea of being on my own for the rest of my life. Is it so hard to understand?"

The president dipped the quill in the inkpot and it scratched on the paper while he made a note.

"It's for a widow to mourn her husband and remain faithful to his memory, not to bring shame on his name. So you admit you led him on."

A tremor ran up her spine. "No. You're twisting my words. I was lonely, but I didn't do anything to attract him. Far from it; at first, I even tried not to admit what I felt for him."

"It didn't stop you from seducing him in the end," said a man who sat on the president's right. "Don't you have any shame at betraying your late husband's memory and leading a simple shepherd astray?"

Valeria twisted her hands. Whatever she said, they distorted it. They made her sound like a praying mantis, lying in wait for an innocent victim.

"Benedettu Colonna may lead a simple life," she said, "but he is far from stupid, and he's capable of making up his own mind. I didn't seduce him. Why don't you ask him yourselves?"

"His opinion is of no importance in this matter," the president replied. "We don't need to ask him. You're his employer and you come from a distinguished family, as well as being the widow of a wealthy man, so the offence is yours and yours alone. Colonna is a simple and innocent man whom you have wronged. In any case, he has been called up for the militia and is no longer in the area."

This was like being lost in a wood, unable to find a path. The more she said, the deeper into the thicket it led her. Benedettu didn't know about the exposure of her pregnancy and the tribunal. Her accusers considered there was no point in finding him, since they already had decided she was guilty, and so it would be inconvenient if Benedettu upheld her story. Everybody was wronged but her: Benedettu, Santucci, her family, Zaronza. She was alone.

"Do you have any more questions?" the president asked.

The men shook their heads.

"And you, is there anything else you wish to say?"

"Yes," Valeria replied. "I'm not ashamed of my love for Benedettu, and I would marry him if I could."

The men looked at each other, eyes wide.

"Are you serious?" one said. "You know that is out of the question. You can't marry him without dishonouring your family. He's not your equal. A wealthy widow marrying her shepherd! The idea is ridiculous."

The tribunal conferred in whispers, and Valeria looked down at her hands. Nothing she could have said would have changed anything.

"Very well," the president said. "We are all agreed that

you are guilty as charged of seducing your shepherd and you are carrying his child. Another accusation has been brought against you and we will gather again tomorrow morning to hear that case and the witness who was absent today. After that, we will pass sentence."

"Aren't you going to tell me until tomorrow what this second charge is?"

The president looked around at the other members of the tribunal. "I can't see any reason not to tell you now. You'll find out soon enough, anyway. You are accused of having poisoned your husband."

CHAPTER 15

The room swayed and the floor tilted under her feet. Valeria struggled to stay upright, and her breath came in short gasps. This was not possible. How could anyone think she had killed her husband? Who could be wicked enough to make such an accusation?

"But it's not true – it's not true. You can't believe this… someone is making it up—"

"Be quiet." The president brought down his hand hard on the table. The inkwell jumped and scattered a few blots over his papers. "You will have a chance to speak tomorrow to defend yourself. In the meantime, I suggest you prepare and pray for God's forgiveness. We will reconvene at first light."

Her chest was ready to burst. She opened her mouth to speak again, but a look from the president silenced her. It was no use, anyway. She took a deep breath, and the Jacopinis approached to lead her away.

Outside, the stars stood out crisp against the velvet sky. Valeria paused a moment to look up. So many times had she seen the milky veil of stars stretch across the heavens, without doubting that a God existed who had created it all. After this, though, it was hard to believe in a just God.

The woman shook her arm and they continued uphill towards her house.

"Do you want some food?" Signora Jacopini said.

"No, only some water. I can't swallow anything else."

The key clicked in the lock behind her. Valeria lowered herself onto the bed, heavy as an old woman, and dragged off her headscarf. The baby moved, and the slow tears spilled over and trickled down her face, seeping into her black dress. There would be no praying that night.

**

The shutters were open, and she turned to look when the first cracks of dawn broke through the morning clouds and scattered light onto the mountains beyond. Where it touched them, they turned from blue to gold.

The lock grated again, and her guard brought in a plate and a jug.

"You must eat something. You'll faint with hunger, otherwise."

Maybe it would be better if she did pass out, since it would make little difference to the outcome. In any case, hunger was the last thing on her mind. Even so, she took the plate and chewed a mouthful of bread, forcing it down past the lump in her gullet.

She handed back the dish.

"Now you must prepare yourself, since they'll soon call for you."

"I am ready."

Signora Jacopini pointed at the headscarf draped over the pillow. Valeria touched her hair. Yes, she had taken it off last night. She rearranged it, tucking in the loose strands, and smoothed her skirt.

Nobody was about when they crossed the square, but furtive movements behind the windows told Valeria the villagers knew everything that was happening. The sun was framed between the peaks of the cape while it rose and chased away the last of the morning mist. In the hallway of the house they waited again to be called. Specks of dust twisted in a shaft of sunlight, and a scent of garlic lingered in the air. Simple things, everyday things you took for granted until you were about to lose them forever. Valeria's heartbeat throbbed in her ears when the footsteps echoed in the corridor, as they had the previous evening.

This morning, the room smelt of cold cinders. The shutters remain closed, blocking out the sunlight and the life outside. On the table stood the oil lamp, which cast a feeble glow. Some of the men's faces were in shadow. The president beckoned her forward. She stood on the same spot as before, and clasped her palms together, slick with sweat.

"I hope you have spent the night in prayer and asked God's forgiveness," he said.

Valeria said nothing. There was little to pray about.

The president drew a deep breath. "We had better start the proceedings. This might take some time. Valeria Santucci, in addition to the crime of seducing your servant, the shepherd, Benedettu Colonna, you have also been accused of taking your husband's life by poison. What do you have to say? Are you guilty of this charge?"

"I know you won't believe me, but I am not guilty, and I'm shocked that someone could be wicked enough to accuse me of this. My husband died of the wasting sickness. I did what I could to help him, but it wasn't enough and the illness took him. I was contented and secure with Santucci. Why should I kill him?"

"Maybe you had a motive. With your husband out of the way, what was there to prevent you pursuing Colonna?

Also, as Santucci's sole heir, you stood to inherit substantial property through his will. Isn't that the case?"

"If that's what you believe, nothing I can say will change your mind. I repeat: I'm not guilty and I did not kill him. He died of an incurable illness."

The president turned to a man at the end of the table. "Ask the witness to come in. We'll see what he has to say."

Valeria turned when the witness was led in. The man glanced at her and then looked away. Her neighbour, Signore Rossi. A cold wave skimmed across her flesh. Of course, she should have realised. The woman couldn't come herself; women didn't appear as witnesses in a trial unless there was no one else. Their evidence was given less weight than men's, anyway. So she sent her husband instead. Everything started to make sense, but one thing wasn't clear. Why was Signora Rossi doing this? What did she have to gain?

"Signore Rossi," the president said. "You have come to bear witness against Valeria Santucci. You are aware, Signore, that these accusations are very serious. Do you wish to pursue them?"

Rossi nodded. Valeria's gut contracted. If only he would drop dead on the spot or be struck by lightning. This was all such a pretence.

"Very well. Take the witness the Bible."

Rossi swore the oath, but the back of his neck was red and he kept rubbing his hands as if to wipe them clean.

"Now, Signore Rossi, you say you have some important evidence to back up your accusations. Please tell us what it is."

"We... I believe Valeria Santucci gave poison to her husband over a period of months and he died because of it. She also called in a sorceress to make sure he wouldn't recover, in my opinion."

"Yes, but what is your evidence?"

Rossi cleared his throat. "Signora Santucci was always going out onto the hillside to pick herbs. My wife saw her on several occasions. Santucci fell ill about the time she started to do it. He lost weight and complained of stomach cramps. He looked terrible. I've known him for years, and he was never unwell before."

"There's nothing wrong in gathering herbs," the president said. "Plenty of women use them both in cooking and to prepare infusions."

"Yes, that's true, but I believe she made poison from these herbs. The night of Signore Santucci's death, his wife called us in because he had collapsed on the floor and was bleeding. My three sons and I carried him to bed and then we left, but my wife sat and kept vigil with his while he lay on his deathbed and he was in great pain. There was a beaker of liquid by his bedside and Signora Santucci made him drink it. After that, he fell unconscious and never woke again. Signora Santucci said it was a painkilling infusion. My wife sniffed what was left in the cup and found it smelt very bitter, and said so. Santucci's wife said later she made it from opium poppies. My wife discovered this can be a fatal poison in large doses."

"What do you have to say to this, Valeria Santucci? Do you admit to making poisons?"

The frustration rose like bile. "I don't deny I tried to help my husband during his illness by giving him calming draughts to relieve the pain and to ease what we believed was indigestion. I learned how to do this in Felicavo. My remedies didn't work, since the sickness had taken hold and was too strong. I don't deny I used poppy, which is well known as a painkiller. If the dose is too high, it can be dangerous, but I never used more than a weak measure. I have never used herbs as poisons."

"We only have your word for that. Signore Rossi says your husband fell unconscious after drinking the potion and never woke again."

"That's not quite true. After he had drunk the infusion, I went for the priest and he woke up and was able to make his confession. Once the priest had left, he drifted in and out of consciousness until he died."

The president scribbled on the paper in front of him.

"It would be very easy to substitute a stronger dose, wouldn't it?"

"Yes, but why should I have done that?" Valeria said. "If I had wanted to kill my husband, there would have been other, less obvious, ways of doing it."

The tribunal gasped as one and an angry murmuring arose, like a swarm of bees. The president raised his hand and the muttering subsided.

"So you admit you are familiar with these other ways and thought of using them? While you could maintain the fiction of the wasting sickness, you could give him these poisoned draughts without anyone suspecting, couldn't you? That was your plan: rather than a sudden death that would raise suspicions, you chose a slow decline mimicking the wasting sickness."

Valeria's mouth was full of thorns, and the sweat broke out between her shoulder blades. This was all going wrong again. They twisted everything she said. How could she know what was the right thing to say? No one was there to defend her, everyone was against her. They waited for her to fall into their traps.

"That's not how it was at all, but you won't listen to me."

"If you won't speak to the tribunal with respect, I'll have you removed from here and we will continue the hearing without you. Now, answer me. Your plan was as I have described, wasn't it?"

Valeria closed her eyes. This was so tiring and fog shrouded her mind.

"My husband was ill, but it wasn't because of me. I have already said I was content with my life and I had no reason to wish him dead. No remedies I know can cure the wasting sickness. I have seen how it works once it takes hold. In Felicavo, an old woman died of it within a few months. Margherita, who taught me all I knew about herbs, tried everything, but nothing could help her."

"This Margherita, she no doubt taught you which herbs can harm as well as those that can cure."

"Of course. It's important to be able to tell the good herbs apart from the bad ones, otherwise you could make terrible mistakes. That must be obvious."

"You made no mistakes when you measured out your husband's doses, did you? You knew what you were doing," the president said.

"I keep telling you, he was ill. The physician, when I could get him to visit, agreed it was the wasting sickness. Why haven't you called him? He would be able to confirm that what I say is true."

"We don't need to call him. He is a busy man and I've already spoken to him. He agreed that your husband's illness looked like the wasting sickness, but he also said certain poisons might cause the same symptoms. He wasn't aware that you prepared so-called remedies for your husband."

Valeria screwed up her fingers and pressed her fists into her eyes. It wouldn't have made any difference if the physician had known about her infusions or not. The darkness in the corners of the room deepened.

"Now let's move to your other piece of evidence, Signore Rossi: the sorceress."

CHAPTER 16

As if the pretence about the poison weren't enough, more was to come. The black dots invaded her vision again. Her skin was clammy and she was cold to the core.

"Please may I sit down? I'm afraid I'm going to faint."

"Very well. Given your condition, you can sit while I question the witness again."

Her keeper brought forward a chair and Valeria sank down onto it. The black spots dispersed.

"Now, Signore Rossi, please tell the tribunal about this so-called sorceress."

Rossi shifted his feet and rubbed his neck.

"Well, I didn't see her myself. My wife did."

"Have you any reason to doubt what your wife said?"

Her neighbour shook his head. "My son saw her, too. It was a few days before Signore Santucci died. I don't quite remember; two, or maybe three. I was still out tending my vegetables with my youngest son. The other two had gone to Pietranera on an errand for me.

"My wife says she was preparing the evening meal when

she heard light footsteps in the alley. Few people pass that way, especially not at dusk. The footsteps stopped across the way. Knowing Signora Santucci was in the house on her own, and fearing for her safety, my wife opened the door a little to see who it was. A tall woman carrying a basket stood there, looked around and tapped at the door a couple of times before Signora Santucci opened it. Our neighbour looked up and down the alley as well before closing the door. My wife thought she recognised the visitor, but couldn't quite place her at first."

So someone had seen the *signadora* – and, of course, it had to be her neighbour. As for being concerned for Valeria's safety, that was complete nonsense. What other lies would this man pour out that his wife had told him to repeat?

"My son and I stayed in our field to profit from the last of the light, but my other two sons returned from Pietranera during that time. My wife says an hour or so passed before the door opened again and the tall woman came out and hurried away."

"What makes you think Signora Santucci's visitor was a sorceress?"

"Well, as I said, I didn't see her myself because I wasn't there, but my wife saw her when she arrived and one of my sons, Pietro, caught a glimpse of her when she left. He too believed he recognised her, and it came to him he had seen her once before, when he went to Cisco. He asked one of his friends who she was and he told Pietro she was a *signadora*. People came to her to have their fortunes told and to find out if the Eye afflicted them."

Some of the members of the tribunal crossed themselves.

"So people used her to heal themselves," the president said.

"Yes, but that wasn't all she was known for," Rossi

continued. "My son's friend explained she was also said to be a *mazzera*. She was often seen slipping out of her house at night and going into the *machja*. Sometimes people whose fortunes she had told not long before died soon afterwards. She preyed on those she had pretended to help. That's how she selected her victims.

"After the evening of the woman's visit, Signore Santucci seemed a little brighter in himself, although he still looked terrible. A couple of days later, as I told you earlier, Signora Santucci asked for our help since he had fallen ill again, and he died the next day. I think that woman helped to finish him off."

This was all so absurd. If Valeria was already murdering Santucci with poison, why would she need to bring in someone else? The woman had tried hard to help, but it hadn't worked, even though she thought it did at the time. Maybe there was no such thing as the Eye after all, and the illness was too strong. It had been rash going to Margherita, and now she wished she hadn't sent for the *signadora*, but she was desperate and couldn't think of any other course. If medicine didn't cure him, maybe magic could.

The president turned to her. "Stand up. What was your intention in consulting this woman, who is known to be a *mazzera*?"

"I did it as a last resort, because my husband was declining fast and I didn't know what else to do. A friend sent for her on my behalf, because she was known to cast out the Eye. If my husband was afflicted by the Eye, she might be able to save him. If he wasn't, no harm would be done. I grasped at any chance to see him recover. As for her being a *mazzera*, I can't believe it. Why would she do good with one hand and evil with the other?"

"It's known that some women are *signadore* by day and *mazzere* by night," the president said. "Isn't it true that you brought in this woman to make sure Santucci wouldn't recover so you could carry out your plan to seduce Colonna?"

She was like a donkey tethered to a threshing stone, condemned to walk around in circles and always to return to the same point. A heavy weight hindered her breathing.

"I've told you several times already: my husband was good to me and I had no reason to want him dead. My only thought was to help him. Benedettu and I didn't start our relations until long after my husband's death. I met him once while Santucci was alive, one day when he felt too ill to see Benedettu, and I had nothing to do with him afterwards until well after my seclusion had finished."

So it went on, back and forth. The president asked the same questions in different words. Valeria gave the same answers each time. From time to time, another member of the tribunal broke in, but the president led the questioning. Would this never end? At last, he sat back and made a few more notes.

"Signore Rossi, do you have any more evidence you wish to bring before the tribunal?"

"No, I think I've told you everything."

"One last question, then. Do you think Signore Santucci had any idea he was being poisoned by his wife?"

Rossi remained silent a moment and pulled at his beard. "It's hard to say. He wasn't the sort of man to complain about feeling ill, although it was clear he was suffering. I can't think of anything, except…"

"Well?"

"He did mention one day that he felt as if someone had put a curse on him."

"Thank you, Signore Rossi. The questioning is finished and you may leave."

Her neighbour reached into his pocket and pulled his hat

on. He nodded to the tribunal and left the room. Valeria watched him go, but he didn't look at her once.

"Valeria Santucci, do you have anything else to say in your defence?"

"No." What else could she say? Nothing she could say would sway them. Now it was over and it only remained to hear her fate.

"You will leave the room while we consider the verdict," the president said.

Signora Jacopini took her arm as before and steered her along the corridor into the hallway. This time, a chair was free and she sat down, leaning her head against the whitewashed wall. The daylight was welcome after the gloom of the tribunal chamber. Dogs barked and cocks crowed in the distance: life went on.

Scenes from her life in Felicavo flashed before her: the time she and Antone careered down the hill, hand in hand, and ate their fill of the cherries from the tree by the stream. He was six and she thirteen. After that, they drank from the brook until their teeth were numb. Antone had eaten too many cherries and he gripped his belly and wailed when they got home. Mother gave him a clout around the ear, while twelve year-old Pietro looked on and grinned.

She pictured Margherita's scent-filled room, crammed with bunches of herbs and baskets of fruits from the *machja*, her soft murmuring while she explained how to make healing infusions or to preserve the bounty she had gathered. Margherita. How much more like a mother she had been to her than her own. She would never see her again. A pang pierced her.

"You're to come back into the tribunal chamber."

Valeria jumped. So soon? They had not taken very long to discuss her case. Surely they had more to say than that. Was no one prepared to defend her? The baby moved when she stood up. She took a step and faltered. Signore Jacopini preceded her along the corridor; his wife followed.

The darkness in the room was almost like a physical presence, threatening from the corners, relieved by the feeble light of the oil lamp on the table. Valeria curled her fingers and dug her nails into the palms. Her heart raced.

"Step forward," the president said.

He leaned towards her. "Valeria Santucci, you have been accused of serious crimes. The first charge is that of seducing your employee, a man whom you cannot marry without dishonour to your family and your late husband's name. You bear his child, the result of your perverted liaison. The tribunal finds you guilty of this crime."

She already knew that, and she expected it from the moment she first entered the room the previous evening. Even so, she clenched her fists harder.

"The second charge is even more serious. You were accused of poisoning your husband over a period of months so you could inherit his wealth and carry on a relationship with his shepherd. You then obtained the services of a sorceress to make sure he had no chance of survival. On the night of his death, you made him drink a final strong draught of the poison and even admitted to your neighbour when questioned that you had used this drug."

He paused. "The tribunal also finds you guilty of this crime."

Valeria closed her eyes. Numbness spread through her limbs, and again it was as if she saw herself from above. She was guilty of loving Benedettu; she was not ashamed of it. The charge of murder was false, and the neighbour had invented it to cause her ill. Signore Rossi had reddened and stammered, and it was clear his wife had put him up to it, but the tribunal still chose to believe his false evidence rather than her defence. The detachment gave way to a slow-burning anger. What had she ever done to deserve this?

"Do you have anything more to say before I tell you the sentence we have agreed?"

She shook her head. Her tongue was like a piece of wood in her mouth.

"In that case, I must tell you we have decided the punishment must fit the offence. Your crimes have tainted the honour of your family and the reputation of your late husband and Zaronza. You must die by poison."

Again, the floor slanted beneath her feet. She had never doubted the sentence would be harsh, but she had chased away the thoughts of death and how hers would be carried out. The bile crept up.

"My baby…"

"The baby will die along with you. You should have considered this before you put your plans into action."

She shut her eyes. The people she loved: Antone, Benedettu, her unborn baby. Didn't it deserve to live? If she could get word to Benedettu, maybe she might have some hope. He could save her, take her away. Perhaps it was possible if she could get a stay of execution. Anything was worth trying. The mist cleared from her mind.

Valeria drew a deep breath and dug her nails into her palms again. "Would you grant me one last request?"

"Tell us what it is and then we will decide."

"I would like a few days before my sentence is carried out. I want my family to be able to visit me so I can make my peace with them."

The president pulled at his beard and spoke in a low voice to the other members of the tribunal. Some frowned and glanced at her. Valeria held her breath.

At last, the president turned back to her. "Very well, we agree. This is an odd request, since you have wronged your family, but we are willing to grant you three days to prepare yourself. Whether they wish to visit you is up to them, but I will send word. The sentence will be carried out at the end of that period."

She bowed her head. There was still a chance, although a slim one, to escape this unjust sentence.

CHAPTER 17

The three days began: three sunsets and three sunrises before she might no longer be in this world. A handful of meals, a few hours of sleep before she ceased to exist, unless she could carry out her plan, and she depended on Antone for that. She had hoped she could stay in her own house, but the tribunal didn't consider it appropriate, and so she was lodged with Signora Jacopini and her husband in their house overlooking the square. For the most part, they left her alone and didn't even bother to lock her in. Where could she go on her own in this condition, anyway?

From the small window in her room at the back of the house, she had a view of the bay and the ever-changing mountains beyond, sometimes bathed in sunlight, sometimes shrouded by clouds. Would she never walk on the hills again, the stones pressing into her soles, the breeze stroking her face, the *machja* brushing at her skirt and leaving its aromatic scent on her clothes? Did she have to die for loving a man whom people considered beneath her, a crime that wasn't a crime? Worst of all, did she have to die for an offence that she hadn't committed?

"Your mother's here to see you."

The guardian stood aside and Valeria's mother jostled past her into the narrow room, her face like stone. The woman shut the door and her footsteps receded down the stairs.

"I almost didn't come. Pietro came with me, but he doesn't want to see you. You've brought such shame on us I can hardly bear to leave the house. We'll never recover from this disgrace."

She didn't expect sympathy from her mother, but it would have been better if she had stayed away. "Why did you come, then?"

"Because I wanted to tell you to your face: I disown you, you are no child of mine and I won't speak of you once you're dead."

Valeria's cheeks flared. "You could have sent me a message to say that. You didn't need to come yourself."

"No, that wouldn't have done, because I have something else to tell you to your face. When they came to tell me about the sentence, I made a decision." She paused. "I will prepare the poison and I will stay while you drink it."

Valeria gasped and clapped her hands over her mouth.

"Mother, how could you? I'm your daughter."

"You're no daughter of mine, not any more. You were your father's favourite, but I was ashamed that my firstborn was a girl. Now you've done some terrible things and you deserve to pay the price. Look at you," she gestured at Valeria. "Your baby is the child of a shepherd, a man who isn't fit to be under the same roof as you." She pushed her face close to Valeria's. "How could you let him touch you? You're nothing but a whore."

Spittle sprinkled Valeria's face. She flinched and clasped her arms around her.

"He may be a shepherd, but I loved him and he was worthy of it."

"Love? You have some stupid ideas, Valeria. Look where love has got you. Where is this shepherd, anyway? It doesn't seem very worthy to me that he disappears with the militia. Maybe you cooked up this plan together and he's afraid of being judged, too."

Valeria took a deep breath. "There was no plan, Mother. Santucci was ill. I didn't kill him, and nothing happened between me and Benedettu until well after Santucci's death."

"You can protest all you like, but you've been tried and found guilty. Now I can't bear the sight of you any longer." She moved towards the door.

"What about Antone? Where is he?"

Her mother turned. "Skulking about on the hills somewhere, I expect. I've given up with that boy, and now, because of what you've done, no one will want to marry into our family. I don't know what I've done to deserve this fate."

A small spark of hope kindled. At least Antone was back in Felicavo. But she had to speak to him. He was the only hope of carrying out her plan.

"Mother, I know you won't want to do anything for me, but I would like to see Antone before... before... one last time."

Her mother shrugged. "He often stays away for days, but knowing him he'll come of his own accord. I'm not going to tell him anything. Now I need to go. Pietro is waiting."

Valeria wrung her hands. "Please." Her mother turned her back and closed the door. The searing tears overflowed and she sank onto the floor and gave way to them.

***

On the second day, not long after first light, footsteps sounded on the bare boards of the stairs.

"You have another visitor," Valeria's keeper announced. The figure of a tall, broad man appeared behind her.

"Antone. Thank God," she cried, and flung herself into his arms.

"I came as soon as I heard, but Mother wouldn't tell me anything. I had to worm it out of Quillina. I came back to Felicavo a couple of nights ago, and I thought the few people I came across looked at me in an odd way, but nobody said anything. What happened? What's all this about poisoning Santucci? I don't understand." His strong fingers bit into her shoulders. "I see you're expecting a child, though." His brow furrowed.

She held him away from her. "We don't have much time. Tomorrow I must die, unless you're prepared to help me. Of course I didn't poison my husband. You know me better than that. You can't possibly believe it. The trial was all based on false evidence, but I did fall in love with a man whom no one thinks is worthy of me. He's in the militia now, and you need to find him and get him to take me away. This is my only chance, Antone. Please help me."

"But where is he? Even supposing I did find him, what could he do? He can't walk in here and escort you out in front of everyone as if you were going for a stroll. You wouldn't get very far, not carrying a baby."

Her heart drummed against her ribs. "You've got to do this for me. Remember all the times I helped you when you got into trouble, all the times I dressed your cuts and bruises, all the times I defended you in front of Mother and Pietro. Remember the time you shot Signore Leca's goat with Pietro's gun and I got Santucci to plead for you and smooth things over with Leca. Have you forgotten? Is your memory so short? Or are you so ungrateful that you won't do

143

something for me now, when I'm in desperate need?"

Antone turned his face away.

"Look at me, Antone. Have you forgotten what I did for you?"

He looked down. "No, of course I haven't. If it hadn't been for you, I don't know what would have become of me. I'm not ungrateful, but I can't see how it will help if I go to look for this man. What if he comes too late?"

"That's a risk we have to take. His name's Benedettu Colonna and he's been in the militia since August, but I have no idea where."

Antone nodded.

"You must go now. There's very little time. The sentence must be carried out at sunset tomorrow." Her brother stared at her. "There's something else you must know. Mother came yesterday. As you might expect, it wasn't to sympathise or to offer me any support." She paused and looked into Antone's face. "She was so ashamed of me and what I had done to the family's reputation that she said she would mix the poison herself."

"What?" Antone's eyes widened. "I don't believe this. I know Mother has never shown either of us much love, but she can't want to do this herself. It's merciless." He smacked his fist into his palm.

"Go now, find Benedettu. Tell him what has happened and make him understand how urgent it is. And say... say I'm sorry about our quarrel. We both said things we didn't mean, and I haven't seen him since."

"I'll do my best."

She took him in her arms and held him hard against her before pushing him towards the door. His eyes shone, and then he turned and was gone. Valeria went to the window to try to catch a glimpse of him, but it faced the wrong way. The outer door slammed and footsteps hurried away across the square. She wrapped her arms around herself and rocked back and forth.

***

The second day passed fast, too fast, and nightfall soon fell upon the mountains over the bay. She could no longer distinguish them from the clouds banking up behind them. No other visitors came that day, nor did she expect to see anyone, except when her keeper brought food. Her thoughts kept swinging back and forth between Santucci, Benedettu and Antone. Snatches of the trial came back to her: the stern group of men, their features distorted by the lamplight; Signore Rossi's red neck and stammering speech; the floor that tilted beneath her feet.

This might be her last night on earth. Still wearing her dress, she lay on the bed and listened to her pulse beating. How many heartbeats did she have left if Antone couldn't find Benedettu? Her guts turned to water at the thought of the next day.

She caressed the mound. "I'm sorry," she whispered. "You deserve to live. You've done nothing wrong, nothing you need to make amends for. My crime is to love where it's not permitted."

Again the spark of hope kindled. It still wasn't too late. Sleep claimed her in the small hours, but the nightmare tore a scream from her when the bitterness trickled over her tongue.

She tried to force herself back into sleep, cradling her head in her elbow, but it was no good. Instead, she turned onto her back and straightened her stiff limbs. The little window had no shutter, and the first inklings of dawn stretched across the sky. The day was stormy, and dark rainclouds chased each other. A squall spattered against the pane. Valeria levered herself up and sat on the bed for a long time, straining to hear the slightest footfall in the square. Before long, a soft tread sounded on the stairs and her keeper entered with a plate of bread.

"I don't want anything."

"As you wish. I'll leave it here on the table, anyway." The woman looked at her and something like compassion flickered in her eyes. "Would you like me to stay with you today?"

"I'd prefer to be alone to prepare myself."

The woman nodded and retreated. The knot in Valeria's gullet was too rigid for food, and the bread lay untouched on the plate. The light extended outside. Every minute brought her closer to her death, and yet she still couldn't believe it would happen. Antone would find a way, he would bring Benedettu and she could escape. Even so, Benedettu would somehow have to overpower the woman and her husband, and they wouldn't have much time to get away. Where they would go after that was too far in the future.

Valeria's thoughts ranged over her life and kept returning to her mother, this bitter woman who was prepared to kill her firstborn for the sake of the family's reputation. It was hard to imagine any mother could do that. She was so stern and unbending. What had happened to make her like that? Few words of endearment had ever passed between her parents, and Mother never spoke of Father after his death. Pietro's role was to be head of the family in her father's place, but Mother ruled the household and took the decisions. All Pietro did was carry them out.

Antone had always been more of a rebel, despite his softness when he was a boy. Maybe that was why Mother seemed to despise him, too. Now he was a grown man and had spent time in the militia, he had more steeliness about him. He no longer needed her protection. Their roles were reversed. The day when he and Pietro had a reckoning of accounts might not be far off, but if Benedettu didn't come in time she would know nothing about it.

The declining light of mid-afternoon slanted though the window. Time was running out, and fear rose into her mouth. She stood and paced up and down the narrow room. Three steps took her from one side to the other. She set herself a goal: cross the room ten times, take thirty paces, and Benedettu would be here by the thirtieth. She counted to thirty again and again, each time recommencing over the uneven floorboards. The light began to fade. No footsteps crossed the square or hurried up the stairs. Her mouth dry, she sat down and rubbed her clammy palms together. What if Antone hadn't been able to find Benedettu? What if he had refused to come? Would Antone himself come to free her? If he did, he would condemn himself for helping a convicted criminal. He would have to take the *machja* and become a bandit, as he used to fantasise in his youth. The reality of life as a bandit must be quite different. They always died a violent death after a relentless pursuit.

Muffled voices from below broke into her thoughts, followed by the tread and creak of several people climbing the stairs. Her heart stopped. Antone had found him – he had come for her. The footsteps paused outside on the landing and further murmuring took place. Valeria closed her eyes. When she reopened them, the president of the tribunal stood in the doorway. He stepped into the room, followed by her two keepers. Valeria pressed her back against the wall. No, this wasn't possible. Someone must be able to save her.

"It's time," the president said.

Valeria looked from one to the other, seeking some sympathy, a chink in the armour that would make them relent, but their faces were blank.

"Where's my mother? She said she was coming."

"She decided not to, in the end. She sent word that she's

147

unwell. But she prepared the poison and wishes to be informed when it's all over."

"What about the priest? Don't I have the right to the last rites?"

"You forfeited that right when you carried out your crime," the president said. "There are no last rites in a case such as yours."

So they wanted to squeeze every last drop out of her and deny her even the most basic comfort – the chance to make her confession and her peace with God. She couldn't believe she would be condemned to eternal damnation. God would know she didn't kill her husband, and her other offence was pardonable if He was merciful. Now I know I must die, she thought.

Summoning the last of her strength, she pushed away from the wall and stood straight. "If I have to die, let it be quick, but beforehand, I want to say I am innocent of the crime of poisoning my husband, and I will meet God with a clear conscience. As for Benedettu Colonna, I loved him and I still do. I have no regrets. My only sorrow is that my baby must die with me, since the child has done no harm to anyone. I hope you can live with yourselves afterwards, for in my eyes yours is the worst crime of all." She covered her face with her hands.

"That's enough," the president said. "You brought this punishment on yourself and you must submit to it."

Valeria no longer made any sense of the words. They passed over her like the breeze, without stopping. She could no longer think, her limbs were like water. If it must be done, let it be done fast.

The woman keeper advanced into the room and with a gentle pressure pushed Valeria down onto the hard chair. Her spine jarred against the back of it. This was one of the last sensations she would feel. She smoothed a hand over her tight belly, where the baby was growing. Why had all this happened? Why had everyone abandoned her?

The president busied himself with something in a bag, but Valeria barely saw or heard what was going on.

"Here," he said, handing her a beaker. "You must drink this to the last drop."

Valeria took the cup and peered at the murky contents. The liquid was blood-red, like the potion she had almost taken to rid herself of the child. She was still glad the baby had not died by her hand, and that she had not taken Delfina's way out. She looked into the president's eyes and found no comfort there.

Now, it must be now. Lifting the cup to her mouth, she raised her chin and swallowed the draught before the taste hit her tongue. When it did, the bitterness made her gag. The dream again, it was the dream, the same acrid tang flowing through her mouth. Was this what Margherita saw in the sheep's bone? The liquid burned like acid. With a shaky hand, she tried to place the beaker on the table, but it caught on the edge and rolled on the floor. A numbness took hold of her limbs and the room revolved around her. Her head was so heavy it kept falling forward. She must fight it, this couldn't be the end.

The people in the room splintered and multiplied until they were a crowd. Eyes surrounded her, terrible things that had never lodged in a human face. The walls pressed in upon her, and echoing voices resonated in her ears. The chair was dropping away. She was falling, sinking, tumbling into the stars that rushed to meet her, and beyond those the blackness that had never known light. It wrapped itself around her like a blanket until the last glowing pinpricks of light died out, one by one.

PART 2

CHAPTER 18

I t was cold, biting cold, and dark. She was jolted about and there was a grating sound, like wheels grinding over stones. Above her, something flapped in a rushing wind. So death was a journey and she had started on the road to – where? – Heaven or Hell? Or was this the way to Purgatory? The road would be long, but maybe time meant nothing on this side. She had no idea how far she had already travelled. A tight band pressed against her temples. The bitter taste of her death was still in her mouth.

Her head juddered against something hard, and she put out a hand to steady herself, grazing the palm against a rough board. A familiar scent that she couldn't place lingered on the air, and behind it another, salty tang. If her head would stop aching so much she could think. The darkness descended again, a curtain reaching inwards across her vision.

A wet object moved over her face and she tried to thrust

it away.

"You're awake, then, sister?"

Valeria snapped open her eyes. A blurred face swam into her vision and she could make out only the shape. The ground tilted and moved beneath her and she shut her eyes again, but it made the dizziness worse.

"I'm going to be sick." A foul substance rose up and spewed from her mouth. She retched until there was nothing left to expel. This must be Hell for it to taste so vile.

A strong arm encircled her shoulders and raised her to a sitting position.

"Drink this and you'll soon start to feel better." A hand pressed a cup to her lips and cool, fresh water trickled into her mouth. A whole river wouldn't have slaked her thirst, and she gulped until the cup was empty.

"Here," the voice said, and a damp cloth wiped her lips and around her mouth.

"Where… Who…?"

"You've been asleep for a long time. I was afraid you would never wake up."

She knew that voice. Antone? No, it couldn't be. Again the face moved in front of her, and the features began to piece themselves together.

"This is some sort of evil trick," she said. "You sound like Antone. You look like him, but he isn't dead. You must be a demon sent to torment me." She pressed her palms to her eyes. The hands lifted them away.

"Look at me. I'm no demon. It's me – Antone." He spread his arms wide.

She put out a hand and touched his face. The beard was soft and thick. She traced his nose and lips with her fingers.

"How can this be? You shouldn't be here." Her eyes widened and her mouth fell open. "You can't be dead, too."

He took her shoulders and shook her a little. "Calm

yourself. I'm no more dead than you are, and you're still very much alive."

"What happened, then? I drank the poison." She shuddered at the memory. "I must be dead."

She shivered again, and Antone fastened a shawl around her shoulders. "We can't stay here in the open much longer. You have to think of your baby."

Her hands went to her stomach. The baby. She had forgotten about it for a while, but the mound was warm and living. Relief flowed through her veins like sweet water, and a bubble of joy rose.

"Can you stand up? We must move on. I'll tell you all about it when we get there."

He helped her to her feet and lifted her into the back of the cart and laid her on a pile of sacking over a bed of straw.

"It's a little rough, I'm afraid, but we don't have much further to go."

She lay back on the sacks and the rhythmic movement of the wagon lulled her into sleep again. When it drew to an abrupt halt, she awoke.

"Here we are," Antone said. "This is the best I can manage for tonight, but it's dry, and I've brought some food. You need to eat."

Valeria climbed down from the cart, and her brother unhitched the horse and let it loose in a small enclosure encircled by a wall. Next to the pen stood a rough building, roofed with split stones. Antone ducked under the low lintel and spread fresh straw inside.

"Come inside. It's much warmer in there out of this gale."

On stiff legs, she staggered to the hut.

"Aren't you going to tell me what happened? I still can't believe I'm alive."

"Eat something first, and we'll talk after that. Here." He

handed her a hunk of bread and goat's cheese. At first, she felt sick at the idea of food, but the tangy cheese made her mouth water and she ate it all. Food had never tasted so good.

Antone wiped his knife on the straw and shifted his back against the wall. "When I left you for what we both feared was the last time, I was so upset I barely knew what to do. That scheme of yours to find Colonna and get him to rescue you wouldn't work; I could see that, even assuming I could find him. After all, he would have been in no better position than I was to get you out of there."

So he never went to look for Benedettu.

"I knew it was useless to track him down. This meant breaking my promise to you, so I had to find some other way to save you. That sentence was such a mockery. I knew you couldn't have killed Santucci. Mind you, you were foolish to take up with your shepherd. It just gave them a motive."

Valeria grimaced, but said nothing.

"I was even more horrified when you told me Mother had decided she would give you the poison. The night after I left you was terrible. I couldn't think what to do, but at least Mother's decision gave me some chance of influencing the situation, so I went home." He paused.

"I suppose Benedettu still doesn't know about the trial and the sentence, unless the news has reached him somehow," Valeria said. "I wanted him to know that I was sorry for our quarrel."

"If I'd gone to look for him, you might well be dead now. Let me explain what I did."

Valeria nodded.

Antone settled against the wall. "When I got home, Mother and Pietro were arguing. She was still disgusted with you, but she'd had time to think about it. She disowned you, but couldn't go as far as killing you. Pietro didn't agree. He was all for you dying by the family's hand, although he wasn't prepared to do it himself. Mother refused. In the end, he took his gun and stormed off. Mother told me to go down to Zaronza and tell the tribunal they'd have to carry out the sentence themselves. This gave me my chance."

He paused. Valeria held her breath.

"As well as what Margherita taught me, I learned in the militia how to bind wounds and ease pain. One of my colleagues, an older man from the Niolu, told me his mother had been a healer."

The image of the *signadora* casting the drops of oil on the water sprang to Valeria's mind. A vision of Margherita reading the sheep's bone slid in behind it. Goosebumps stippled her flesh.

Antone continued, "Some of his mother's remedies included a draught of bittersweet that puts a patient into a deep sleep and allows them to heal. In the right amount, it can feign the signs of death: too much, and it's fatal."

Valeria smiled. Margherita would have been proud of him.

"I still had some of the powder my militia friend gave me, so I made up the mixture, hoping I'd got the dose right, and took it with me. I handed it over, pretending it was the poison Mother had mixed. I didn't tell them anything about her change of heart, except to say she had decided to let them give it to you, since she wasn't feeling well."

He paused and drew breath. "There was no way I could warn you about what I'd done." He bit his lip. "I'm sorry you had to believe it really was poison. It pains me to think of the terror you must have gone through, but it was the only way. I'm sorry."

Valeria's mouth twisted. "The potion was certainly foul-tasting. That made it easy to believe it was poison." She hesitated. "I don't understand how you managed to take me away. Didn't they want to get rid of me?"

"That was the trickiest part. Mother didn't want to know about it, as long as it was all over. She thinks they got someone else to prepare the poison. But I had to convince the president to release your body to me. I was afraid in case I'd given you too big a dose of the sleeping draught and you really were dead. They were all for burying you at the corner of the wood, where your grave would be unknown, but I argued that you had brought dishonour on the Perettis so you didn't deserve even that."

"And the president believed you?"

"In the end, he decided to wash his hands of the whole thing and avoid the bother of burying you. He agreed I should take your body and dispose of it as I saw fit. If he hadn't, the whole plan might have failed."

A chill passed through Valeria. She might have been buried alive. If she had woken up in the grave, the soil would have filled her mouth and stifled her. She put a hand to her lips and chased the thought away.

"You took a big risk that they wouldn't let you do it."

"Yes, but what else could I do? Anyway, they did, so you're here now, alive."

She put a hand on his arm and squeezed. "You can't imagine how grateful I am. I owe you everything. Without you, I would now be lying in a grave with my baby, to be forgotten in a corner and trampled over. I'll never be able to thank you enough." Again, her hand went to the mound that started to tighten her skin like a drum.

"What happens now?" she continued. "I can't go back to Zaronza or Felicavo. I can't even go to Oresta, Benedettu's village, since they might know about it, too. Where will my baby and I be safe? And what about Benedettu?"

Antone hesitated for a long moment. "I think you have to

forget him. I don't know the man, but he's brought you nothing but trouble and misery. If you hadn't taken up with him, you'd still be living in comfort as a respected widow in Zaronza. Now, you've lost everything. All you owned is forfeit, and you can't turn up and ask for it back. Everyone thinks you're dead and your body has gone. You have to disappear, Valeria. You have to leave Corsica."

She gasped. "Where can I go? What would I do?"

"That's a chance you have to take. Every minute you stay on the island puts you in danger of discovery – and me, too. Imagine what would happen to me if they found out I helped a convicted criminal. They would hang me. Do you want that?"

"Of course not, you know that. But I'm a woman on her own, carrying a child. It's hard to see where I could live or be safe. You didn't think of that when you saved me from execution."

He snorted. "You didn't think of it, either, when you begged me to go and find Colonna. Where would you have gone with him – if he had agreed to take you away in the first place? There's nowhere on the island the pair of you would have been safe. Maybe he would have agreed to go abroad with you, but I wonder about that. In any case, my one concern was to save you and worry about what would happen later."

She looked down. "I'm sorry. We mustn't quarrel. You're quite right: I shouldn't put your life in danger. What about Benedettu? I doubt if he even knows our baby is still alive. He thought I should get rid of it, since we couldn't marry."

"I've said you're better off without him. If you want me to, I'll try to find him and tell him what has happened, although I'm not sure it's a good idea. You have to try to forget him and take your chance somewhere else. He can't,

156

and no doubt won't, follow you. You have to face up to it."

She swallowed and bit back the words. Antone was right. When she started her affair with Benedettu it could never lead anywhere, but she ignored that. She only had herself to blame. If she could relive the past few months, would she do it all again? It was too soon to answer that.

"Now we'd better try to sleep. Tomorrow I'll take you to Isola Rossa, and you can find a passage to the mainland. I can't risk doing any more."

"You've already done more than enough. Thanks to you my baby and I are still alive. We have a chance."

Antone stretched out on the straw and turned on his side. Soon, his breathing deepened. Valeria made a nest and curled up around the baby. Trying to sleep was futile, even though heavy weights dragged on her limbs. The wind howled around the hut trying to wrench off the slates.

***

At first light, Antone harnessed the horse between the shafts and they set off again. The wind had dropped. It had chased away the clouds and polished the sky to a silvery blue. A whitening of frost lay in the hollows. The mountains loomed blue-grey in the growing daylight. The island had never looked so beautiful, and yet she would have to leave Corsica and might never see it again. She had never known anywhere else, barely even left her own village or Zaronza, and couldn't imagine what the lands beyond Corsica might be like. She tried to conjure up Benedettu's face, but already it was less sharp, as if seen through gauze. Only the blue purity of his eyes stayed with her, all she had to hold on to through the days to come.

The cart jolted along the track, the horse picking his way between the stones. Nobody was about yet, and the route Antone had chosen skirted the villages and dwellings. In the

157

distance, white hamlets clung like barnacles to their hillsides, and the silvery-green leaves of the olive trees trembled in the light breeze.

Nothing was left to say and they travelled in silence. Before long, the path flattened out and the shimmering mirror of the sea appeared between the hills. They passed the first houses of a small port wedged on the flat land between the mountains and the sea.

"Where are we?" Valeria said.

"Isola Rossa. I'm told one can get a passage from here to France."

It was all so vague. Once in France, what would she do for a roof, food? Another thought struck her.

"How will I pay for the journey? I have no money, nothing."

Antone reached into a goatskin bag and pulled out a small purse. "Here. I've been able to save some money from my time in Corte. I don't know if it will be enough, but it's better than nothing."

The purse chinked in Valeria's fingers. A twist of guilt weaved its way through her. She put her hand over his. "Your savings. It's all you have. One day, I'll find a way to repay you if I can."

He nodded, and his Adam's apple rose up and down. The cart clattered down the cobbled streets towards the small harbour. A few fishing boats bobbed on the waves, which smacked against the breakwater. A larger vessel was at anchor a little further out. The only person in sight was a fisherman mending his nets outside a cottage on the quay.

"I'll ask him what he knows of that ship," Antone said.

The men exchanged a few words. Antone returned to the cart.

"He says you can usually find the captain in the house over there, taking his breakfast. You'd better stay here. It wouldn't do for you to enter a place like that."

Valeria pulled the shawl over her and drew it around her. After a few minutes, her brother emerged with a swarthy, thickset man. A grizzled beard straggled below a gaunt face criss-crossed with the marks of weather and salt.

"Here's my sister, Signora Santucci, Captain."

The man nodded. "Signora," he said in a strange, thick accent.

"Captain Alvarez has agreed to give you a passage to Marseille in France, which is nearly two days' sailing from here. You must pay him his price."

The man named a fee. With each coin Valeria dropped into his hand the reality of leaving Corsica grew, and she smothered the tears that threatened to flow. At least some money was left.

"We set sail when the tide turns, in a few hours' time."

"Where can I find shelter in the meantime, Captain? It's too cold to stay outside."

He pointed at the fisherman. "His wife will look after you and give you something to eat. She's used to doing it for the few passengers we get passing through here. I'll send one of my men to fetch you when it's time." He turned on his heel and crossed the quay to the tavern.

"I told him you're a widow going to the mainland to live with our sister," Antone said. "He didn't seem to care one way or the other, provided you paid up. I think you can rely on him not to ask questions. He seems a close sort of man."

Antone led the way to the house of the fisherman, who called his wife, a round, apple-cheeked woman with eyes that looked in different directions.

Antone drew Valeria aside and whispered, "Now I must leave you, sister. I've stayed away long enough. Mother's used to me roaming about, but she might start to be suspicious if I don't return soon. I shall have to report what happened and how your body was disposed of. There's nothing more I can do for you here, and we must part."

His eyes shone. Valeria's throat was too thick to speak. She pulled her brother to her and clasped him tight.

"Goodbye, Valeria."

"Farewell, Antone," she whispered. He stepped up onto the cart and turned the horse towards the cobbled alleyway. She stood there, a hand raised, until he was lost to view, and then entered the house.

The kitchen was dark but warm. The woman bustled about preparing food. She asked where she was going, and Valeria gave a short version of the story Antone had told Captain Alvarez.

"When is your baby due, Signora?" She didn't miss anything.

"In a few months."

"Ah. Such a pity, you being a widow. Your child will miss having a father. How did your husband die?"

"He had an illness."

The woman clucked. "It's not often a lady travels alone like you, but at least you have relatives on the other side who can look out for you. How many children does your sister have?"

Would the woman never stop asking questions? Valeria gave short answers until at last the fisherman's wife turned away and left her in peace. No doubt she didn't have much female company here, but the last thing Valeria wanted to do was talk. The final view of Antone when he disappeared up the alleyway was imprinted on her memory. It was all she would have of him for the rest of her life, perhaps. She had lost all those she loved, but she still had the baby.

The ship's man came for her and took the goatskin bag. It contained some food, a sheepskin fleece and a few items of men's clothing, all Antone had been able to gather together at short notice. It would have been impossible to get any of her own clothes, so she would have to make do with what she had.

"Is this your only bag, Signora?" the man said.

"Yes, a few things for the voyage. My brother will send my box on after me."

The man nodded and said nothing. He helped her into a small skiff and rowed across to the ship, where two of the hands descended the ladder to fetch her up. The baby was starting to restrict her movements. They showed her to a narrow cabin, where she sat on the makeshift bed, her thoughts whirling but her emotions numb.

The trial, so recent and yet so far away, was receding into a nightmare, something not lived in reality. Amid the mist swirling in her mind, a face was taking shape. Signora Rossi's hooded eyes materialised, always watching her, waiting for her to make a fatal mistake. The woman had wanted her dead. Why had she hated her so much? Valeria turned it over and over in her mind, unable to find an answer.

She was alive, thanks to Antone, and the life surged in her. Even so, the bitterness wedged like a lump in her gut. Signora Rossi had committed a crime far worse than anything Valeria had done, yet she would go unpunished for it. Valeria would carry the burden, but she could do nothing about it and must look to the future. A momentary dizziness took her at the idea of that unknown void, and her fingers gripped the wooden bunk, hard and solid.

A short while later, the ship weighed anchor and glided out of the harbour. Valeria had never been on the sea before, even when she lived in Zaronza, and the boat rolled and creaked under her feet. She went up on deck and stepped around the coils of rope, keeping well away from the side. At the stern, she clung on tight. The fragrant scent of the *machja* accompanied her for a while, carried on the offshore breeze. The purple mountains dwindled, until they disappeared altogether into the haze, and Corsica was lost to her.

At that moment, the baby stirred, and along with the movement came a flutter of hope.

"One day, we'll return. I promise."

CHAPTER 19

Marseille: November 1762

The boat from Isola Rossa had an uneventful, if choppy, passage across the Mediterranean. The wind whisked up the silvery-blue sea into a greenish swell that rocked the vessel from side to side. After the last sight of Corsica, Valeria kept to her cabin and took her meals there alone, afraid to be pitched over the side if she ventured on deck. She was not going to risk her life now, after her close brush with death. Captain Alvarez and the crew were polite but distant. Most of the time, she stretched out on the bunk and rested, quelling the occasional tide of nausea that threatened to engulf her.

On the second day, a crewman tapped on her door. "We're not far off land now, Signora. The sea's calmer, so the captain said you might like to come up on deck and take a look."

She heaved herself upright, giving thanks that the nausea had subsided.

Captain Alvarez approached when she went up on deck.

"Good morning, Signora. The wind is with us, so we should make the port by midday." He pointed over the bow. "You can just see the land now."

On deck, Valeria shaded her eyes against the sun and strained to catch a glimpse of Marseille. The grey clouds that accompanied them out at sea had peeled away to leave a brilliant blue sky, which arced over the horizon. Now, the implications of what she was doing came home to her. Her stomach shrank. Throughout the voyage, she had avoided thinking about what she would do when they arrived, but the need to make a decision wouldn't go away.

She had half a mind to ask Captain Alvarez to take her back to Corsica on his next voyage, but, of course, that was absurd. Maybe he could suggest a place to stay, but she would have to be careful. Antone had told him she was going to live with her sister. It wouldn't do to suggest she was alone. True, nobody would be looking for her in Corsica, and certainly not in Marseille, but a lone woman might raise suspicions. The habit of secrecy from her upbringing was her protection.

"Captain, my sister lives some way outside the city. She won't know which day your boat docks. Could you recommend a decent place to stay, so I can rest before I travel to her tomorrow?"

A glint appeared in his eyes, somewhere between awareness and amusement. His gaze travelled up and down the simple dress in which she spent her last days in Zaronza. All she carried with her was a small bag. She could almost hear his mind work. Had he given a passage to pregnant women from Corsica before? The heat rose up her neck. Alvarez fingered his beard and appeared to consider the matter.

"Well now, a lady wouldn't be comfortable in the sort of places the crew and I are used to."

He chuckled, and the warmth broke out in Valeria's cheeks. She had led a sheltered life, but she could imagine what he meant. The village women and the elders of Zaronza said she was no better than a whore. A momentary vision of Benedettu passed across her thoughts. No, it wasn't like that with him.

She ignored Alvarez' innuendo and looked him in the eyes. "I need a decent house where I can get a clean room at a fair price. You, or your men, must know somewhere, even if it's not the sort of place you favour."

His face closed up and he looked over her shoulder. "I'll get one of the men to show you once we've docked, but you'll have to wait. We need to unload the cargo, and I can't spare a man until we've finished."

"I don't mind waiting as long as there's somewhere I can sit."

"You can stay aboard or wait on the quayside, as you wish."

Alvarez swivelled on his heel and shouted to a crewman about the preparations for landing the vessel. Valeria approached the ship's side and leant her weight against the wood to ease her ankles. The land was still distant but now quite visible. The problem of the first night ashore was solved, but she would have to be careful with the remaining money.

The ship docked in a large port, where the buildings stretched in all directions. The city was built on a hill with mountains beyond it. Valeria had never seen so many people in one place. Gulls screamed overhead, and a constant hubbub arose, as if the place itself were talking. She stayed on deck for a while and watched the perpetual movement, until the sun became too hot. The weather had changed during the voyage. She sought refuge in the cabin again and lay down on the bunk.

It took a while to unload the cargo, and she nodded off several times, only to wake with a start a few minutes later. Each time, her body tensed at the awareness of where she was. A headache fanned out over her temples and she pressed her eyes shut to ease it. The figures of Benedettu, Signora Rossi and the village elders marched across her vision, but she brushed them aside.

At length, someone tapped on the door.

"The captain's asked me to take you to a place he knows, Signora."

"I'm ready."

The crewman picked up her bag and she followed him down the gangplank and onto the crowded quayside. Without papers, Valeria expected to be stopped at any moment, but no one seemed interested in her. Alvarez was nowhere to be seen, but she hadn't expected him to wait to say goodbye. The man shouldered his way through the crowd and Valeria stayed close behind. If he disappeared with her bag he would find little of value in it. She had sewn the purse under her dress. From time to time, the man turned to see if she was following and then set off again.

"Is it far?" Valeria asked, almost faint with the fatigue of the past few days.

"No, Signora, not far."

He led her along a maze of small streets away from the harbour. It would be difficult to find her way back. This was all so different from Felicavo and Zaronza. The stonework was chipped and soiled. Limp washing hung on lines stretched between the windows above, and grimy children squatted in the gutters or ran to and fro yelling. A salty, fishy odour filled the air, with a stronger, sour reek beneath it. From the upper windows, women called to each other in a strange tongue.

At last, the man stopped before a solid door with a

knocker in the shape of a closed hand around a ball. The house seemed to be better-kept than its neighbours.

"Here you are, Signora. This is Madame Pons' place. The captain said to mention his name."

He was still hanging on to her bag, and Valeria gave him a coin, although few remained. He flashed her a toothless smile, handed over the bag and loped off, no doubt relieved to be rid of her and anxious to spend his money after being at sea.

She rapped on the door. Almost at once, a stout woman with white-streaked raven hair opened it. A deep line ran from the side of each nostril to the edges of her mouth. The woman said something which Valeria didn't understand. Madame Pons spoke again, louder. Valeria shook her head and said in Corsican, "Captain Alvarez sent me. I'm looking for a place to stay."

Madame Pons frowned and said, "Italian, are you?" She stumbled a little over the words. The language was strange; not Corsican, but very similar. A warm surge of relief flowed through Valeria.

"No. I come from Corsica. I'm a widow and I'm going to live with my sister, but I need somewhere to stay for a few days. Captain Alvarez said you might give me a bed."

Madame Pons' gaze dropped to Valeria's stomach.

"A widow," she repeated, as if it were doubtful. "Well, you'd better come in. You're in luck. I've one room at the back. It's small, but that means it's cheaper. Payment in advance." She mentioned a price.

Valeria strained to understand. She didn't know the money Madame Pons spoke of, so she held out a few coins. The landlady took one, inspected it on both sides and bit it.

"Yes, I'll take those; they're as good as any. How many nights?"

Valeria thought fast. "Three, to begin with."

167

Madame Pons selected five more coins from her outstretched palm.

"Good thing for you I'm honest. Now, I'll show you the room."

Madame Pons' bulging hips preceded Valeria up three flights of a narrow staircase and she stood aside at an open door. The room was tiny, with just enough space for a bed and a small table with a basin and a ewer. Valeria crossed to the window and looked down onto an enclosed courtyard. Above, a square of sky was visible. Her heart plunged when she thought of the Corsican views and sunsets. At least the room was clean and tidy. She turned back to Madame Pons.

"Yes, this will suit me."

Madame Pons nodded. "A few rules. I keep a respectable house and I don't allow men friends to visit. I don't do meals, but I'll provide a soup in the evening for two sous extra. The rest you have to find elsewhere. I can suggest places where a woman can eat in peace."

"In that case, I'll pay for a soup this evening."

Madame Pons turned to go.

"I'm so glad you speak Corsican," Valeria said in a rush.

"It's not Corsican, it's Italian. My father came from Livorno."

She nodded again and went downstairs. Valeria shut the door, put her bag on the floor and lowered herself onto the bed. Children's screams and a woman's scolding tones floated up from the courtyard. Valeria massaged her aching temples. She was bone-tired, but the first test was over. She had somewhere to stay, and could make herself understood. Maybe this was a sign that everything would work out. Then the inevitable reality flooded back in. The money wouldn't last for more than a few days, and Madame Pons didn't seem like the kind of woman to take pity on her when it ran out. The next day, she would have to find work.

CHAPTER 20

When Valeria awoke from a dreamless sleep, the morning was already well advanced. She rubbed her face with a damp cloth and shook out her dress, which was several days in the wearing, stained and dusty from the journey. She picked up her bag, but decided it would be a burden. Even if Madame Pons was not as honest as she made out, there wasn't much in it worth stealing. She tucked the remaining money into the pouch inside her dress and went downstairs. Her stomach felt like a cavern. She hadn't eaten anything since the soup and bread the night before.

A door opened and Madame Pons peered out. "Oh, it's you. I was wondering when you were going to appear. I don't like my residents staying in bed all day. They get in my way."

"I'm sorry. My ship came in yesterday and I was so tired that I slept longer than I meant to. I'm going out now and I won't return until this evening."

Madame Pons pursed her lips and her glance strayed again to the bulge in Valeria's dress. Valeria wondered if she should ask where she could get work, but decided to say nothing. She went out into the street. Which way? By instinct, she turned in the direction of the harbour.

The sun was already high, and it was much warmer than in Corsica. Before she did anything else, she needed to find food. She wandered along several alleys with nothing but houses. After turning a corner, she came into a square where a woman carrying a loaf of bread emerged from a door. The shop was dark, but once Valeria's eyes had adjusted to the dim light, an array of bread and pastries was spread out before her on the counter. The savoury aroma made her mouth water.

A plump woman with floury hands came out of a back room. Valeria pointed to a pie like the ones they ate in Corsica. The woman spoke, but Valeria shrugged and held out her palm with a few coins. The shopkeeper indicated two. The money would run out too fast if she took the pie. The hunger urging her, she pointed at a smaller, flat pastry topped with olives and what looked like tiny fish, and made signs to ask its name. The woman frowned, but at last she understood.

"*Pissaladiero.*"

Valeria worked hard to mimic her. She handed over the single coin the pastry was worth. The saliva filled her mouth.

"*Merci,*" the woman said.

Valeria guessed this meant thank you, and said it in return. The woman smiled. She had learned two words already.

Once out of the square, she took a bite of the pastry. A hot mantle of shame descended on her. People didn't eat in the street in Corsica, except for children who thought their mothers weren't looking. Once she had taken the first mouthful, she had to finish it. The salty pastry took the edge off the hunger for the moment.

There remained the problem of finding paid work. Wandering about wouldn't help. The alleys were shady on one side, but the heat bore down when the sun reached its highest point, and Valeria's armpits grew clammy and sticky. The houses were shuttered, and people were no doubt taking their midday meal. She was thirsty, too. She came to a fountain shaded by a tree and sat on the parapet, dragging her fingers in the water. It reminded her of the fountain in Zaronza, the scene of her disgrace.

A woman carrying a jug came out of a nearby house and approached the spout.

"Can I drink this water, Signora?"

The woman stared at her and then frowned and shrugged. Valeria pointed to her mouth and to the water. The woman's brow cleared and she nodded, holding her jar under the silvery jet. She returned to the house. Valeria waited until the door had closed and leant over, scooped up the water and gulped it down. Once she had drunk her fill, she sat enjoying the comparative freshness under the tree.

"What am I going to do? I don't speak the same language as the people here. How can I find work if they can't understand me?"

A cloud of despair descended. It was no good escaping death if she couldn't find a way to live. The only person she knew in this hostile place was Madame Pons, and the woman was as soft as granite. Sitting by the fountain, pleasant as it was, wouldn't solve her problems. Her talents were limited. She could sew, cook and keep house, and knew a good deal about the medical uses of herbs, but Marseille no doubt had plenty of physicians to tend to people's illnesses. Perhaps a clothing workshop would have work for a seamstress. Or maybe a rich person might need a housekeeper.

Valeria sighed and pushed herself up from the parapet. She dragged up and down the sweltering streets until her ankles swelled. Despite the water, her mouth was dry. Through an open door, rows of women were seated at long tables sewing great sheets of cloth. They laboured in silence. Valeria tapped on the doorframe. A dozen pairs of eyes gazed at her. A thin middle-aged woman with an air of authority, dressed in black, stood up. Valeria pointed at the tables, made sewing movements and pointed at herself. The woman looked at Valeria's pregnant bulge and spoke again, this time to the women around the table.

"Oh, please," Valeria said in Corsican. "I need to get work. I'm a widow and I haven't any money. You needn't worry; I'll work hard, I promise."

One of the women looked hard at Valeria, and then approached. Her face was very pale, and white blonde hair escaped from her headscarf. She could have been anywhere between twenty and fifty.

"You are from Italy?" she asked in halting tones.

"No, I'm from Corsica, but I think I understand Italian, if that's what you're speaking."

"I speak it a little bit. I think you ask for work and have no husband anymore?"

Valeria grabbed her hand.

"Yes, that's right. Could you explain to this lady?"

The girl (for she couldn't have been more than twenty, despite her bent back) turned to the supervisor. The older woman frowned, shrugged and pointed to Valeria's belly before replying.

"She don't have spare work just now and you have a baby to come. She can't have a baby here."

"Oh, but I could work from home and look after the baby there. I wouldn't be any trouble. I'm used to hard work."

The girl turned and related this to the woman, who

shrugged.

"I'm sorry. She say even if you don't have a baby she don't have any work to give you." The girl gave a fleeting smile and patted Valeria's arm. The supervisor swept the other women with her gaze and they bent their heads to their sewing.

"I'm sorry," the girl repeated.

Valeria stumbled unseeing towards the door. People saw her baby and not her.

"Wait," the young woman called out and hurried after her. "You look like a good person. I want to help. I work at another place before I come here. You can try there. Rue des Treize Pierres."

Valeria repeated the meaningless words.

"Bérengère!" a sharp voice called from inside the *atelier*.

Bérengère looked around and then back at Valeria. She pointed down the street. "That way, near the sea. Say them I send you. Bérengère." She ran back inside.

A chink of light pierced the dark cloud hanging over Valeria. Even in the crowded streets of this city, one could feel alone. People were busy with their own affairs; no one cared about a pregnant widow. But some people wanted to help, and a few spoke a language she could understand. She had felt an instant rapport with Bérengère. A friend would make all the difference.

She had to ask passers-by the way, repeating the strange syllables of the Rue des Treize Pierres until they understood. The keening of gulls and the briny tang of the sea were in the air. The sun was now at its height, and swelled the odour rising from the gutters. Valeria put a hand over her nose to quell the wave of nausea. She longed for the clean-smelling *machja* and the scent of scrubbed wood and stone.

More hopeful this time, she approached an *atelier* and rapped at the open door. This time a man came and looked

173

her up and down. She went through the same motions of asking for work.

"Bérengère, Bérengère," she said and pointed back in the direction of the other *atelier*.

The man's face clouded at the mention of Bérengère's name, and he gave a scornful wave of his hand. As before, he spoke in a language she didn't know, and nobody here seemed to speak Italian or Corsican when she tried it out. The man spread his hands in a helpless gesture. The baby again. He shrugged.

Yet again, Valeria left, head bowed. A cold wave travelled through her body, despite the heat. No one wanted a woman with a child. Maybe they were right. For a moment, she sensed bitterness towards the baby she was carrying.

The sun was sinking when Valeria made her way back to Madame Pons' house. The afternoon's search had turned up nothing else.

"May I have a bowl of soup again this evening?"

Madame Pons grunted and didn't ask what she had done all day.

Valeria dropped onto the bed. The bag had been moved from the floor to the table. No doubt Madame Pons had taken a good look inside. What would she have made of the men's shirts, which were all the clothes Antone had been able to gather at short notice? If she hadn't been so weary, she would have smiled, but even that was an effort. Before she fell asleep, Valeria resolved to wake much earlier the next day and to try harder.

CHAPTER 21

"**Y**ou're up a bit earlier this morning," Madame Pons said, her mouth pursed in a wintry smile. Valeria pushed down the reply that came to her lips. "I'll be out all day, so I won't bother you."

The creaking stairs and closing doors showed that the other residents rose early and returned late. Maybe she could find out about work from one of them. The language would be a problem, but she was already learning how to get around it.

"Don't forget," Madame Pons said, when Valeria opened the front door, "you paid for three nights and you've already had two. If you want to stay after tonight I expect to be paid in advance tomorrow. Perhaps your sister will turn up?" The lines beside her nose deepened.

"Of course," Valeria said, struggling to master her expression while a cold fist gripped her. The lighter mood in which she awoke that morning trickled down like the sand in a timer. Madame Pons must have guessed at her pinched circumstances from the dress worn every day and the few things in the bag. Valeria stood tall, nodded at her landlady, and shut the door hard behind her.

She walked all day in a sultry autumn heatwave that pressed down on the city. Wisps of hair escaped from her headscarf and stuck to her damp brow. The baby kicked hard. Women flung water on the alleys to lay the dust, but it coated Valeria's tongue and settled in her nostrils.

She tried shops, *ateliers*, even taverns near the waterfront, but nowhere had work. Entering such places would have been frowned on in Corsica, but there was no choice. With a mixture of relief and regret she left unsuccessful each time. The sailors eyed her askance, and one or two winked in a suggestive way, but she ignored them and moved with all the dignity she could muster.

If Santucci could have seen her begging for menial work, it would have been a personal affront to his honour. He had left her enough to live on, even if life as a widow in Zaronza was arid and lonely. She cursed herself for not resisting Benedettu. She cursed him, too, for abandoning her when she needed him. Most of all, she cursed Madame Rossi for the lies she'd had no chance to prove false.

Dusk gathered in the street corners when Valeria made her way back to the pension. Madame Pons was prowling in the hallway, like a giant spider in the middle of its web. Didn't the woman ever go out? The smell of cooking, stale as it was, made Valeria ache with emptiness.

"Soup?" Madame Pons asked.

"Yes, please." Valeria had enough coins for that and maybe for a meal the next day. After that, nothing would be left. Nothing at all.

"Don't forget, I want to be paid in advance if you plan to stay any longer."

Valeria turned and faced her, looking her in the eyes. "I'll tell you tomorrow morning, Signora Pons. I must decide whether I need to stay for a few more days. I have some business to see to here."

Madame Pons snorted and headed towards a back room. "Business," she muttered.

Valeria passed a sleepless night. The room was stuffy, even with the window open. No air circulated in the cavernous courtyard. City night sounds floated in. Where would she stay tomorrow night? At last, she fell into a sleep populated by dreams where half-known faces appeared before her. They dissolved again when she tried to make out their features.

Waking with a start, she saw dawn was rising and a grey light filtered through the tiny window. The intense blue sky of the previous days had disappeared, replaced by a milky white, mottled with grey. Shafts of sunlight pierced the clouds for brief moments.

Valeria had to make a choice between the room and food. If she left without paying, Madame Pons would let the room to someone else. If she gave Madame Pons all her money, she wouldn't be able to eat. She must eat, for the baby's sake. Maybe she could slip out and claim later she couldn't find Madame Pons when she wanted to pay. She decided to leave her bag as proof of her intention to return. It would be a burden, anyway.

From the top of the stairs, Valeria could see the front door. Madame Pons emerged from the back room, muttering to herself, and crossed the hallway. Her heavy footsteps receded down the street. Valeria sped down the staircase, careful not to trip on the uneven treads. Opening the door a crack, she peered out to right and left. She hurried to the end of the street and turned the corner.

Ranks of purple clouds massed behind the buildings, and with a stab of alarm Valeria remembered her shawl, left behind in the bag. It was too late to go back. She would have to find shelter if a storm broke.

No work was to be had that day, either, not for a woman who would give birth within a few months. The rain held off, but the heat continued to build until it must surely burst out. Valeria spent the last of the money on food and had a few small coins left. Not enough to pay Madame Pons for another night. Life was reduced to where she would sleep and how she would eat for a day. All thoughts of Corsica, Benedettu, Signora Rossi and the rest were consumed by the bare need to stay alive.

Unsure what to do, Valeria wandered down to the harbour. Crates littered the quayside and crewmen hurried here and there. Ignoring them, she crossed to the water's edge and looked down at the sea, which splashed against the wall. Flotsam bobbed up and down in the grey, scummy water. What would it feel like to slide into the waves, draw the water over her like a blanket and let it rush into her lungs, crowding out the air? She took a step forward, right against the edge of the quay, and closed her eyes. It would be so easy. Just another step…

The baby fluttered. She stepped back as if scalded. What was she thinking of? She owed it to Antone, who had risked so much to save her, to protect her child. In spite of everything, she wanted the baby, to whom she was bound now. It was no longer only one life. She couldn't do what Delfina had done.

"No," she murmured. "This is not where I'm going to die."

Once she had taken the decision, the darkness lifted a little. She walked back towards the city.

***

When she approached the *pension*, the first fat drops of rain fell, leaving spots the size of coins in the dust. The storm gathered itself and unleashed the full force of a downpour like a waterfall.

"Oh no," Valeria said, and quickened her pace.

The rain washed into her eyes and her hair was soon wringing wet. She ran the last few steps to the house and pulled up short. Her bag had been slung on the step, and some of her possessions had spilled out. She picked it up, stuffed back her belongings and hammered on the door.

After a while, a flint-faced Madame Pons opened it.

"Oh, it's you. I told you it was payment in advance. You're lucky I didn't keep your things."

Valeria was now dripping wet, but Madame Pons blocked the doorway.

"I'm sorry; I couldn't find you when I went out this morning, so I left my bag. I hoped you'd realise I would come back. Couldn't I stay one more night?"

"If you pay the price, yes. I haven't let the room yet."

"Well… but, you see, for the moment I'm bit short of money. I was expecting to have some today and I'm sure I will have it tomorrow."

"Tomorrow's no good. No payment in advance, no room."

"Please. I haven't anywhere else to go. I promise I'll pay you tomorrow."

"You should have thought of that earlier," Madame Pons replied. "I knew this tale about going to live with a sister was a load of nonsense. Well, it's no good giving me some hard-luck story. And I don't accept promises."

"I'm pregnant and it's raining. You can't leave me out on the street."

"I don't give charity. I let my rooms to respectable people who pay me. If you can't pay, you can't stay, and there's no more to be said. Try one of the taverns by the harbour. They're less particular about who they take."

179

She pushed the door closed. Valeria tried to push back, but Madame Pons was heavier.

Valeria pounded on the door. "You're a cruel woman. Don't you have any pity?"

No answer came from within. Valeria sank down onto her knees on the wet step, regardless of the damp soaking through to her skin. It would have been better to keep money for the room rather than food. Now where could she go? A bubble of panic swelled, and she gave way to the tears of anger, frustration and fear that stung her eyes and mingled with the rain.

After a minute or so, she felt calmer and stood up. First, she rummaged in the bag and pulled out the sheepskin fleece and the shawl. At least those garments were dry, for the moment, but she shivered under the damp dress and pulled the shawl tight. The temperature had dropped with the storm's arrival.

If she went back to the *atelier*, Bérengère might agree to take her in for a night or so. If it came to it, she would sleep on a floor. Anywhere was better than walking the streets in this weather. Warmed by the idea, she set off towards the *atelier*.

The teeming rain made the going hard. The dust had churned into mud, and puddles had collected in the uneven streets, lapping over her shoes. The shawl and the fleece beneath it were soon weighed down with water, and the bag was heavy despite its meagre contents. Hunger was overtaking her; the little she had eaten during the past few days wasn't enough. She struggled on until she came to the street with the *atelier* and quickened her pace.

The workshop was locked up. No one came when she banged on the door. She slid down onto the step. The street was empty. Everyone was indoors, shutters closed against the weather. She could try knocking on doors, but doubted anyone would take her in. Perhaps one of the taverns, down by the waterfront? Yes, it was a last resort, but worth trying. She would do anything now.

When she stood up, a cold wave ran through her and everything wheeled around her. Black dots appeared before her vision, and grew larger until they merged into one another.

CHAPTER 22

Faces swam above her, but their features were blurred. They jabbered away in words she didn't understand. Hands were on her, shaking and pushing her back and forth. Her arm was shoved in one direction and pulled in another. For a moment, she thought she was back in Zaronza by the fountain, with the women spitting and jeering at her while Signora Rossi spurred them on. She fought to escape their grasp, but firm hands held her down. After a while, she gave up and the blackness fell again.

***

Valeria opened her eyes and everything was much clearer this time. Where was she? The last thing she remembered was standing up from the cold, wet step of the *atelier* before the black patches covered her vision. It came back with chilling clarity, like a plunge into an icy stream. She had no money, no work and nowhere to live. All she had were her wet clothes and the baby.

The baby. Her hands moved to her abdomen with its swollen mound, and a gentle prod met the pressure of her palms. She shut her eyes and breathed out, rubbing her arms. The sleeves were dry; she had been wet through.

With a start, she sat up and stared around her at a dingy room. A copper-haired woman peered at her and spoke but, as usual, it was gibberish.

"Oh, not again," Valeria said, the tears springing to the corners of her eyes. "I can't understand." She gestured at the room, the bed. "Where am I? What's happened? If only I could talk to you."

The woman put a finger to her lips, gave Valeria a glass with a syrupy liquid in it, and then left the room. Moments later, the woman returned, followed by another, taller one with black hair and an olive complexion. She signalled to Valeria to say something.

Would it make any difference? "My name is Valeria Santucci. I don't know where I am, and I can't understand what anyone says."

The tall woman sat down on the edge of the bed. She had dark, almost black, almond-shaped eyes.

"You speak a language that's close to Italian, but not Italian. Where do you come from?"

Valeria breathed out. Thank God; someone who spoke a language she could follow. "I come from Corsica, and I've learned the two languages are not far apart. You know Italian, then?"

The other woman babbled at the dark one, who silenced her with an imperious wave and spoke in a sharp tone.

"I am Italian," the woman said, switching her gaze to Valeria. "My name is Francesca. I'll tell you later how I came to Marseille. For the time being, I think you should rest until you feel stronger." She made to get up, but Valeria put a hand on her arm.

"Please, before you go, can you tell me where I am and who you are?"

183

"This is where we live, Arlette and I. We both work in the soap factory, just around the corner in the Rue Sainte."

Valeria had no idea what soap was, but she didn't want to look ignorant, so she nodded.

"I must admit when we found you in the street, Arlette and I thought you might be a prostitute," Francesca said. Valeria gasped. "But I couldn't leave you lying there. Anyway, you don't seem the type."

So they had assumed she sold her body for money. For a moment, the indignation threatened to get the better of her. Still, what else could they think? She was out on her own, in a seedy part of the city, on a filthy night, wearing a soiled and shabby dress. Once a respectable married woman, she had become a penniless vagrant carrying an illegitimate child. Other women no doubt had similar stories to tell. How many of them did it because they wanted to? If it hadn't been for the baby, she might have had to do the same. She might still have to.

The anger leached out of her. She lay back against the pillow.

"I can imagine how it must look, but I haven't had to sell myself yet. I hope it won't come to that. My life in Corsica was quite different."

Francesca smiled and patted her arm. "Now, get some rest. We'll talk later, and then you can eat something."

The two women left the room. Valeria pulled the rough blanket over her and allowed sleep to claim her.

***

"What time is it?" Valeria asked when Francesca brought her a plate of food.

"Mid-morning. You've slept for some time. At least it's Sunday. Arlette and I don't have to work today."

Valeria devoured the food, while Francesca watched her.

184

"Feeling better?"

"Much," Valeria said.

"Now, if you feel strong enough, tell me why you left Corsica and how you come to be here."

Valeria studied her hands for a moment. How much should she tell? Knots tightened in her temples. She couldn't go back to Corsica to face her sentence again, but the desire to unburden herself was too strong. The only other person who knew her story was Antone, and even he didn't know everything. Something about Francesca invited confession, so she pulled herself upright in the bed and spoke.

When she described the trial, Francesca took one of her hands and squeezed it tight. She frowned. "So unfair," she said. She kept hold of Valeria's hand.

At last, the tale was finished. A feeling of great tiredness came over her, but also one of peace. She was emptied out, purged. Tears slid down her face and she dried them with her sleeve.

It took some time before Francesca spoke. Her eyes shone. "What they did to you was terrible, cruel. You may have been unwise to follow your feelings, but haven't we all done that? The woman always gets punished for it, never the man. I don't think for a moment you were a murderer. How could they have believed such lies?"

"Are you going to tell Arlette?"

"I'll tell her what she needs to know, but it might be safer for you if we left out the part about being accused of murdering your husband. The fewer people who know about it, the better, but I can keep a secret. I'll say you were chased out of Corsica for having an affair and becoming pregnant. Neither of us is in a position to judge you for that. Another thing. If I were you, I would change your name. Arlette didn't hear it: she didn't understand. What was your maiden name?"

"Peretti."

"Revert to that, then, but keep your first name."

Valeria nodded. Keeping secrets had become second nature.

"Now," she said. "What about you? I've told you my story. I'd like to hear yours."

Francesca looked away as if into the far distance. "I was also foolish when I was younger, and I've more than paid the price for it."

Valeria waited while she gathered herself, and then it all came out in a rush.

"I suppose I was rather spoilt but also rather naïve. My father was a professor at the University of Firenze. I started seeing one of his students, a Frenchman, in secret. When I told Papa I wanted to marry Louis, he fell into a rage and wouldn't hear of it. He said Louis wasn't good enough for me. So we decided to elope." She paused and pulled at one of her earlobes. "I was very stupid, but I believed I was in love. Louis persuaded me to steal some money from Papa, saying we could pay it back later. And, of course, I was so love-struck that I did it, but once we were in France, the bastard abandoned me and ran off with the money." She sniffed. "I was desperate, so I wrote to Papa and begged him to take me back. He replied and said he no longer had a daughter. My parents told everyone I had died during a visit to a relative."

Valeria listened, open-mouthed. Parents could be so unforgiving to their children. Look at her own mother. Valeria would be much more understanding with her own child, whatever he or she did. She caressed her swelling abdomen.

"How terrible for you. How old were you?"

"Seventeen. I'm twenty-six now."

Nine years ago. "What happened after that?"

186

"There's not much more to tell. I tried to get work as a cook or a seamstress, but as the daughter of a professor, I had very few skills in that line." Her jaw tightened and she looked down. "In the end, there was nothing else I could do but sell myself. I had to work in a brothel, and those places are like Hell on Earth. It was either that or starve. Believe me, I didn't want to."

She looked up again and frowned. Valeria swallowed. So Francesca had followed that road. That was how she'd sensed Valeria wasn't one of them. Similar places existed in the Corsican ports, she was sure, but none in the villages she knew. Men in Corsica were faithful to their wives. For a moment, her stern upbringing grappled with her sympathy, but she couldn't blame Francesca.

She placed a hand over Francesca's. "I'm sorry you had to do it, but I can see you had no choice. How did you get out of… that work?"

Francesca shuddered. "It was a terrible life, terrible. The men often handled us roughly, but when my friend Nana was murdered by a drunkard with a knife, I realised I had to get out before the same happened to me, even if it meant starving. They locked us in at night, but I knotted some sheets together and climbed out of a window."

Valeria looked down. Again, she wondered what Santucci would have made of all this. He had been a good man, but she doubted if he would have had any sympathy for either of them. As for her mother and Pietro… Even Antone would have disapproved. But she admired Francesca's spirit.

"Even now, I still can't believe how lucky I was," Francesca continued. "Not only for getting away, but also for finding work. They took me on at the Savonnerie Mistral as a stamper and packer. It's hard being on my feet all day, but it's good, honest work."

"And Arlette?"

"She does the same work, but she's been there much longer. I was lucky there, too. I moved in here because she couldn't afford the rent on her own."

One thing still wasn't clear. "You're going to think I'm very stupid, but I'm afraid I don't know what soap is."

Francesca stared at her for a moment, and then tilted her chin and gave a silvery laugh. "Well, you'll soon find out. What did you use in Corsica to wash clothes?"

Valeria shrugged, and the treacherous heat rose up her cheeks. "Ashes from the fire. Doesn't everyone?"

"Maybe in the countryside, but here in the town women use soap more and more. It's made out of olive oil and other things, and it hardens and it's cut into cubes. You rub it on the wet clothes, or you can grate it and mix it with the washing water."

Valeria frowned. How could you make olive oil hard? She had so much to learn. Francesca must think they were very simple in Corsica.

"Well now," Francesca said, pushing herself up from the bed. "We have to decide what we're going to do with you."

A ripple of dread ran through Valeria. Would they turn her out into the street? It would have been kinder to have let her die in the rain.

Her panic must have shown on her face. Francesca sat down again.

"Don't worry," she said. "While we've been talking, I've thought about it, and I wonder if I have a solution. People come and go at the *savonnerie* and I might be able to persuade Madame Crespin to take on another packer. We could do with one. Her husband owns the factory, but she's in charge. She's a bit rigid and doesn't often smile, but she's fair. Stay overnight and come with us first thing tomorrow. I'll talk to her. It may not be full-time, though."

"As long as I can get some work, I don't mind, but I don't have anywhere to live." Valeria couldn't imagine earning enough to pay Madame Pons' prices, even if she wanted to go back there.

Francesca looked at her for a moment. "Listen, I'll talk it over with Arlette. It'll be a tight squeeze, but you could pay something towards the rent. I've got another idea. Can you cook?"

"Oh yes, I'm a good cook. I did it before and after I was married."

"Well, I can't cook, and Arlette can't be bothered. We live on bread and fruit, or what we buy from street-sellers. Maybe you could cook for us. It would help to pay for your keep. How does that sound?"

A few weeks ago, Valeria wouldn't even have considered working in a factory and living in a cramped space. Now, they sounded like answers to her prayers.

"What about my baby? It's due in a few months."

"You just have to work as much as you can while you can. I'm not sure what will happen when the baby is born, but we'll deal with that later. Arlette has... Well, never mind. I'll talk to her."

"What about the language?" Valeria continued. "I don't speak French, except for a few words I've picked up. Does Madame Crespin, or any of the others at the factory, speak Italian? I'm afraid they'll think I'm stupid because I don't understand."

"Stop thinking of problems. A few of the other workers speak it a little, and Madame Crespin knows a few phrases, since they sell the soap to places over the border. You'll soon learn French, you know. A lot of the words are quite similar, and I'll help you."

Valeria leant back against the pillow. She was reassured, but the prospect of meeting Madame Crespin made her stomach churn.

"It won't give Madame Crespin a good impression if I come in dirty clothes. What's happened to my dress?"

"You can't wear that; it's still hanging up to dry, and with this weather it will take some time. We dressed you in one of my chemises when you were brought in. Although you were weak, you put up quite a fight. I can't imagine who you thought we were." Francesca chuckled. She seemed to find everything amusing.

"I supposed I was back in my village, but I've left that behind."

Francesca's grin turned into a smile of sympathy. "I can lend you something." She sprang off the bed, rummaged on another couch in the corner, and thrust a dress at Valeria.

"Here. It's probably a bit big for you, but if you wear the chemise underneath it'll be better."

Valeria turned up the sleeves at the cuff. The dress was lower cut than any she had ever worn in Corsica, but this wasn't Corsica. She pulled up the chemise to hide the gap, crossed the room and wrapped her arms around Francesca. The tension of the past weeks broke. She sobbed on Francesca's shoulder, her chest heaving.

CHAPTER 23

Early the following morning, the three women walked the short distance from the tenement building to the Savonnerie Mistral. The sluicing rain had stopped the previous day, but the cobblestones were still slick with damp. A strong breeze drove ragged clouds across the sky.

"Here we are," said Francesca.

The *savonnerie* was a cavernous building set around a courtyard, reached through a high gateway. Men unloaded heavy barrels from a cart, while the horses snorted and steamed in the sunshine. A strong scent of boiling oil greeted Valeria. She swallowed. What if Madame Crespin didn't need another worker, or refused to take her on because of the baby, like everyone else?

Arlette opened a door into a smaller building set apart from the rest. Inside, a handful of women stood in front of piles of flat trays containing green cubes. The smell of oil was even stronger in there. A few of them looked up, greeted Arlette and Francesca and peered at Valeria.

An inner door opened and a short woman, almost as wide as she was tall, was framed in it for a moment. Her cloud of white hair made her look like a kindly grandmother, but her bright eyes darted everywhere and saw everything. You didn't cross this woman. Francesca ran up to her. Valeria didn't catch anything of their rapid speech, but she could tell from the way Madame Crespin looked her up and down that she wasn't yet convinced. She approached Valeria and watched her while Francesca transmitted her questions and Valeria's responses. At length, Madame raised a hand, moved closer to Valeria and stood for a moment, her sharp gaze crossing Valeria's. Valeria was carried back to the day she met Santucci for the first time, and felt like a sheep being valued. The same spark kindled, but a warning look from Francesca made her soften her expression.

Madame Crespin nodded and said something to Francesca.

"She says she's willing to take you on, even with the baby. You'll help with the stamping and packing on Mondays, Tuesdays and Fridays, and she'll see how you manage. At the slightest sign you can't keep up, you'll be out. She wants to know if that's clear."

Valeria inclined her head. "*Merci, Madame.*"

The ghost of a smile flitted across Madame Crespin's lips and she turned away to inspect one of the tables.

The air exploded from Francesca's lips. "She took some persuasion, and you have to be careful not to annoy her, but now you have a job, at least for the moment. You can work with me and I'll show you what to do."

Francesca spoke to three other women who stood around a pile of trays and stamped the green cubes. They nodded and smiled at Valeria and took furtive glances at her. The work didn't look difficult, but could she stand all day? Maybe she could sit down sometimes, but it wouldn't be good to show any sign of weakness in front of Madame, and the others might resent her if she received special treatment.

At the end of the first day, Francesca said, "Come on, I'll show you where they make the soap. Then you'll know a bit more about it."

She led Valeria across a passage between the packing building and a much larger one. They stood at the top of the steps leading down to the factory area. It was like an immense church, with a high ceiling and windows set high up in the walls. The echoing space magnified every sound. Huge open vats were ranged down the middle, and men in aprons stirred their steaming contents with long poles. The smell of boiling oil mingled with a harsher, acrid one, and the humid heat was intense. Valeria had never seen anything like this.

"What's in those cauldrons?" she asked.

"That's where they put the oil and the other soap ingredients. They have to heat it up until it's boiling and then do other things to it. When it's finished, the liquid runs off through those openings in the wall into flat trays. It hardens and has to dry out thoroughly before they cut it up into cubes."

"It's like magic. I can't see how oil can turn into a cube."

"Well, I don't understand all about it, but it takes several days to make the soap. This is the first stage."

"Isn't it dangerous with all that hot oil?"

Francesca shrugged. "Sometimes the men get splashed, but they know what they're doing."

Valeria shuddered. How terrible to stumble and fall headlong into one of those boiling vats. She turned away. Her ankles were puffed up and her armpits were clammy. The heat and odour made it worse. Thank God she didn't have to work in this part of the factory, which was more like her idea of Hell than a church.

***

From the start, Madame Crespin watched Valeria. Despite her bulk, she could appear at Valeria's shoulder without making a sound. Once or twice, Madame took the cake of soap from her and said, "No, like this." Valeria soon learned, and her work appeared to satisfy Madame. The other women got used to her. Francesca told them Valeria was a widow who had no relatives in Corsica and had to leave to find work. Whether they believed this or not, they soon accepted Valeria as one of them. With Francesca's help she started to pick up French words and phrases.

As she had expected, staying on her feet all day became harder as the baby grew. By the evening, her ankles throbbed and her back screamed. At those times, she shut her eyes and tried to recall the blue mountains of Cap Corse, the calls of the buzzards and the scent of the *machja* after rain. In spite of everything that had happened there, Corsica still held her in its grip. She wondered if Paoli was succeeding in his efforts to oust the Genoese. She had no way of finding out.

On the days she worked, she was almost too tired to prepare an evening meal, but she soon learned to make soups and stews in quantities to last several days. Even more trying were her first outings to the market to buy food. The first time, Francesca came with her early before going to the *savonnerie*. The stalls were piled high with multi-coloured produce from abroad, as well as from the countryside behind Marseille. The stallholders vied with each other to attract the customers' attention. Accustomed to the Genoese blockade, Valeria gazed at the unfamiliar fruits and vegetables.

"A fruit?" she asked Francesca, holding up a knobbly brown object encrusted with earth. She had never seen them in Corsica.

"*Une pomme de terre*," Francesca replied. "I'll show you what to do with them when we get home."

The next time, Valeria went on her own and her hands trembled when she approached the stalls, but the stallholders were used to foreigners in the city. Now she understood the value of the coinage, and Francesca had explained what the produce was worth. Still, she could only point at what she wanted, and the vendors raised fingers to show how many coins to pay.

Valeria settled into a routine as the days slid towards Christmas, and she tried not to think about what would happen when the baby came. Her ripe belly protruded by the day. Madame Crespin hadn't referred to it again, but that didn't mean she had forgotten. Valeria's thoughts were interrupted by one of the women, Eugénie, who doubled up and exhaled between gritted teeth.

"What's wrong with her?" Valeria asked Francesca.

"Eugénie has a problem every month. Her courses are very heavy, and she has terrible stomach cramps and backache. She can never seem to find a way to ease her pains."

"In Felicavo, my friend Margherita gave the woman an infusion of thyme and basil, which helped them a lot. If I'd known, I could have bought some in the market yesterday. I'll do it first thing tomorrow and bring the infusion straight in for Eugénie."

"You seem to know what to do with herbs."

"Yes, Margherita taught me, and I've found a girl in the market who sells all kinds of herbs from the hills around here. Perhaps I could make a batch of infusion and bottle it. I expect some of the other women suffer in the same way."

At the herb seller's stall the next day, she pressed her nose into the bunches of silvery and green leaves and inhaled. The scent of Corsica. A wave of longing broke over her, but she brushed it away and took the herbs home to make the infusion. In a short time Eugénie declared the pains were easing, and kissed Valeria, patting the bulge. All the women did that. Soon, Valeria was besieged by the others, who claimed a share of the potion and asked her what other remedies she had. Margherita had taught her well, and she could make cures for most minor ailments.

Valeria became a regular customer at the herb seller's stall. She was a lithe goatherd of around seventeen who came down from the hills every week, her donkey loaded with sacks of thyme, sage, sarriette, rosemary, mint and strange roots from the hillsides. Between customers, she played a pan pipe. Valeria loved to hear its strains. The girl wore a broad-brimmed hat and an old black velvet dress that was too big for her, covered by a thick woollen shawl. Inside her clogs, her feet were bare, even in the raw chill of winter.

She always greeted Valeria with a wave and a bright smile and moved around the stall like a dancer, even with clogs on. Like the women at the *savonnerie*, she patted the baby's bulge. She has very little, Valeria thought, but she's contented with her life. They communicated in signs and a few words, but that was good enough. She was a friend.

***

The baby was now so big Valeria could no longer see her feet. She had to lean backwards when she walked, and a trapped nerve gave her a constant pain in her hip. The baby turned about and butted like a goat. It became more and more difficult to stay on her feet for long, and she had to sit down to work. Sometimes, she caught Madame Crespin's eyes on her and her gut shrivelled.

"What are you going to call it, then?" Francesca asked, pointing at the bulge with a cake of soap.

Valeria hadn't given it much thought, but answered without hesitation, "Antone."

"Your brother's name?"

"Yes."

"Not after… the father?"

"No. He's lost any right to pass on his name to my baby. I don't think about him any more."

"What if it's a girl?"

"It's a boy, I feel sure."

Francesca raised her eyebrows but didn't argue. Instead, she laughed. "Well, if it is a girl, you can call her after me."

Valeria smiled. "If it's a girl, I promise I will. I'm sure it won't be, though."

As her time approached, she was more and more anxious. Margherita had explained to her all about childbirth, but she had never seen it nor helped with it. The pain, the danger of infection… Would the baby be born alive and sound? It took up her whole world now. Francesca promised to fetch a midwife at the first signs, although Valeria was doubtful about a strange woman who might not be clean.

Alone in their rooms one evening, she was seized with a furious desire to clean the floor, and with difficulty got down on her knees and started to scrub the floorboards.

"What on earth are you doing?" Francesca had just arrived home and rushed into the room and grabbed her under the armpits. "You'll harm yourself and the baby."

Valeria passed a hand over her face. "I don't know. Something made me do it. I had to scour the boards."

Francesca tutted and shook her head. "Sit down and be quiet or you'll have a stillborn baby."

Valeria obeyed, a chill rippling through her, but the baby kicked again. This one was very much alive.

When it came, it happened fast and there was no time to send for the midwife. By chance it was a Sunday, and both Francesca and Arlette were there. Waves of pain like nothing she had ever known tore Valeria apart for what

197

seemed like days, but were only hours, she learned later. She called Benedettu's name, but in anger, not in longing. He did this to her.

"I can see the baby's head," Arlette cried. She seemed to be taking charge. "Push now, push."

A final searing agony, then something gave way and slithered out of her. She heaved a huge sigh and lay back. Somewhere, far away, a slap resounded, followed by an outraged cry. A hand brushed the hair away from her brow and wiped her temples with a cool, damp cloth.

"Little Antone has excellent lungs," Francesca whispered in her ear.

A warm wave pulsed through her. "Where is he?" She raised her head. Arlette busied herself between her legs.

"We'll just clean him up a little and then you can hold him," Francesca said.

Antone was still yelling when they put him in her arms. He had a wrinkled walnut face like an old man, as if he brought with him all the knowledge and cares of the universe. Valeria traced his features and smoothed his shock of black hair with her finger.

"Hello, Antone," she whispered.

Arlette bustled about. "Now she says she has to bind your tummy," Francesca said. "You're not to go to sleep. You have to be watchful for any pains or bleeding."

A few tears gathered in Valeria's eyes at the thought of her brother.

"This isn't a time for crying. You should be happy," Francesca said.

"I am. That's why I'm crying."

At length, they laid Antone in a basket beside her bed, where she could see him, and went into the other room, but Arlette looked in on her from time to time. Valeria's body was drained of strength, but filled with peace and warmth.

The baby was asleep now, his tiny fingers curled up tight. What did life hold in store for him? They had managed to get this far, but the future remained clouded.

Even so, she sensed this baby was a survivor.

CHAPTER 24

Marseille: February 1763

After a few days, the agony of childbirth sank into her memory. Antone was long-limbed and healthy, and sought her breast, suckling well. Francesca and Arlette had to leave her alone during the day, but she didn't mind. The danger of childbed fever was past. She drifted in and out of sleep and cuddled and fed Antone. Staying in bed much longer was not possible. Francesca's attempts at cooking left much to be desired, and Valeria felt stronger and would soon be able to work again. Would the *savonnerie* want her back? What would she do with the baby? These problems troubled her for much of the day.

"How does Arlette know so much about childbirth?" she asked Francesca.

Her friend hesitated and kneaded the blanket between her fingers. Was it such a difficult question? Francesca looked away and then back at Valeria.

"She comes from a big family and helped to deliver some of her brothers and sisters." She paused. "But also... She told me not to tell anyone. I've kept my promise up till now, but you have a right to know. You're one of us. When I first came here, Arlette was pregnant. She got rid of the baby, against her will, but she couldn't see a way to keep it. At first, she found it hard to accept you, but she's got over it now. She couldn't throw you onto the streets when she nearly ended up there herself. You mustn't say I've told you."

Valeria's heart clutched. What it must have cost Arlette to lose her baby and then allow her to stay. The taste of the angel-making potion was on her tongue. She would have to make it up to Arlette somehow. But for now, another concern was more pressing.

"Do you think Madame Crespin will take me back?"

"Well, she hasn't replaced you. She knows you've had the baby, of course, but she hasn't said anything to me and I daren't ask. She can be very close when she feels like it. The best thing you can do is to go and talk to her so she'll see you're keen to work."

"What about Antone?"

"I don't know. She might let you keep him with you. Another woman did that with her baby, but he cried so much it disturbed our work and she had to put him with a wet-nurse."

Valeria gasped. "I can't do that. I wouldn't trust anyone else with him, and I'm sure it would cost too much."

Francesca nodded. "I can understand that, but your Antone is such a good little thing, maybe it will be all right." She paused. "I don't like to mention this, but, you know, some women have to give up their babies when they can't afford to keep them."

An icy wave surged through Valeria. "Give up Antone? After everything I've gone through to keep him? Never. How could you even suggest it, Francesca?"

The baby woke up and whimpered. Francesca put a hand on her arm. "I'm not suggesting it. I know how much he means to you. Let's see how things go. You mustn't upset yourself or your milk will go sour."

The baby started yelling. Francesca picked him up.

"He's a hungry one, that's for sure. You're going to grow up into a big, strong man, aren't you?"

Antone bellowed even louder and waved his fists. Francesca handed him over.

***

Valeria's pulse pounded in her temples when she approached the *savonnerie*. Antone was asleep, tucked up in his basket. As soon as she opened the door into the stamping and packing room, the women flocked around and wanted to look at the baby.

"Francesca, please tell them not to make so much noise. They'll wake him up."

At that moment, the inner door opened and Madame Crespin clapped her hands. The women scurried back to their places.

"Ah, it's you." Madame Crespin looked down at the baby and pursed her lips. A stab of alarm pierced Valeria. If Madame refused to let her have the baby with her, she would have to give up her job and throw them on an uncertain future again. She held her breath.

As before, Francesca translated.

"I expect to start work again tomorrow or even today, if you like," Valeria said. "The baby won't be any trouble. He can stay beside me in his basket and he won't interfere with my work."

Madame's piercing gaze held hers. "He'd better not. We had another one who cried all day, and if he does that, he has to go. It suits me to have you here part-time, and you

202

know the work, so I don't see why you can't keep him with you, provided he doesn't make a nuisance of himself." She looked around at the others. "Don't think the rest of you can get round me." Her gaze switched back to Valeria. "I expect you to work as hard as before. Harder, in fact, since you're not pregnant any more."

Francesca rolled her eyes behind Madame's back.

"You won't have anything to complain about, Madame."

Madame Crespin puckered her lips again and left the room. She hadn't even asked Valeria how she felt, but at least the problem of Antone was solved for the time being. Valeria swept away the thought of what would happen when he grew. In some ways, Madame Crespin reminded her of her mother, but she wasn't as hard-hearted. As the image of her mother crossed her mind, the bitterness rose. And yet, she must have had her reasons to behave as she did. Valeria had never seen it like that before, but it was still impossible to forgive her.

She took up her place by the trays and set down Antone's basket at her feet.

***

With the baby's arrival, the atmosphere in the workroom lifted. The women wanted to take turns to hold and pet him when he was awake, until Madame appeared in her soundless way and scolded them. At least she didn't make Valeria take him away.

Her days were full, too full, but it kept her from thinking about the future. To give the other two some peace, she moved her bed into the other room, even though it was poky and dark, and kept Antone as quiet as possible. In any case, the tenement building was full of children, and the nights were punctuated by wails and shrieks. The harbour area was noisy at night, too, the air rent by screams and shouting.

On the days when she didn't work, Valeria shopped and cooked and washed. She had to wash out Antone's soiled napkins at the wash-house two streets away, lugging the baby's basket and the pannier of washing there and back. She also cleaned and mended clothes for Francesca and Arlette. Working in the *savonnerie* had one advantage: she had all the soap she needed. Sometimes she collapsed into bed tired to the core at the day's end, but she worked herself hard to repay her friends. Without them, she would have no roof and no job.

On occasions, Arlette looked at her and Antone with a light in her eyes and her mouth twisted as if in pain. Arlette had seemed quieter since Antone's birth, and shook her head when asked if she wanted to hold him. Valeria worked even harder to try to make up for it.

She grew used to the other women asking for herbal remedies for this or that ailment. Things became more serious the day she came across Philomène, one of her workmates who spoke some Italian, sniffling behind the packing cases in a secluded corner of the courtyard. The front of her dress was damp.

"What's wrong?"

"I don't know what to do. I'm pregnant."

"Are you sure?"

"Of course I'm sure." Philomène raised a blotchy, red face. "I haven't had my courses for some time and I'm sick every morning. I know the signs. I can't look after a baby and I'll lose my job. Then it'll be the street for me."

Valeria had seen enough of life in Marseille to know Philomène would end up coupling in doorways with men who would refuse to pay, and beat her or even kill her. No one would bother to track down the murderer of a whore. Their lives were worth nothing.

"What about the father?" Valeria said. "Couldn't you

marry him?"

"Ha! Until I told him about the baby, I had no idea he was already married. He couldn't get away fast enough, and I haven't seen him since. I don't even know if the name he gave me was the real one." She shrugged. "No, I can't expect any help from him."

Philomène grabbed her hand. "I can't have this baby. I have to get rid of it. I've tried jumping off walls and drinking eau de vie, but it hangs on. You know all about herbs and potions. There must be something I can take to end it."

Of course Valeria knew how to end a pregnancy. If she had drunk the bitter mixture, no one would have known and she might still be in Corsica, but her son wouldn't be alive. And a foetus was a living thing. She had no right to take its life, but if she refused, Philomène might go under. Margherita had practised as a taker, as well as a giver, of life, although she didn't publicise it. She had no trouble reconciling the two.

Valeria remained silent while she grappled with her conscience. Noble ideas counted for very little against the raw reality of life in this city. Even so, would she damn her soul and Philomène's by helping her? The arguments pulled her to and fro.

She frowned. "Are you sure this is what you want? To kill your baby?"

Philomène tightened her grip. "It's not what I want to do; it's what I have to do. It's all very well for you. You've been able to keep your baby. I'm all on my own and I can't afford to. Madame won't have two in the workroom, she said so. The least you can do is to help me."

Valeria bent her head at the appeal to her conscience. She shut her eyes for a moment and made her decision.

"Very well. I'll get hold of the herbs I need, but I have to warn you: what I give you may make you very ill for a while, and it doesn't always work. Don't blame me if it doesn't. You must promise not to tell anyone."

Philomène's face altered in an instant and she kissed Valeria's hands, but Valeria couldn't share her relief. Instead, she was sinking, sliding down to a new level of shame.

Her friend in the market supplied the plants she needed. The girl hesitated a moment when Valeria asked her, and then nodded. She asked no questions. The following week, the herb was hidden in a large bunch of rosemary. Valeria made an infusion and gave the bottle to Philomène, with strict instructions to wait until the evening to take it, but for no more than a few days.

"It should have an effect within that time."

Philomène came to work as usual for several days and gave a small shake of her head in reply to Valeria's raised eyebrows. She didn't appear on the fourth day.

"Where is she? What's the matter with the girl?" Madame Crespin said.

Valeria pointed to her stomach. "She ate something bad."

"Stupid girl, always eating from street sellers. You never know what filth goes into their pies. She'd better be back tomorrow or she's out."

Valeria's heart jolted. As soon as she could get away, she snatched up Antone in his basket and hurried to the tenement building where Philomène lived. Her tiny room was not much bigger than a cupboard, and stank of vomit and diarrhoea as well as the coppery smell of blood.

Valeria rushed to the bedside. Philomène's brow was hot and clammy, and a dark, sticky mess had oozed from between her legs. Valeria mopped the girl's brow and prayed she hadn't got the dosage wrong. What if Philomène died? She would have to live with it for ever. After a couple of hours the girl's fever abated, along with the nausea. The infusion had worked, but Valeria felt no relief, only bitter guilt that she had put the girl through this ordeal and that her baby was dead.

Philomène opened her eyes. "Has it worked?" she whispered.

Valeria nodded. "Madame Crespin thinks you had a bad stomach. Drink this. It will help with the nausea. I'll bring you some broth later."

She picked up Antone's basket and went to the door on unsteady legs. She had saved Philomène, but at what cost?

***

Philomène had promised not to say anything, but another woman at the *savonnerie* confided to Valeria that six children were already enough and she was afraid of losing her job. She drank the infusion too. Having agreed to help Philomène, Valeria couldn't very well refuse. She was angry with Philomène, but maybe she hadn't let on, and the others just trusted in her knowledge of herbs. Whichever it was, Valeria's activities were criminal, and she lived in fear of Madame and the authorities finding out.

Against her will, Valeria became an occasional angel-maker. She couldn't confide in anyone, not even Francesca, and it weighed like a stone. This was the price for having a place to live and enough to eat, and for having kept her baby.

A small church stood at the edge of the marketplace. Valeria took to entering it each time she went to the market. It was shadowy and cool inside, even during the heat, with a faint musty smell. Motes of dust turned in the shafts of sunlight, which were tinted by the stained glass. The cries and bustle of the market filtered in through the heavy doors, but were remote, far away. The church was still, peaceful,

207

welcoming.

Valeria hadn't been to a church service, let alone confession, since she left Corsica, but she prayed in her way.

"Mary, Mother of God, forgive me," she murmured. "I do what I can to help these women, although I didn't want this burden. Is it so wrong? Tell me what I should do."

No one answered.

When she went out of the house, she tied Antone to her back in a sling, as Corsican women did in the fields. In the church she released him and placed him on a chair next to her, where he could kick and gurgle. With some dismay, she noticed how much he began to resemble Benedettu. Antone had the same long limbs, the same startling blue eyes, and the same thick black hair. He was a daily reminder of Benedettu. That was another price she had to pay, although a warm wave passed over her each time she looked at her baby.

Sometimes she took a different route to the market, past the *atelier* where Bérengère worked. Now she had more French words, perhaps she could talk to her and they would become friends. Much as she loved Francesca, she could be overwhelming and bossy at times, and Arlette was aloof. Bérengère had seemed calm and gentle.

Taking her courage in her hands, she rapped at the door. "Is Bérengère here?"

"No, she's gone," the supervisor said.

"Where did she go?"

The woman shrugged. "I don't know, and it's none of my business."

Valeria cast a questioning glance at the other women, but they ignored her and continued with their sewing. Her shoulders slumped. She would probably never see Bérengère again.

CHAPTER 25

Marseille: late summer 1764

Antone became a kind of mascot in the *savonnerie*. Francesca in particular spoiled him.

"Come to your *Tante* Francesca." She grabbed him, lifting him up high and making him swoop down again. "You're a big bird, an eagle."

He squealed and beat his arms, making her do it again and again.

"Don't over-excite him, Francesca," Valeria said. "I can't get him to sleep afterwards."

Even Madame seemed to soften a little towards the baby, but once he had started to crawl, Valeria could no longer bring him with her to work or take him to the market. At home, she could keep him amused with wooden spoons and rags, but at the *savonnerie* she couldn't divide her attention between the baby and the work. The problem kept her awake at night, and fatigue and anxiety lay heavy on her limbs.

Help came at last from an unexpected quarter. Valeria's

neighbour on the landing was a stout woman with a clutch of children, whose husband worked at the docks. At first, she frowned at Valeria and turned her back, no doubt judging her for not having a man.

One of her children developed a persistent cough and his rasping and whimpering carried through the wall.

"That child keeps me awake every night," Francesca said. "Antone's crying is more bearable. Don't you know some remedy for it?"

"A few of the children in our village got it, and Margherita gave them a mixture that helped. I've been thinking of offering her some, but Madame Robert doesn't seem to like me."

"Never mind. Just do it. I can't bear much more of this." Francesca put her hands over her ears.

Valeria rapped at her neighbour's door.

Madame Robert flung open the door, releasing a strong odour of garlic. She folded her arms across her full bosom. "What do you want? Come to complain I suppose."

"No, no. I want to give you this, for your little boy."

Valeria held out a jar of greenish liquid. Madame Robert eyed it and wrinkled her nose.

"What's this? It looks like poison."

"Not poison. It's coltsfoot, and it will help his cough, I promise. Please take it."

Madame Robert held the jar between her fingers as if it were a snake, and then nodded and closed the door in Valeria's face. *She might have thanked me,* Valeria thought, and heat rose up her neck.

That night, the child still coughed, but less often, and after a couple of days the rasping sounds had subsided.

"Thank God," Francesca said.

The next evening, Madame Robert was waiting for Valeria on the landing. Valeria lifted her chin, ready for a quarrel, but the woman smiled.

"I'm sorry I was a bit rude. The fact is, I was worried about my little boy. Other people in the building had already complained about the noise. He was getting worse and we can't afford the physician. But whatever was in that potion worked, and I can't thank you enough. Is there something I can do for you?"

An idea began to form. "Perhaps there is."

Madame Robert agreed to look after Antone when Valeria was at work and at the market. In return, Valeria kept an eye on the Robert brood when their mother had to go out, and supplied remedies when they needed them. The situation wasn't ideal, since the Robert children could be rowdy, but they were clean and well looked after, and it was better than losing her job. How long could this continue, though? Her son was growing up without a father, and their future was still uncertain.

***

A sultry summer followed a damp spring, and Valeria emerged with some reluctance from the cool church to do her marketing in the early morning before the heat became unbearable. While she stood at the bottom of the steps and surveyed the stalls, a man dashed past and knocked the basket from her hands.

"Oh!" she exclaimed.

He almost fell headlong when he stopped. "Please excuse me, Madame." He picked up the basket and thrust it at her. He said something in rapid speech she couldn't quite follow, but she caught the words "physician" and "urgent".

"No harm done," she said, smiling. "At first, I was afraid you wanted my money."

He looked harder at her, frowning a little, touched his hand to his hat and rushed off down one of the alleyways leading from the square. She watched him until his wiry figure disappeared around a corner and his footsteps receded. When he stared at her, her skin tingled and her pulse beat in her temple, like it had the first time she saw Benedettu at her wedding to Santucci. Why did this man frown at her? Perhaps he thought he knew her. Or maybe he noticed her accent and her imperfect French, although she had worked hard to learn it. His eyes had the intensity of Benedettu's, but they were hazel, not blue.

None of that mattered. Time was getting on, and she still had to buy food and then go home to relieve Madame Robert.

Leaving the hubbub of the market behind, she hurried along an evil-smelling narrow street, a short-cut to the house. She didn't use it as a rule, since cut-purses were said to lurk there, who would slit your throat as well as your purse if you put up a fight. Every dark doorway might conceal a thief, and her heart pounded. She quickened her pace and breathed with relief as she approached the end of the alley, when a bundle of rags launched itself at her from the shadows with a cry.

Valeria screamed and dropped the basket. Fruit and vegetables rolled away into the gutters. She panted as she fought off her attacker.

"Get off me!" she shouted and grabbed the figure by the arms, afraid it might carry a knife. It struggled for a moment and went limp. Thinking this might be a feint, Valeria held on tight, but her fingers enclosed the wrists of a child. She slackened her grip a little. No, this wasn't a child; it was a woman, tiny and shrunken, with no more strength than a new-born baby.

The woman raised her grimy face to Valeria. A black and yellow welt bloomed on her left cheek. Valeria drew in a sharp breath and released the woman's hands.

"Oh please don't turn me in. I'm sorry; I shouldn't have rushed at you, but I'm so hungry. I only wanted some money." The last words trailed off into a hacking cough and the woman doubled up.

Valeria waited while it subsided, the anger burning. "Frightening people half to death isn't the best way to get money from them. Aren't you ashamed of yourself?"

The woman looked up again, her eyes brimming. "I didn't know what else to do."

Where had Valeria seen the woman before? A sea of faces floated before her, around a table covered in fabric.

"Bérengère. You're Bérengère."

"How do you know my name?" she peered at Valeria's face. "I don't see so well these days."

"We met almost two years ago. I came to the *atelier* looking for work, but there was nothing. I was pregnant."

"You. The Corsican lady who couldn't speak French. You speak it now."

"Yes. You tried to help me and I remember it. I went back to find you, but they said you'd left."

Bérengère's face darkened. "That filthy bitch," she spat, but this brought on another spasm of coughing.

"You're not well," Valeria said.

Bérengère waved a hand and her gasping ebbed away. "It's nothing, just a cough I've had for a while."

It sounded like more than nothing. Valeria considered for a moment. She couldn't leave Bérengère, who had shown her kindness when she was in need, here in this foul street.

"You'd better come with me. Wait while I pick up these vegetables. They'll need a good wash." She picked the produce out of the gutter, wrinkling her nose at the foetid water trickling along it.

The house wasn't far from the alley, but she wondered if they would ever get there. Bérengère had to keep stopping to catch her breath. Valeria half-carried the tiny figure through the door and up the three flights of stairs.

Madame Robert knocked at the door and came into the room leading Antone by the hand. She gasped at the ragged figure on the bed and raised a hand to her mouth. Antone tottered to his mother and grasped her legs.

"Would you mind keeping him for a few minutes longer, please? He shouldn't stay in here. Go with Madame, there's a good boy." She stroked his head.

Lost for words for once, Madame Robert nodded and took the struggling Antone back to her rooms. Valeria heated a pan of water.

"Let's clean you up. I remember a pretty face underneath this."

Poor thing, Valeria thought, that bruise covers half her face. She wrung out the cloth and dabbed at it. Bérengère winced, but smiled.

"It's a long time since I had a wash," she said in a feeble voice, and fell asleep almost at once. Valeria fetched Antone and put him to bed in the other room.

"Who's she?" Francesca said, when she returned in the evening.

Valeria gave a short explanation. Francesca whistled. "She's fallen on hard times since then."

Bérengère's face was a ghostly white beneath the grime. Her eyes stared from over-large sockets. Valeria helped her to eat some broth, in which she had soaked bread. She coughed a few times, but a little colour returned to her cheeks. It reminded Valeria of the time, two years ago, when Francesca had picked her out of the gutter and brought her here.

"Now, if you want to, tell us what happened."

Bérengère struggled upright in the bed. "Monsieur Anglade owned the *atelier* and his wife was the supervisor. I

214

hated him. He'd come up behind me while I was working and put his hand on my shoulder or stroked my neck, and even touched my breasts." She shuddered and choked a little before wiping her mouth. "I tried to shake him off, but he wouldn't stop. Late one evening, he got me into a corner when everyone else had left. I struggled, but he was too strong for me. He had his hand up my skirt when his wife came in. She got rid of me on the spot." The coughing resumed.

"Pigs," she exclaimed. "I tried to find work in one of the other *ateliers*, but they put word around that I was lazy and dishonest, so no one would take me on. I couldn't pay for my room and my landlady threw me out." Her eyes flashed.

"What did you do then?"

"What could I do? All I had left to sell was myself." A hectic flush rose up her face. She took a deep breath. "Not that I earned much, and sometimes nothing at all. They don't always pay, you see. You wouldn't know anything about that."

Valeria and Francesca exchanged a glance. "We know more about it than you think."

Bérengère frowned. "What do you mean?"

Francesca explained, and Bérengère's eyes widened. She opened her mouth to speak, but Valeria raised a hand.

"No more questions for now. You need to sleep and get strong again."

In the other room, Valeria picked up Antone and bounced him on her hip.

"What's Arlette going to say when she gets back?" Francesca said.

"We'll worry about it later," Valeria replied. "I don't like her cough. What she brings up is a nasty colour, but I don't see any blood, so I don't think it's consumption. It might be serious, though. I can give her something to ease the cough,

215

but I don't know if I can cure it. She needs a physician."

"A physician? But that costs money. Where do we find one at this time in the evening?"

Valeria frowned. She had very little money left over by the time she had paid her share of the rent and the food. The rare coin or two to she had to spare was spent on things for her son.

"I want to help Bérengère. She was good to me when I first came to Marseille, and she doesn't deserve what's happened to her. I just don't know where I'll find the money."

"I'll pay," Francesca said.

"You? How?"

"I've still got some jewellery I brought with me from Italy. At least that bastard left me something. I can pawn it at Mont-de-Piété."

"You might need it one day, Francesca. I can't let you do it."

"Look, I never wear it, anyway, so it's not much good to me," Francesca replied. "Believe me, it's no loss, and you can pay me back one day."

My chances of paying it back seem slim as things stand, Valeria thought, but there was no other solution she could see. She took Francesca's hand and squeezed it.

"We need to fetch the physician. Could you go? I left Antone with Madame Robert all morning, and I can't expect her to take him now."

"Yes, but which one? I heard that old sawbones Viguié was ill himself. A lot of good his potions have done him."

"Well then, I don't know. Could you ask around in the *quartier*? There must be someone."

"I'll try, but I might be some time," Francesca replied.

An hour or so passed. Valeria looked in on Bérengère, who was in a deep sleep, curled up on her side, snoring a little. Francesca was taking a long time.

Antone was asleep in the other room, and Valeria's head was nodding when the door opening roused her. Silhouetted in the door frame were Francesca and a tall, lean figure.

"Oh," Valeria said. The man who had jostled her outside the church stepped over the threshold. He took a pace back and stared at her.

Francesca looked between the two of them. "Do you know each other?"

"We've encountered each other," he said. He smiled the first time in the market, but now his angular face was clouded and severe. His eyes swept over Valeria and her flesh tingled. She tried to ignore it and led the way to Bérengère's bed. She was sitting up, still deathly pale but with a brighter expression.

"I haven't slept so well for a long time. Who's this?" She pointed to the man.

"My name is César Puget and I'm a physician." He removed his hat and laid it on the bed. "Your friends have called me in. I'll have to examine you, so if you... ladies would leave us, I'll get on with it."

The loaded pause was not lost on Valeria. "Please call us if you need anything," she said in a chilly voice. He didn't reply.

"So where did you encounter each other?" Francesca said, elbowing her in the ribs.

Valeria rolled her eyes. "It's not what you think. This morning in the market he almost knocked me flying in his haste and picked up my basket for me. That's all."

"He's a nice-looking man, this Doctor Puget. A bit thin for my taste, but your cooking would soon fatten him up."

"Oh stop it, Francesca." Her friend's bantering made her head ache. "He's not going to be interested in me with a child in tow. I expect he thinks we're all whores. In any case, he's probably married. I've had enough of men."

A small smile played over Francesca's mouth. Valeria pressed her lips together. Women didn't tease each other like this in Corsica, where you married the man your parents chose for you; a serious matter. But she swallowed her impatience and smiled back. After all, Francesca had offered to pay, and she already owed her so much.

At length, Doctor Puget called them back and asked for a basin of water to wash his hands. He ignored the cloth Valeria offered and shook his fingers, spraying the table.

"Well?" Francesca asked without ceremony.

"She's very ill, malnourished and wasted. Her time on the streets has taken its toll. I've sounded her chest and ruled out consumption, but she's feverish and it looks like the winter fever. In her weakened state, she may not survive. The next few days will be critical, and I think it would be dangerous to move her now. If she improves, I'll get her admitted to the Hôtel-Dieu."

Valeria looked at Francesca. This would be hard on them all.

Puget turned a stony gaze on Valeria. "She told me you gave her some potion that eased her cough and helped her to sleep. It could have been very dangerous in her condition. What was it?"

The familiar embers glowed. How dare he speak to her like that? With all of Margherita's experience behind her, she knew what she was doing.

She drew herself up. "Monsieur, I know the herbs that help people with bad lungs. What I gave her was good. It was meadowsweet." She stumbled over the words. Her French always failed her when she was angry, and it had to do it now.

He gazed at her as he had in the market. "You're not French."

"No." As if it were any of his business.

"Well," he said, waving a hand, "I also know about herbs, and what you gave her can't do any harm. It may possibly do some good. Even so, you should have waited for my judgement."

What faint praise. Of course it did more than good, she knew that. She glared at him. At that moment, Antone's strident cries filled the air, and he tottered out of the other room and buried his face in Valeria's skirt.

Puget's face softened. "Who's this little fellow?"

"Antone. He's my son." She smoothed down his unruly hair.

His face clouded again. "I see. Well, he looks healthy enough. He has a good pair of lungs on him, at any rate."

At least he didn't accuse her of being a bad mother, whatever else he thought of her.

"What do we owe you, Doctor?"

"Nothing. I don't charge for the first visit. I'll need to come back, and then we'll have to see."

Valeria said nothing. She wasn't going to thank him. With a gruff farewell, he let himself out.

Valeria stretched out her arms on the table. "What a day."

"It hasn't finished yet," Francesca said.

CHAPTER 26

"This isn't a sick house," Arlette exclaimed. "We might catch something. She has to go. There isn't room, anyway." She jabbed a finger at Valeria. "Before you came, we were two and now we'd be five, counting the little one."

"She has nowhere to go, and the physician said we mustn't move her. She'll die if we do."

"We might all die if she stays. You made a big mistake bringing her here like this, Valeria."

"Doctor Puget says there's little danger of catching her illness. Do you think I'd risk my little boy's life?" Valeria paused.

"Bérengère was working the streets when Valeria found her," Francesca said. "I know what it's like. We can't put her back out there. You must see that, Arlette."

Arlette waved her arms and shouted, "Are you going to take in every stray in Marseille? You can't help them all, you know. It's cramped in here as it is." She pointed at Valeria. "It was bad enough when you brought her and her baby back, Francesca, you know that, but I've got over it now. This one can't stay."

The argument went back and forth, with Francesca breaking into impassioned Italian from time to time. At length, Arlette's shoulders slumped.

"Oh, all right. It's like arguing with a scorpion. She can stay until she's well enough to go to the Hôtel-Dieu, but don't expect me to care for her."

She swept them aside and the outer door slammed behind her.

Valeria breathed out and sat down. "That was hard work. Thank you for your help, Francesca."

"If we don't look out for each other, who else will?"

***

Bérengère lay suspended between life and death for several days. Valeria sat beside her and wiped her face with a damp cloth, changed the bed, spooned broth and infusions into her mouth and sang her Corsican lullabies in a soft voice. When Bérengère slept, Valeria tended her cooking pot and kept Antone amused so he wouldn't clamber onto the bed.

César Puget came several times and instructed Valeria in her care. She had decided to remain distant and cool with him, and never looked him in the eye. He was like a marble statue, anyway, except that he moved. Each time she dropped the coins into his hand he nodded, put his hat on and left without a word. She brushed away the sense of loss, like she did the fluttering in her stomach every time he arrived.

Once Bérengère was over the worst, Valeria allowed her to sit up in bed, and then told her she would have to move to the hospital soon. Bérengère's face lengthened.

"I know Arlette doesn't want me here. I heard you arguing with her the first night, when you thought I was unconscious. If I hadn't been so weak, I would have got up

221

and left. You've already been so good to me, and I don't want to be a nuisance to everyone. I don't know how I can repay you and Francesca, but I'm worried about what will happen once I'm well enough."

"Believe me, I wish it could be different," Valeria said. "Perhaps Madame Crespin will take you on in the *savonnerie*. Try not to worry about it now. You need to get stronger, and then we'll see." She smiled at Bérengère to cover her concern.

César Puget came for the last time. "She doesn't need my care anymore, unless she falls ill again. I'll arrange for her to be admitted to the hospital in a few days."

Something died a little in Valeria. She paid him. "Thank you, Doctor."

He opened his mouth as if to say something, but closed it again, rammed on his hat and left. Valeria stormed about and clattered the supper plates onto the table.

***

The humid, stormy summer turned into a glorious autumn, hot during the day but cooler at night, not unlike the weather when she arrived in Marseille two years before. Much to Valeria's relief, Bérengère recovered, and the nursing sisters kept her on in the kitchens at the Hôtel-Dieu. They even gave her a small room in the hospital. Valeria's breath caught at the thought of what might have happened to Bérengère if she hadn't taken the short cut that day.

In her mind's eye she often saw the seasons changing on Corsica and the shifting light on the mountains. Sometimes, during a rare free moment, she walked down to the harbour and stood with the breeze lifting her hair, looking out to sea in the direction of the island. She couldn't go back, and had no idea what was going on there. Now and then, columns of French soldiers boarded ships that set sail towards the south, but they could have been going anywhere.

Her ears strained for the sounds of Corsican speech on the quayside, but all she heard were Italian and French and plenty of other tongues she didn't understand. Once, she caught sight of Captain Alvarez, and started to walk towards him, but checked her stride. He might know what was happening in Corsica, but it was more than her pride could bear to ask him.

On a blustery early November day, the wind buffeted her from behind while she scanned the horizon, and carried snatches of conversation with it. The language was so familiar she thought nothing of it for a moment, and then she whipped round. Two men were talking on the quayside not far away, in Corsican. Her heart bounded and, without thinking, she hurried up to the men, who recoiled. Women didn't do that in Corsica.

Remembering herself in time, she said, "Excuse me, Signori, for approaching you. I left Corsica two years ago and I've had no news since."

"Who are you? What do you want?" one of them said, his face like a hatchet. "Whatever you're selling, we don't want it."

They must think I'm a whore, Valeria thought. She waved a hand. "No, no. I'm not selling anything. I only want some news of the island. Have you come from there?"

"What are you doing in Marseille? It's quite a surprise to see a Corsican woman here."

"I'm a widow and I left Corsica to live with my sister two years ago." The old half-lie dropped from her lips without even thinking about it. She almost believed it herself. Francesca wasn't the only one who could tell a convincing falsehood.

The men's features relaxed. "In that case, Signora, I can tell you times are still troubled. The General has done many great things, but he has to deal with enemies on all sides. The Genoese still hold the major ports, but are too frightened to venture into the interior, and so they've called on other allies, like the French, to help them. What's more, there are traitors within who question Paoli's authority. The bad harvests have added to the misery caused by the blockades."

Valeria went cold. The situation seemed hopeless.

"Despite all this, the General fights on, and we have our own coinage now. I believe he'll win in the end."

"Do you have news of Cap Corse? That's where I come from."

The man's face darkened. "My brother and I are from Corte ourselves, but I believe the whole of the cape rallied to the General and we were building our own fleet at Centuri. Unfortunately, the French occupied the cape this summer. We still hold Isola Rossa along the coast towards Calvi. Paoli is making it an important port."

"Have you heard anything about Felicavo, or Zaronza?"

"No, Signora. I can't tell you any more."

Valeria bowed her head a little and thanked them. She didn't ask what they were doing in Marseille, a hostile town. Very little had changed in Corsica during those two years. Maybe it had been too much to hope that an island could overthrow its masters with a small band of patriots, above all when other powerful countries had become involved. She knew nothing of how these things worked, but wondered if Paoli had an impossible task.

The sun-steeped mountains of Corsica shimmered before her eyes, and she had no idea where her steps took her until she found herself outside the church in the market square. She pulled up with a jolt. France was now an enemy of Corsica, and she lived in its midst. With dragging steps, she climbed the stairway into the church and slumped down on the first chair. All the memories of Corsica, joyful and bitter, flooded back.

A muted cough brought her back to the present. César Puget stood inside the door, his hat in his hands. Her spirit soared, but she ignored it. Whatever effect he had on her, his country was at war with hers.

"I'm sorry to disturb you, but I followed you in here because you looked unwell and I wondered if you needed help."

"I'm not ill."

He stepped closer.

"I know your name, and I knew from your speech when I first met you that you weren't French. Apart from that, I know nothing about you. Are you Italian?"

"No. Corsican."

He nodded. If only he would go away and leave her alone, but he continued to stand there.

"I've asked myself many times what a woman like you is doing in a place like that. I must admit I was surprised to see you there when I came to tend to your friend."

"You made it obvious. You can think what you like, but I'm a widow and they took me in and gave me a home and found me work at the Savonnerie Mistral. My real home is Corsica, and you French are trying to take it away from us."

"But...," he began.

Valeria stood up and swept him aside. "Excuse me. I have to go."

Without a backward glance, she stumbled down the steps of the church and flew around the market like a whirlwind.

"Look out, Madame. You nearly upset the whole stall," a ruddy-cheeked woman said, rebuilding her pyramid of tomatoes.

By the time she returned to the house, Valeria's face was on fire and her back was moist with sweat.

"What's the matter with you?" Francesca said when she returned from work.

"Nothing. I just need to be left alone." She snatched up a protesting Antone and slammed the door behind her.

CHAPTER 27

"Someone to see you," Madame Crespin said, her face etched with disapproval. "He was wandering about in the courtyard looking for you."

César Puget appeared behind Madame's shoulder and towered over her. Under other circumstances, it would have been amusing, but Valeria wasn't in the mood for laughter. The desire to be left alone wrestled with her lifting spirits. After a few hours, she had cooled down, but Francesca remained short with her. It wasn't César Puget's fault that Corsica was now fighting France as well as Genoa. Even so, she didn't want to see him. It would only complicate things.

"I'll leave you, then," Madame said, and bent forward to hiss, "I don't like men friends coming here. You'd better not take long."

Valeria frowned at her, but Madame Crespin had already turned rigid shoulders on her.

Conscious of the other women's eyes on her, above all those of Francesca, Valeria said, "Come into the courtyard."

César removed his hat and turned it around in his hands.

"I owe you an apology."

Valeria took a deep breath. "I think it's the other way around. I was upset the other day and didn't know what I was saying."

He brushed her words aside with his hand. "I shouldn't have intruded on you, but you looked pale and I was afraid you might faint. Earlier, I thought you were a... loose woman. Can you forgive me?"

Valeria nodded. "I realised that, and I admit I was offended, but it's not your fault. What else could you think, when I live where I do?"

The corners of his mouth lifted. "It does seem strange. You're so far from Corsica. Why did you leave? Of course, you needn't tell me if you don't want to."

She looked down. She wanted to unburden herself, but the whole story might be as off-putting as the idea that she was one of the workers here.

"It's a long story, so I'll be brief. Madame won't be pleased if you stay long." She took a deep breath. "I am a widow, as I said, and in Corsica I was accused of something I didn't do, so I couldn't stay there. I came to Marseille by chance and was without work and homeless. One night I collapsed in the street. Francesca – she's the one who came to find you when Bérengère was ill – brought me here. That was two years ago, and I had my son, Antone, here in Marseille. He'll be two in February."

She chewed her lip. None of this was a lie, but she hadn't told him the whole truth.

César was silent for a while. His eyes searched her face. At last he spoke. "You've been very courageous. It can't have been easy to adapt to this life. I've never been to Corsica," he continued, "but I did have the privilege of meeting Pietro Paoli and his father in Naples when I studied there. It was just before he returned to Corsica to run the

228

government. I found him a fine man, very learned for one so young, but full of fervour and patriotism for his country."

"I met him once, too," Valeria said, "when he visited my husband's village. He has given himself to Corsica, but with the French now on Genoa's side, it will be a hard struggle." She sighed.

"You mentioned something about it in the church," César said. Valeria looked up and grimaced. "Don't worry, I understand. Your patriotism does you credit. I don't follow these matters very much, but I'd like to see Corsica gain its freedom. I hear Paoli's doing great things against the odds. If courage and determination were all that were needed, Corsica would be its own master."

Madame Crespin hovered at the outer door.

"You'd better go," Valeria said. "Thank you for coming. I was glad to have the chance to apologise."

"Yes, of course. As I said, it was for me to apologise, but I would very much like to hear more about Corsica, if you can bear to talk about it."

Her heart expanded. "I'd like nothing more, but you can't come here. I go to the market every Wednesday and Saturday. Sometimes I have time to spare. If you don't find me there or in the church, I'll be down by the sea."

He grinned and put his hat on the wrong way around.

"Valeria!" Madame's sharp voice rang behind them. "Don't you have work to do?"

"Coming, Madame."

"I don't want him coming here and interrupting your work. This isn't a public place, you know. Do you understand?"

"Yes, but don't worry. He won't come back, I promise."

Madame turned away.

Her mood lighter than for some days, Valeria regained the workroom and started to stamp the soap cubes again.

Her movements grew slower and slower. Far from being a marble statue, César was a man of fine feelings, and he seemed sincere in his respect for the General. What was he doing in a down-and-out *quartier* of Marseille, when he could have been a physician to rich people in a better place? Maybe he had his secrets, too.

A cold hand touched her. She hadn't told him anything about Benedettu, so he must think Antone was her late husband's child. Could she put that right at some point? Maybe it didn't matter? She couldn't be anything to him. He only wanted to talk about Corsica. Even so, she wouldn't tell anybody about her meetings with him, not even Francesca, assuming they took place at all. A pang of unease struck her. She wasn't truthful with anyone, except herself.

***

The following Saturday, she lingered at the market stalls as long as she could. Perhaps César had gone straight to the harbour, but there was no sign of him there, either. The church bell struck eleven. She couldn't wait any longer. He never intended to come, she told herself. He was just being polite and had far more important things to do than to waste time with a worker from the *savonnerie*. What was she thinking of, anyway? In Corsica, an unmarried woman was dishonoured if she so much as spoke to a man outside the family. The images of Santucci and her mother rose up before her. They had gone to great lengths to preserve their honour. A dark cloud hung over her for the rest of the day.

When César didn't come the following Wednesday, Valeria resolved to wipe him from her thoughts and turned to go home. A shout made her look around. A tall, lanky man elbowed his way through the grumbling matrons with their baskets, who stared after him. He waved his hat.

"*Madame*! Wait!"

César halted in front of her, red-faced and breathing hard. She couldn't stop the smile spreading across her lips.

"I ran all the way, hoping to catch you. I meant to come last Saturday, but a physician's time is not his own, you know. I hope you can stay a little."

She wondered if he could hear the beat of her pulse. "I don't need to go home yet."

"Would you walk a little way with me, then? I'd like so much to hear more about Corsica. Let's go down to the harbour. Here, let me take that."

She surrendered the full basket and they strolled towards the street leading to the quayside. She was careful to keep an arm's length from him. They walked in silence for a few minutes.

"Do you come from Marseille?" Valeria asked.

"No, I'm a country boy. I come from a village near Avignon, but I wanted to work in the city, although I must admit I crave the quiet of the hills sometimes."

"What made you choose Marseille? It must be very different from where you were brought up."

"It is. I decided to come and work here when I studied in Naples. There are some similarities between the two places: they're both big ports with a varied population and plenty of newcomers all the time. They are also alike in being places of great poverty and want. When I was there, I became interested in the link between poverty and illness, in particular the spread of diseases. My theory is the better fed and housed people are, the less likely they are to succumb to illnesses. Consumption is a good example, which is far more prevalent in the poorer *quartiers* of the city than it is in the wealthier areas. Only yesterday…" he broke off. "I'm sorry, once I start on my favourite subject I'm like a runaway horse. Let's just say I felt I could do more good here than in a well-to-do suburb, although I earn much less. With only myself to keep, I have more than I need, anyway."

"I find it very interesting," Valeria said. In truth she still had difficulty following some of the words, but she picked up his last sentence well enough.

"How did you find out about the medicinal properties of herbs? I have to tell you it's forbidden to practice medicine if you haven't taken the examinations." Valeria gasped. He smiled and said, "Don't worry. I won't report you to the authorities. On the contrary, this is another aspect of medicine I find fascinating. The common cure for everything is bloodletting, and I grant you it has its uses, but I don't believe we should abandon the old remedies."

She told him about Margherita and her mixtures, and explained that some of the women at the *savonnerie* came to her when they felt unwell. The fire rose in her cheeks, although she didn't name their specific complaints. The other things she had helped with, the ones against the law, had to remain unspoken. He seemed sympathetic and understanding, but she didn't know him well enough to cross certain boundaries. So many secrets.

They had reached the quayside and looked out over the sea, where veils of rain obscured the horizon. She shivered.

"Are you cold?" The wind was biting from the north that day.

"No. I was thinking about Corsica."

"Tell me about the island."

"I only know a small part of it, where I was brought up, and where I lived with my husband and after his death."

She described the mountains, the view across the bay, the scent of the *machja*, the houses and the churches. A pang of longing struck her.

"It sounds like a Paradise on Earth," he said.

"In some ways it is. In others, it can be harsh and unforgiving."

He said nothing, but she knew his eyes were on her face. A church bell nearby rang the hour.

"I have to go," he said. "I've enjoyed our talk this morning. I hope it didn't upset you to tell me about Corsica."

She gave a small shake of her head. He handed back the basket, touched his hat and set off with his usual loping stride. The cries of seagulls and the rot of seaweed crowded in on her senses as if she had been held in a bubble that burst when he left. He didn't say anything about seeing her again.

***

The weeks went by. Valeria spent as much time outdoors as she could, beneath December's flashing blue sky and radiant sun. The mornings were chilly, and she walked to the market at a brisk pace, gathering her shawl around her. César Puget seemed to have disappeared, and she gave up hope that he would come to seek her out. No doubt he found her ignorant, and had better things to do with his time. To expect anything else was pointless, and she had too many secrets, too many things in her past. Even so, she returned from the market each time with a sense of regret. It remained, even though Antone yelled with delight and flung out his arms to be picked up.

At last, one frigid Saturday, she spied the familiar figure topped with its broad-brimmed hat at the edge of the market square. She bent over the produce and pretended not to see him. The heat rose in her neck and crept up her face.

"Ah, there you are," he said. "I hoped I'd catch you today."

She stuffed a bundle of leeks into her basket and counted out some coins for the stallholder, taking her time. He needn't know she had been waiting for him every week.

"I hope you're well." He blew on his hands. "It's turned

cold, and I'm afraid it will mean more customers for me."

She looked at him but didn't say anything.

"Speaking of which, they've been keeping me very busy of late, and I had to go to a medical colloquium in Montpellier for several days, otherwise I would have come to resume our talks. There are so many things I want to ask you." He gave a crooked grin, exposing slightly jumbled teeth.

Warmth flowed through her and she smiled back.

"I've been very busy, too, what with everything I have to do. They seem to rely on me more and more, and my little boy grows by the day. I don't often get any time to myself."

"He's a fine little fellow, robust and well made. Does he take after his father?"

Valeria swallowed. "A little."

César rubbed his hands together. "It's too cold to walk down to the harbour. If you have a moment, perhaps we should go into the church. At least we'll be out of this wind."

He took her basket, and they climbed the steps and pushed open the heavy door. The scent of incense was heavy on the air. She crossed herself with her thumb, in the Corsican way. He didn't, but made a vague nod towards the altar. They sat down on rush-seated chairs near the back. Again, she took care to keep her distance from him.

"As I said last time we met, I'm very interested in your experiences with herbs and simples. I was wondering if you could write down for me some of your receipts, in particular those to do with chest ailments."

Valeria closed her eyes. "I'm sorry. It won't be possible."

"I know you're very busy, but I don't think it would take too much of your time," he replied.

She shook her head. "It's not that. It's..." Her hands

made tight fists. This was so embarrassing. "I don't know how to write. They didn't teach women where I lived." She looked away.

"Oh. I see." Even in the gloom, the lengthening of his face was visible. This must have confirmed his view that she was ignorant and pitiful.

"I do apologise. Sometimes I get carried away, and don't think before I speak." He waved a hand. "It doesn't matter at all. You could tell me, and I could write it all down. Would you mind doing that?"

"N… no." The burning tears were in danger of falling at any moment, but she blinked them away and straightened her back.

César's features relaxed. "Excellent. Perhaps we could start next time we meet. I don't have much time today." He paused. "Before I go, I hope you won't mind my asking, when I came to the *savonnerie*, you said you were accused of something you didn't do. I don't want to pry, but I've been wondering what it was."

She stared into a deep, black well. At the bottom, the faces of her accusers and judges appeared, reflected in the water. The burden of it weighed her down, and she had never spoken of it to Francesca after the first time. Let him judge her as he would.

She sat up straight and looked him in the eyes. "I was accused of poisoning my husband."

CHAPTER 28

"What?" he exclaimed, and sat back as if winded, his mouth open.

"I thought you'd take it like that," she said. "I shouldn't have told you, but I couldn't keep it a secret any longer. I didn't do it, but I don't suppose you'll believe me. No one else did, except for my brother."

César was silent. She turned away. "Now, I expect you'll want to hand me over, so they can send me back to Corsica."

Still, he said nothing. She stood up and made as if to leave, but he put his hand out to block her way.

"Please stay. I admit this was a shock, but if you say you didn't do it, of course I believe you. It's impossible to imagine you killing anyone. I saw the way you cared for your friend when she was ill. You didn't spare yourself. And I've seen you with your little boy. No, I can't accept it. You're not a murderer." A deep furrow appeared between his eyes.

"How can you be so sure?" she said, with a bitter laugh. "I don't suppose all murderers are wicked." She thought of the children who would remain unborn because of her; only a few, thank God, but they were enough.

He looked at her for a long moment. "Do you want to tell me about it?"

"Here? Now? But your work…"

"It can wait a little longer. This is important. Tell me, please."

His knees were so close to hers that she could feel the warmth of him. She shut her eyes for a moment. The votive candles flickered before the altar, and the scent of incense filled the air. The silence of the bare church weighed on her, but comforted at the same time. This was like being in the confessional: the same sense of relief, of sharing a burden, and of hope for forgiveness, except she had done nothing to forgive during her life in Corsica. Even her time with Benedettu, foolish though it was, hadn't been such a terrible sin.

Looking at her hands in her lap, she told him everything, including her affair with Benedettu and her brother's rescue of her. César didn't flinch, except when she described the sentence for her so-called crime, and then he clasped his hands together so the knuckles blanched.

"Santucci was a good man. I didn't love him, but I was fond of him and I would never have hurt him. I tried to ease his pain. I'm not even sure now if I loved Benedettu, but we needed each other at that moment. Nothing I did was enough to deserve their punishment. There. You know everything. You, my brother Antone and Francesca are the only people who know I didn't die in Corsica."

César nodded. "From what you've said, it seems he had the wasting sickness. Your mixtures would have helped him, but not cured him." He paused. "This is all a terrible injustice. It must be put right. That woman should be made to pay for her lies and your good name cleared. As for the shepherd, I'd kill him for abandoning you if I had the chance." His voice took on a harsh, angry tone she hadn't heard before.

She put a finger to her lips. "Please. One day, I may try to do something, but it's too soon. If I went back to Corsica now, they would still believe her rather than me. They think I'm dead, so it would put my brother in danger for saving me. Anyway, things in Corsica are different from here. They also accused me of seducing a man who was beneath me, and they won't forgive that. I must wait. I haven't any choice."

He flung his arms wide. "There must be something I can do to help you. This is all so unfair."

She raised a hand. "You've done enough by listening to me. It's been like a rock pressing down on me. Maybe I was wrong to put my burden on you as well... Now you know I'm no better than the women you see on the street corners here."

"It's not for me to judge. Don't you think I've come across every possible kind of human behaviour in my work? People do what they do out of necessity. As far as I can see, you've never committed any offence, except perhaps against the morals of your country. Injustice is a far worse crime, in my opinion. I'll admit I was surprised when I first came to your house, and for a while I allowed my prejudices to sway my judgement. I also admit I was relieved when I understood you didn't do a certain type of work."

"Don't you think badly of me for having the child of a man who wasn't my husband?"

He shrugged. "You made the decision to keep him, and that was a brave one. I'm sure with your knowledge you could have ended the pregnancy if you'd wanted to."

He gave her an intense look. She swallowed. The one part of her story she hadn't revealed was how close she came to drinking the angel-making potion. No doubt he had

238

an inkling of what she did in secret to help the others. You couldn't live and work among people in this *quartier* without being aware of those things. Even so, she would never speak of it.

"My main concern," he continued, "is that your little boy is growing up without a father, and in a less than ideal setting for a child."

The indignation rose in her throat. "What choice do I have? They took me in. Without Francesca, I'd be dead now, and Antone, too. Don't you think I wish it were different? My son wants for nothing. I make sure of that."

He raised his hands in a calming gesture. "I'm not criticising you, just stating a fact. I know you do the best for your son."

The anger subsided.

"Now I must go. I'm sorry. I would have liked to stay and talk more about this, but we'll have plenty of other opportunities."

She sat up straight. "You still want to see me, even after everything I've told you?"

"Why shouldn't I? It doesn't make you a different person, and I always enjoy our talks. They take me out of myself. Until next time."

He stood up and bowed a little, and strode to the door. It creaked on its hinges, and for a moment the noises of everyday life flowed in, until it swung shut. Valeria sat for a long time, numbed, unable to think. She was like an empty pitcher, from which all the water had drained. No longer being alone was a good feeling.

***

During the following year or so, Valeria met César as often as he could get away. She was relieved that he seldom mentioned her confession in the church. He seemed to have

239

abandoned the idea of overturning the injustice. Instead, she asked him about his work and found a growing interest in it.

Antone grew fast, and she often took him with her, in case he was becoming too much for Madame Robert. He was a favourite with the stallholders, but she had to fashion a makeshift pair of reins from an old belt to stop him running off and getting lost.

At first, when César approached, Antone hid his face in the folds of Valeria's skirt and she had to coax him out, but this phase didn't last long. Soon, he pointed and shouted, "Man's coming."

"Not man; César," Valeria said.

"Sissa."

César remained Sissa. Valeria was pleased they took to each other so well. When they walked down to the harbour, César swung Antone up onto his shoulders, making him squeal with delight, and pointed out the ships and the swooping seagulls.

Sometimes, when they parted, Antone hung back and pulled at Valeria's hand.

"I want to go to Sissa's house."

"Shush. We can't go there because we don't live there. We have to go back to our house."

She dragged him after her, his heels digging into the cobblestones. In truth, she too would have liked to see where César lived. He told her he had a small set of rooms, but she had never been there. That wouldn't be right. They always met in the market, the church or the harbour.

Valeria revealed to Francesca that she sometimes saw César. A slow smile spread across her friend's face.

"I knew it. When he first came here, I suspected there might be something between you two."

The treacherous heat rose up Valeria's neck. "It's not like that. He's a friend, and we talk about his work and my herbs and remedies. Nothing else."

"Oh, really?" Francesca said and narrowed her eyes. "So it's your medical knowledge he's interested in? Hmm. I wonder if there isn't more to it than that."

"Don't be silly. He doesn't think of me like that at all. Anyway, he wouldn't want to take on another man's son. He gets on well enough with Antone, but he doesn't have to live with him."

Francesca didn't say anything, but continued to grin in her knowing way. Valeria busied herself with the pot over the fire to cover her unease. Her feelings for César went well beyond friendship, and she experienced the same swell of longing each time she saw him. It had been more intense with Benedettu, but not so deep. César had touched her soul. He didn't feel the same; it was obvious. He was wedded to his work.

She stopped stirring the stew. She was thirty: no longer young, but not old. An image of herself crossed her vision, toothless, grey-haired, bowed, and still standing at the trays of soap in the Savonnerie Mistral. What would happen to Antone? What was his future? Her everyday life was so busy she hadn't given this much thought before. Even so, she wouldn't want César to take them on out of kindness. She couldn't live with that.

***

"I've got some excellent news," César said, flushed and out of breath. "I ran all the way to tell you."

"Good morning," Valeria said, raising questioning eyebrows at him.

"I'm forgetting my manners." He swept off his hat. "It's very exciting. I've been offered a position at the Hôtel-Dieu hospital. It seems my work on the spread of maladies has come to the attention of the professor. This is in addition to

241

my work in the *quartier*, which they want me to keep on because they complement each other." The light shone from his eyes. "I'm going to be very busy."

"I'm pleased for you. You've worked hard and deserve to do well." She smiled, but she was numb inside. This was the end of their walks and conversations. He wouldn't have time for that, for her, any more. Antone would be sad, too. Sissa was his best friend.

"When do you start?" She gave the lettuces a close examination.

"In a week's time."

"Well, congratulations. Now I must go. I'm late already."

"Oh, but—"

She pushed past him and walked away fast.

"Valeria, wait." Footsteps rushed up behind. He stopped in front of her. "There's something I must talk to you about."

She turned away so he wouldn't see her expression.

"Is something the matter?"

"I've got a headache, that's all."

His brow furrowed. "I'm sorry to hear it, but I did so want to speak to you… And maybe what I have to say will make you forget it, if you have a minute or two."

She couldn't imagine what might be so urgent, but she bent down and placed the laden basket on the ground.

He took her hands in his. She started and looked around. For a man to touch a woman in public would be unthinkable in Corsica, but no one else was in the alley. She resisted the temptation to pull away.

César cleared his throat. "I've wanted to tell you this for a long time, but I realised it would be selfish of me when I could barely keep myself. Now I've been offered the position at Hôtel-Dieu, everything has changed."

She raised her eyebrows. His meaning wasn't clear.

"I'm now able to take a wife."

Her heart shrank. A vision came to her of him with a pretty, homely woman in a neat house, bouncing a baby on his knee. He was going to get married. Let him tell her, instead of prolonging this torture.

"Oh dear," he continued. "This isn't going at all as I'd planned. I'm no good at fine speeches. You must know that by now, so I'll tell you in plain words I want to marry you, Valeria. Please say you will. I can't imagine a life without you."

She held her breath. A thousand thoughts ran through her mind.

"Are you sure you want to marry me? What will people say about a physician marrying a woman who works in a *savonnerie*? A woman who already has a child, who has no money, and was convicted of a crime in Corsica?"

His hands fell to his sides. "You raise so many objections. Perhaps you don't want to marry me. Nobody need know about your past or your background," he ticked them off on his fingers. "As for Antone, you know I adore the little fellow. I'd like nothing more than to become his Papa. I don't care if you don't have any money. It's you I want to marry, not your possessions." He hesitated. "Of course, I understand if you want some time to think about it."

A warm sensation started deep inside and radiated outwards. "I don't need to think about it. What date should we plan for?"

César's lop-sided grin spread across his face. "You say yes, then?"

"Of course I say yes. I must admit, this isn't how we do things in Corsica, where the families arrange everything."

"Well, this isn't Corsica, I'm glad to say… in that respect at least… and neither of us is under our parents' thumb." He took her hands again and squeezed them. "I was so afraid you might say no, and I don't know what I'd have done then. You've made me so happy."

He gave her a peck on the cheek. She gasped and recoiled.

"I suppose that's something else you don't do in Corsica."

"Certainly not, but I might get used to it."

***

Marseille: April 1766

On a blustery April day, with billows of clouds scudding across the sky, Valeria married César in the church by the market. Behind them, Antone clapped his hands and chuckled, restrained by a beaming Francesca.

This was so different from the hot May day in Corsica more than ten years earlier. Then, she had been tense and fearful. Even today, beneath her joy, she was pricked by a twinge of regret for her brother, but she couldn't make contact with him. The old bitterness against Madame Rossi and the others still festered, and always would while the stain on her name remained. For the moment, she could do nothing about it, but one day she would have her chance.

César clasped her arm and she looked up at him and smiled. She would see that nothing ever blighted their life together.

PART 3

CHAPTER 29

Bastia, Corsica: April 1786

Valeria stood by the ship's rail, watching the press and weave of the people on deck and on the quayside below. The day was warm, but the gusty April wind made the temperature dip when the sun went in. She tightened her shawl around her shoulders. The ship's pennant bearing the colours of the Kingdom of France snapped in the breeze. Driven by the wind, the vessel had docked with some difficulty in the narrow harbour of Bastia. The air was filled with the tang of brine and rotting seaweed.

A troupe of French soldiers disembarked and marched away towards the garrison, their gleaming rifles like a moving forest. In the meantime, the ship's hands emptied baggage and packages from the hold, and rolled barrels along the quayside, accompanied by much shouting.

The other passengers, official-looking men in formal dress, straggled down the gangplank. They jostled each other and sought their luggage. A gaggle of muleteers stood by and eyed with apparent indifference the band of new arrivals. Some of the passengers approached the muleteers. Others tossed a few coins to deckhands. Valeria caught snatches of curt instructions to bring their baggage on a cart to their lodgings or to the main square.

She raised her gaze to the hazy mountains that loomed behind Bastia and stretched up Cap Corse as far as the eye could see. Further up the cape, the clouds obscured the peaks and ridges. Beneath the harbour odours was another, more elusive, scent: aromatic, vegetal. Her spine tingled. She would recognise the perfume of the Corsican *machja* anywhere.

She turned to her son, who leant forward with his elbows on the rail, his brow furrowed. Thick black hair curled around his temples. Her heart swelled with pride and affection, as it always did when she looked at him. How serious he was now. He had laughed more as a child and was never much given to crying, but he had become more solemn as he grew. She sometimes wished he were a little less so, but she smiled. He was a true Corsican.

She put a hand on his arm. "Are you ready, Antone?"

He turned to her, a faint smile on his lips. The startling blue of his eyes always took her by surprise. They never ceased to remind her of another life, another time. She took a deep breath. Had she done the right thing to come back?

"Yes, Maman. I'm sorry. I was looking at the view. You've described Corsica to me many times, but nothing can compare with seeing it for the first time. I still can't believe we're here."

"Can you smell it?" she said. "The *machja*?"

He lifted his face to the offshore breeze.

"Yes, I think so."

He bent and picked up the bag that stood at his feet. Valeria took his outstretched arm and smiled again. He was a full head or more taller than she was. They were the last passengers to descend the gangplank.

While Antone dealt with the port hands, Valeria looked around at the town, from which France governed the island. She had never been in Bastia. When she was a young woman it would have seemed like a great city to her. All she had known were the villages of her birth and her marriage. Now, after the bustle and crowds of Marseille, Bastia was like a provincial backwater. She had convinced herself she was doing the right thing, but now she had set foot on Corsican soil again, she wasn't sure. Too late now to go back to Marseille.

"When are we going to visit Corsica?" Antone had kept asking, ever since he could understand.

"When you're old enough," she'd always replied.

Her son's voice broke into her thoughts, and she shook herself out of her reverie.

"I'm sorry, Antone. What were you saying?"

"I said it's all settled, Maman. This man will bring our bags to our lodgings. They're not very far from the port, I understand. Can you walk, or should I try to find a carriage?"

She laughed. "Of course I can walk. Don't forget I was raised running up and down the hillsides. It will do us both good to get some air after that stuffy ship."

She adjusted her hat, shook out her skirts and took Antone's arm. They set off through the narrow streets of the town. The worm of doubt burrowed into her again, but she tried to ignore it. Instead, she drew her son's attention to the buildings and the people, more to distract herself than to entertain him.

Drained by the crossing and the emotions stirred up by her return to Corsica, Valeria went to bed early. She hoped the wine with dinner would send her to sleep, but it had the opposite effect, and she turned to and fro, unable to settle. With heightened senses, she was aware of everything in the town. Distant, melancholy singing rose up from somewhere near the harbour, carriage wheels grated on the streets, and the other residents of the guest house shifted and murmured. Sleep wouldn't come if she tried to force it, so she lay still and let the past wash over her.

More than twenty years earlier, she had travelled towards a future cloaked in mist. She resolved then to return to Corsica one day. In the meantime, her main concern was to live, and for the baby to survive. They had been given a chance. At first it was hard, but she and Antone had found happiness and security with César. He was now a professor at the Hôtel-Dieu, but retained his boyish humour, even though his gangly frame had filled out. To their great joy, their daughter Francesca was born a few years after their marriage, and was now a lively girl of fifteen. She resembled her godmother and namesake in many ways. Valeria smiled in the dark. Her friend had found herself a physician, a colleague of César, and had raised a noisy brood of her own.

When she looked at her daughter, Valeria often thought about her own mother and her bitter severity. How could Mother have believed she had poisoned Santucci? How could she have brought herself even to think of killing her child? Family vengeance wasn't uncommon in Corsica, but Valeria couldn't imagine any situation in which she would condemn her own children.

She rarely talked to César about the past. She assumed time would lessen the old injustices, but they weighed on her even more as she grew older. The only way to purge the

248

bitterness was to make Signora Rossi know she had lost. César was uneasy about her return to Corsica after so many years, and insisted that Antone accompany her. Valeria gave in. She could no longer deny Antone the chance to see the land of his ancestors, but was determined to deal with things in her own way.

***

The carriage made slow but steady progress up the hill and away from Bastia. The chill of the clear night was still in the air, and the dew pearled the cobwebs that festooned the *machja*. The day promised to be hot, and the sun rising over the bay was already dispelling the threads of mist drifting just above the ground.

Valeria watched the scenery go by, her chin in her hand. The other passenger, a well-dressed man with a prosperous paunch and outsize buckles on his shoes, had handed her into the carriage.

"Are you travelling far, Madame?" he said in French.

"To Zaronza."

"Ah. In that case, we shall accompany each other as far as Casabianca, where I believe you must change."

"Yes, I know."

Was he going to keep this up all the way? She needed to think, and could do without the distraction.

"I'm continuing to Saint-Florent, where I have business. This is my first visit to Corsica. I like it well enough, and Bastia seems a pleasant town, but I must admit it's a little modest compared with France. I imagine a lady of your obvious refinement must feel the same, Madame."

"No, I'm Corsican."

The man's already ruddy face darkened further. He opened his hands.

"Ah. I had assumed… Your French is…" He stuttered to

a halt.

Valeria gave him a pale smile to stem further conversation and turned her attention to the open window, which let in a fresh breeze with the scent of the *machja*. She avoided looking in his direction, but could see him dart an occasional glance at her. His assumption that a lady of refinement couldn't be Corsican was infuriating. After so many years living with the French, she should be used to their assumed superiority, but it still rankled.

Her thoughts turned to what she planned to do. Antone had wanted to come with her to Zaronza, but she insisted that she had to settle old scores on her own. His presence would make things more difficult. With reluctance, he had stayed behind in Bastia.

She shivered.

"Are you cold, Madame? Would you like me to close the window for you?"

"No. I'm glad of the fresh air."

Valeria turned her attention again to the view. She had never travelled this way before, despite living on the other side of the cape for half her life. A country girl could have no business in Bastia. Corsica had exchanged one master for another, and her life had taken turns she could never have imagined during her simple existence in Felicavo. Underneath it all, though, Corsica was still the same. The French had conquered the land, but they would never douse the Corsican spirit.

At points on the road, a vista opened up. The backbone of Cap Corse rolled away to the north, the mountain tops obscured in places by grey plumes of clouds. This was her country. Felicavo couldn't be far away, and a jumble of childhood memories invaded her.

She tried to focus on the task ahead, but the memories crowded in: the track from Felicavo down to the coast and

250

along to Zaronza, the sparkling May morning, so similar to this one, the hazy marriage ceremony, the first glimpse of Benedetto's startling blue eyes, Santucci's illness, and the events afterwards. The gloomy tribunal room swam before her, the men's faces lit from below by the lamp, Signore Rossi's red neck while he gave his false evidence, and the monotonous voice pronouncing the sentence. Valeria set her jaw and clenched her fists. The thought of the unjust accusation dispelled any doubts.

The carriage jolted over the rough road and slowed on the final ascent to the Col de Teghime. The driver stopped the stagecoach at the top to give the horses time to recover before the descent. He suggested Valeria and her fellow passenger should stretch their legs for a few minutes. She was happy to leave the confined space with its hard-sprung seats and odour of musty leather. The sun was warm on her face, but a cool westerly breeze swept the exposed col and stung her eyes. In the distance, a silvery sea lapped the mountains that reared up behind, and she could make out the contours of a far-off town fringing a bay.

The man appeared at Valeria's elbow. "I believe that's my destination, Saint-Florent."

"I expect so. I have never been there." She turned and got back into the carriage.

They set off downhill around a series of steep bends. Valeria was tempted to laugh again when the Frenchman turned pale beneath his ruddy complexion and clung onto the seat. It wouldn't do him much good if the carriage did tumble over the edge and down the mountainside. If he planned further visits to Corsica, he would have to get used to the roads.

Several hours after leaving Bastia, they arrived in Casabianca. The French passenger handed Valeria down.

"Don't you have a box, Madame?"

"No. I return to Bastia tomorrow." She raised the small bag she carried.

"Well, bonne route." He bowed.

Thank goodness they were parting company. At least he hadn't imposed himself on her once he knew she wasn't French.

The only way to get to Zaronza from Casabianca was by donkey cart. Valeria had to wait until the carter had finished his errands. She sat in the shade of a plane tree in a small square dominated by the church. Doubts about what she was planning beset her again, but she quelled them. She had come too far now to turn back.

At last the carter and his donkey clattered into the dusty square. The heat of the day was waning, but the mid-afternoon sun was still strong. The journey to Zaronza took another two hours along the twisting coastal path. It was so narrow in places that Valeria could see straight down to the shore below. They rounded a hill, and the village came in sight, perched on its rocky pinnacle. Paoli's Tower raised its jagged grey-green fist to the sky. The place looked the same as it had all those years ago. Valeria drew in a deep breath.

CHAPTER 30

The cart rolled into the village and stopped near the church. Valeria handed the man a few coins and turned to look around. No one was about in the late afternoon heat, and she crossed the square towards the alley where she had once lived, gazing about her. She avoided looking at the house of her imprisonment and intended execution, but the gooseflesh stood up along her arms. The lane was silent, all the houses shuttered. At the end stood Santucci's house, which she had never thought of as her own: square, unadorned, severe – just as she remembered it.

The house appeared empty, abandoned. The shutters were closed, and weeds and fig saplings sprouted from the base of the walls. As the sun dipped towards the horizon, it exposed small holes pocking the stonework and the shutters. Bullet holes? What else could they have been? Something had happened there, but it must have taken place a long time ago. Whoever owned the place now didn't care very much about it. The house was unkempt and desolate. She supposed she had been dispossessed after her fictional execution, and the injustice of it rose like bile in her mouth.

"How could they?" She beat her fist against her thigh.

Her gaze switched to the house opposite, where Signora Rossi and her family had lived. Her enemy, whose prying eyes belied her honeyed words and false shows of concern. Who had sent her husband to lie for her at the trial, shifting from foot to foot and twisting his hands. What a sham that so-called tribunal had been. Anyone with half an eye could have seen Rossi wasn't telling the truth, but they preferred to believe him. They had already branded her a criminal. The verdict, and the sentence, had been decided long before the hearing.

The force of the pent-up bitterness struck Valeria like a physical blow. Her legs almost gave way, and she struggled to control her breathing. Steadying herself against the wall, she took several deep breaths and composed her face. If she was to confront her enemy, she must be cool and unemotional. The house, like Santucci's, looked closed and unoccupied. Perhaps they had gone away. So many things had changed in her absence.

A man Valeria didn't recognise walked past and gave her a curious look. As ever, a stranger attracted attention.

"Are you looking for someone?" he asked, his gaze travelling up and down her clothes.

"I've come to visit Signora Rossi. Does she still live here? The house seems unoccupied, although I haven't knocked yet."

"You'll just about have come in time," the man replied. "She's ailing, got the wasting sickness, they say. I haven't seen her in months; she hasn't left the house in that time. Relative, are you?"

Valeria looked the man in the eye and nodded. "In a way, but I haven't seen her for many years."

"You'll find her a bit changed." He nodded, and moved off to climb up the hill opposite her former house to the tower. She watched him for a moment and then turned to Signora Rossi's door. She wasn't too late. On reflection, she could perhaps use this illness to her advantage.

She gave a couple of light taps on the door and waited. Footsteps approached the door, which opened a crack. A young woman's face peered out, frowning a little.

"Yes? Who is it?"

"Good evening, Signora. I hope I'm not disturbing you. I've come to visit Signora Rossi."

"This isn't a good time. She's been ill, and," she lowered her voice to a whisper, "she isn't expected to last very much longer."

"I see." Valeria took a deep breath. "I had heard about her illness and wanted to visit her. It's a long time since I last saw her – before her marriage, in fact. I'm sorry, I should explain. I am a cousin on her mother's side."

"Mm." The woman hesitated. She looked in her mid-twenties, so Valeria had no fear of being recognised. In any case, she herself had changed. Catching sight of herself in the mirror that morning, little was left of the bony young woman she had once been. Now, she looked like a prosperous French matron, fuller in the face and figure. Her nose and chin were less prominent as a result. Only her large, dark eyes might give her away.

"I've come all the way from Bastia. I was so hoping to see her."

"In that case, you'd better come in. I can't see it will do any harm, and maybe it will cheer her up to see an old relative. You can leave your bag here by the door if you like."

"Are you from the village?" Valeria asked in a casual tone.

"Oh no, I'm from Casabianca, but my husband Giovanni has lived here all his life. I've been here for three years,

255

since we married. The village women take it in turns to look after Signora Rossi. It seems to be my turn more often than the others."

Her face darkened. So, Valeria thought, she'd found out what it was like to be an outsider in Zaronza.

"What about her family? Can't they help?"

The woman lowered her voice. "There's no one left. Signore Rossi died of a stroke last year. Struck down he was, while he worked in his field. I don't know about her sons. I heard two of them were killed in some battle, and the other one left to go to France and nobody knows where he is."

"Ah," Valeria said. "Well, we haven't kept in touch, so I knew nothing about this. It's only by chance I heard of her illness." She pressed her lips together. It would be better not to say too much.

She felt a fleeting sympathy for Signora Rossi, dying alone without her sons around her. At least she, Valeria, had her Antone. Losing not one son but two must be unbearable. Signora Rossi's third son was all but lost to her. Valeria's resolve almost wavered, but the surge of bitterness washed over her again when she remembered this woman was her enemy, and had sent her on purpose to a fate she didn't deserve.

"May I see her now?"

"Yes, I'll go and find out if she's awake." The young woman disappeared into another room and returned a few moments later.

"You can go in. She doesn't seem to remember any relatives in Bastia, but you know, with this illness..." She tapped her forehead with a finger.

Valeria entered the room and the woman closed the door behind her. The light through the tiny window was fading, and the room was dim, save for a candle by the bedside which shed a yellowish glow onto the pallid and shrunken face beside it. Valeria crossed to the bed and stood over it, looking down at the woman she hadn't seen for so long. Madonna, the years hadn't been kind to her. Her plump cheeks had withered, and the hands grasping the blanket to her were like hooks.

"Who is it? I can't see you in this light." The quavering voice was a frail old woman's, but Signora Rossi was only ten years or so older than she was.

"Don't you know me?" Valeria asked, settling herself in a chair next to the bed so the candlelight shone on her face.

Signora Rossi raised her head a little to peer at her, and then shrank back on the pillow, her eyes widening.

"No. It can't be. You're not her. She's dead. They killed her years ago with the poison." She raised her shaking, mottled hands to her mouth.

Valeria nodded. "Yes, that's right. They killed me with the poison. They shouldn't have done, because I wasn't guilty, was I? You know that better than anyone, don't you?"

"No. It's not true. I saw her give her husband the poison. She made him ill and he died. She was carrying on with her shepherd and she wanted the husband out of the way. That's what we told them. You can't be her. She's dead." She paused. "Unless…"

Signora Rossi's face grew even whiter, like a laundered chemise. Her eyes stood out of her ravaged face. She opened her mouth but a strangled whimper emerged. Valeria spoke again, her voice steady.

"Yes, unless…You did something very wrong all those years ago, and you've already been punished. God took your sons and your husband. But it wasn't enough, and you'll suffer if you die without making the truth known. I've been sent to tell you that you have one last chance before God."

"I didn't… My husband, he gave evidence against her."

"Yes, but you sent him to do your dirty work for you, and he always did what you told him. Now he's dead, but you were the guilty one."

Her face now hot with anger, Valeria stood up and bent low, close to Signora Rossi's face, and hissed. "You sent an innocent woman to her death. Don't you have any shame? Haven't you felt any remorse all these years?"

The woman shrank further into the pillow. Her lips trembled and she swallowed, but still the fire kindled in her eyes.

Signora Rossi waved a limp hand. "Santucci should have married me, all those years ago when his first wife died. My father even talked to him about it, but he wasn't having any of it. It was all, 'Oh, my poor wife, I must remain faithful to her memory. I can't even think of marrying again.' My father was offended, and I was shamed in front of the village. More than that, I was wounded. I wanted him. He should have been mine. A few years later he went and married her."

She almost spat out the last few words and then subsided into a coughing fit. Valeria waited while Signora Rossi gasped and wheezed until it was over.

"He married her," she resumed. "When he should have married me. I had to marry Rossi and endure him and bear his sons. I should have borne Santucci's children, but I had to live here, right near him, knowing that."

She paused, and a stray tear meandered over her cheek, unchecked. Again, Valeria felt sorry for her, but dismissed the feeling. The woman still didn't seem to feel any regret for her actions. Whatever the outcome, Valeria had to get her to admit it.

"If I was poisoning my husband and you knew about it, why didn't you stop me while there was still time?"

"Of course I know she didn't poison him, and the business with the shepherd didn't start till after Santucci died. But he would have deserved it after he rejected me. It was so unfair, she got everything, inherited everything, and it should have been mine. I had to punish her."

Valeria's chest tightened. So much bitterness and hatred, nurtured and fed like a Christmas Eve bonfire all those years, never dying out.

"Why did you wait so long after Santucci's death to denounce me?"

"I had to have proof of her liaison with the shepherd. It gave her a motive for doing away with her husband, otherwise they might never have believed us about the poisoning. I got my proof the day she fell over in the square and showed us all what she'd been getting up to. She'd been clever enough hiding it up till then. Even I hadn't noticed, and I'd been looking for ways to catch her out."

Valeria nodded and drew herself up to her full height. She looked down on the frail woman in the bed.

"Very well. You're on the verge of death, and yet you don't show any sign of repentance for murdering me. I told you, I've been sent to tell you that if you don't atone now, you'll suffer once you're dead. Do you realise what that means?" She paused. "You will be damned for eternity."

Signora Rossi's pallor increased, and she inhaled sharply. She made the sign of the cross with her thumb, and covered her eyes with her palms.

"God help me, I know what I did was wrong, but I loved him so much. I couldn't bear her having him and then everything of his once he was dead. I'm sure she didn't love him. I hate her still, but I can't go to Hell for her." She looked up at Valeria. "Tell me what I need to do."

"First, you must confess to the priest – confess everything. You must then send for the notaire and explain it

259

all to him. He'll write it down and you will sign it in the presence of a witness. Instruct him to give your confession to the authorities so they pardon me publicly. Do this now, today, or it may be too late. Remember what I said."

Signora Rossi's eyes took on a glazed look, as if she was already staring into the flames of Hell. She nodded.

"Now I must go, and you won't see me again."

Valeria closed the door behind her, trembling so much that the latch rattled. The young woman, who was stirring something over the fire, stood up and wiped her hands on her apron.

"Did she recognise you?"

With a supreme effort, Valeria brought her attention back to the room.

"I don't think so, but she talked about something she did in her life that was very wrong. I didn't understand, but she muttered about calling the priest and the notaire. She was quite insistent. If I were you, I would do as she asks. I don't think she has much longer, and she seems to want to get this matter off her conscience."

"I'll go in and check on her and after that I'll call the priest. The nearest notaire is in Casabianca. All this had to happen while I was watching her, but we have to respect dying people's wishes, don't we?"

"Of course. It's only right."

Nobody had respected Valeria's wishes when she was condemned; no final confession or last rites for her. The fire burned again, but she smiled at the woman.

"Now I must go. Thank you for letting me see her."

The young woman nodded. Valeria picked up her bag and opened the front door. She paused on the threshold and looked back. The woman had already disappeared into Signora Rossi's room, from which a soft murmuring emerged.

Out in the alley, Valeria leant against the house wall for a moment, closed her eyes and breathed out. It almost seemed she had been holding her breath while she was with Signora Rossi. She looked around. Zaronza seemed emptier than it had when she lived there. No doubt the convent just outside the village would offer her a bed for the night.

Before going there she turned towards Santucci's house, but it was too much to bear to look around even the outside. Instead, she took the steep path up to the ruined castle and the tower. The sun was dipping in a blaze of crimson and ochre over the hills across the bay. The walls of the tower reflected back the heat of the day, and Valeria sank onto a flat stone overlooking the sea. The place was deserted.

Many years had passed since she had last sat there, but the view was the same, changing with the light. Her body sagged with relief that the confrontation was over, and she massaged her aching temples. Had she overdone it with Signora Rossi, pretending to be her own spirit? Was it wicked to torment a dying woman? Would she be punished for it in turn? These nagging questions kept rising to the surface. She was not a cruel woman, but the things other people did had hardened her. The rational side of her brain kept turning over these thoughts, but she could feel no pity for Signora Rossi, who had felt none for her and still didn't. Valeria had no doubt her repentance was skin-deep; her one concern was to save her own soul. With luck, she would be scared enough to carry out Valeria's instructions.

She sighed and took a last look at the view, which she would never see again. Fatigue settled on her limbs. She was empty, drained of emotion. It was time to go to the convent and ask for food and a bed. Dusk was falling when Valeria picked up her bag and went downhill, stumbling once or twice on the loose stones scattered over the rough path. At the bottom, she paused and ran her eyes over the façade of

Santucci's house. She would never come back. Too many things had happened here. Still, she could not tear herself away.

While she stood there, the door of Signora Rossi's house opened and a priest emerged, followed by the young woman. Valeria shrank back into the shadows.

"She has made a full confession," the priest said to the young woman, "but it's not time for her to go yet. I think she'll linger a few days. She insisted the notaire should come. Don't worry, I'll see to it. I'll send a message this evening and ask him to come tomorrow, as soon as he can."

The woman muttered something inaudible. The priest nodded, raised his hand in a blessing and strode away across the square to the church, his soutane billowing behind him. The church door closed, and Valeria came out from her hiding place. A wave of relief washed over her, and the exhaustion lifted from her limbs. So, Signora Rossi was scared enough to comply. Valeria wondered if she had said anything to the priest about the ghost, but doubted it.

Her mood lighter than for many years, she turned her steps towards the convent. She would sleep well that night, but one more thing remained to do before she returned to Bastia the next day.

CHAPTER 31

The next morning dawned grey and misty. Valeria knew the sun would burn off the cloud cover within a short time to reveal a vivid blue sky. Getting out of the narrow bed in the guest quarters, she dressed, refreshed in both body and mind.

The nuns had given her a bed and a simple but satisfying meal. Valeria repeated her story about being a visiting relative of Signora Rossi.

"We don't get many visitors here these days," said the guest sister. "I'm sorry about that. I like to have news of the outside world. Zaronza suffered during the war with the Genoese and then the French, and both sides considered Cap Corse an important prize to fight for."

"What happened here?" Valeria asked. "When I visited Signora Rossi, I couldn't help noticing damage to the stonework of... the house opposite." She almost said, "Santucci's house," but bit her tongue in time. Being a stranger, she wouldn't have known him.

"Ah, yes. Well, all that happened back in '63 – or was it '64? I don't quite recall. At any rate, it was when Saint-

Florent was besieged and a troupe of French soldiers came up here because they wanted to take the tower, which commands the strait. The General had it built a few years earlier as a watchtower, you see."

Valeria nodded. Of course, she remembered Paoli's visit and the building of the solid turret not long afterwards.

"It was terrible. They bombarded the village from the sea. Mother made us all go down to the cellar. We huddled down there on our knees praying amid the cannon-fire and gunshots. Some of the villagers joined us. We found out what had happened afterwards. The General's garrison in the tower ran away, all except their captain. Although he was wounded, he devised a way of firing several muskets at once, and the French believed our soldiers were still in there. When he finally came out, the French were astonished. Instead of taking him prisoner, they escorted him back to the General."

"What a story," Valeria said. No wonder the place seemed more derelict now. Santucci's house, beneath the tower, took the brunt of the bullets.

"Yes, indeed. That will go down in history as one of Zaronza's finest days."

Valeria smiled. She thought nuns were not supposed to concern themselves with politics, but there was no doubt about this one's allegiance: "Our soldiers... the General". She was a Paolist to the bone. Santucci would have approved. Valeria could almost imagine her taking up arms herself, a strapping woman with a spirit that glowed in her eyes.

Valeria hesitated, but her curiosity got the better of her. "Who owns the house at the end of the alley off the square, opposite Signora Rossi's? It doesn't look lived-in."

"Oh, it's been empty for years, since before I took my vows. I'm not sure who owns it now, but I heard it once

264

belonged to a wealthy man who died and his widow lived there for a while. There's some story about her being executed for poisoning him." She shrugged. "I don't know more than that. May God rest both their souls." She crossed herself.

Valeria fought to stop the flush rising in her neck and face and to blurt out the true story, but the nun was clearing away the breakfast plate and cup and didn't look at her. Valeria said nothing. If the plan had worked, everyone would know the truth within a short time.

"I expect if anyone was interested in buying it, they could. It's a pity to see the place empty."

The bitterness welled up again. The house should have been hers, even though her life there had been threaded through with sorrow. Now, it would be very complicated to remedy. As far as the authorities in Corsica were concerned, she was dead, and it would be hard, if not impossible, to unravel the fabric of a pretence that had lasted half a lifetime. But at least it looked as if the stain on her name would now be wiped away.

"Well, I mustn't keep you from your work any longer. I have to be away myself."

"Going back to Bastia, are you?"

"Yes."

"A lot of Frenchies there now, I hear. I don't know if that's better or worse than the Genoese. I suppose time will tell. At least out here they don't bother us too much."

The nun escorted Valeria to the convent's outer gate. A man riding past on a horse called, "Good morning, Sister. Good morning, Signora."

The nun raised a hand in response and Valeria nodded to him.

"Who was he?" she asked, when he had continued on his dusty way.

"Oh, he's the notaire from Casabianca. I understand your relative, Signora Rossi, has called for him, no doubt to settle her affairs before she dies, poor soul." The nun touched the crucifix around her neck.

News travelled fast in Zaronza, as it always had. Valeria hid a secret smile of satisfaction. She thanked the nun for her kindness, and walked back along the sandy track. As she expected, the sun broke through the clouds and the day promised to be hot again. Already, the cicadas were trilling in the bushes by the road, and fell silent when she passed. The unmistakable scent of the *machja* accompanied her into the village, where she had hired the carter for a further journey.

***

They took in reverse the stony track she had descended on her wedding day, more than thirty years before. Little had changed along the way, except for the occasional crumbling house, no doubt a casualty of the French war. The cart rounded a corner and the *campanile* of Felicavo came into view, towering over the terraced village. The alleys were empty and most of the shutters closed. Here and there, a curl of smoke rose. A dog lying in the road raised its head and gave a half-hearted bark.

Valeria asked the carter to set her down at the edge of the village.

"Should I wait for you?"

"No. I'll make my own way on from here."

The cart trundled away along the track leading to Casabianca. Valeria stood for a moment and looked up at the jumbled houses. Here, she had learned to keep secrets and to suppress her inner self. Moments of joy had punctuated her life in Felicavo, too.

Picking up the bag, she took the path behind her old

266

house by the cork oaks, now neglected and ragged. The trees screened her while she looked down at the house.

Why had she come? All her family, except for Antone, believed she was dead. She couldn't turn up after all this time, but maybe she'd catch a glimpse of her brother, and it would have to be enough. She couldn't return without giving herself that chance.

A sudden movement made her shrink back behind a tree. A man came around the side of the house, walking with a stick and carrying a basin. He tossed the contents onto a heap where a few chickens chuckled and scratched. His beard was grizzled, but his height and broad shoulders gave him away.

"Antone," she whispered. He looked up and she stepped out from behind the tree and rushed down the bank. She stopped in front of him and flung her arms around him. For a moment he stood rigid, then dropped the basin and the cane and clasped her so hard she thought her bones would break.

"Valeria! What in God's name are you doing here? I didn't even know if you were still alive, it's been so long."

The tears coursed unchecked down her cheeks. "My little brother. It's so good to see you. I can't believe it."

She looked around her and whispered, "Where's everyone else? Mother, Pietro? They mustn't see me. I'm supposed to be dead."

Antone shook his head. "It's only me here now. You'd better come in. We can't stand out here like this."

The house was dusty and smelt of damp. Objects littered the floor.

"If I'd known you were coming, I'd have tidied up a bit." He grimaced, sweeping clothes off a cane-seated chair. "Here, sit down. I've only some bread and goat's cheese to offer you."

"Later. We have a lot to say to each other first."

"You start," he said.

Valeria described everything that had happened to her since they said goodbye in Isola Rossa. The sun's rays lengthened as the day drew on.

"I'm sorry I couldn't do more for you at the time," Antone said. His mouth turned downwards. "It must have been very hard at the start."

"Yes, but you gave me a chance, and in the end it worked out well. I miss Corsica, though. And you."

His face brightened when she told him about young Antone and about her daughter, Francesca.

"So I was an uncle to them and didn't know it. I wish I could meet them."

"Maybe one day you can. Now, it's your turn to tell me everything. What happened to the others? And I see you walk with a stick."

Antone's eyes left her face and looked through the window. He rubbed his lame left leg.

"Where shall I begin? We had such high hopes of the General, and things seemed to go our way for a while. We even took back the isle of Capraia from the Genoese. But what could we ever do, a small island on its own? Behind our backs, Genoa sold us to the French." He spat on the floor. "Even against them, we had some success, and they were routed at Borgo. It didn't last. They just sent more troops and they crushed us at Ponte Novo."

"I know," Valeria said. "When César told me, it was like a knife in my back."

"Pietro died there. He fought like a lion. We all did, but we were outnumbered. Imagine the Hell the priest used to threaten us with. Well, it was ten times worse. Smoke everywhere, cannon fire, men shouting and crying out. And the blood..."

Valeria put a hand to her mouth.

"A musket ball hit my leg." Antone winced and rubbed his thigh again. "I collapsed, and someone else fell on top of me. That's how I was saved. After the battle, my friends dragged me away and they bound up the wound as best they could. For a while, I expected to die, but I didn't. It's left me with this souvenir, which aches when the wind blows from the north."

Valeria closed her eyes at the thought of Antone's pain. And Pietro was family, after all, even if she had never felt close to him.

"Paoli managed to flee," Antone continued. "I heard he left the island, and went first to Italy and somewhere else after that. After Ponte Novo, the spirit went out of us, although some fighting still went on in places. Paoli was a great man, but he couldn't lead us in battle. Now we're no better off than we were under Genoa." He looked down at his hands.

"And Mother?"

"She's dead, too, although not that long ago. Quillina took Pietro's children and went back to her own village, so I was left to look after Mother. She never got over the dishonour she said you'd brought on the family, and stayed in the house all the time, avoiding the neighbours. When Pietro was killed, she started to lose her mind, although it brought us closer in some strange way."

An image of Mother, straight-backed, rigid, stern, dressed in invariable black, crossed her mind. She had always behaved as if Valeria were a burden, and rarely had a soft word for her, even as a small child.

"In her last days, she rambled a lot, and kept speaking to someone called Gian'paolo, over and over again. She said several times he should have married her and not the other one, since she was the one having the baby, so she had to marry Francescu. That was Father's name, wasn't it? None of it made much sense to me, though. In one of her lucid moments I asked her who Gian'paolo was, but she said, 'Nobody,' and wouldn't tell me anything else. I never found out."

Valeria kept very still while the meaning of Antone's words seeped into her mind. She was the first-born. Did Mother take out on her all the sour resentment of this Gian'paolo? Had she lived a lie all those years? So all Mother's talk about family honour and correct behaviour was a sham. For a moment she felt nothing, before the anger boiled like an unwatched pan, and then subsided again. A picture came to her of her mother, young, pregnant and unable to tell anyone, taking the only solution, like a drowning soul clutching at a spar of timber. At least Mother had found a way out, unlike Delfina... and unlike her. Such bitterness; such regret. Still, she could never forgive her mother for the way she had treated her, and would always bear the scar. She rubbed her forehead.

"What do you think that was all about?" Antone said.

"I have no idea." She wouldn't share her suspicions with him. That's all they were, in any case. "My husband tells me old people often ramble towards the end. Their brains are confused and what they say is nonsense. Anyway, she's gone, so now we'll never know."

"There's one more person we haven't talked about yet," she continued. "My son's father." She couldn't bring herself to say his name.

Antone's face darkened. "After what happened to you, I could have killed him. I don't know if he ever found out about your so-called death. I suppose he must have done, although I doubt if he wanted to show his face around Zaronza after that. I never went after him. What was the point? Even if he had known you were still alive, you were

270

far away and not likely to come back. I hope he felt the weight of guilt on his shoulders. He deserved to."

"Don't you have any news of him?"

Her brother frowned. Valeria held up a hand.

"Don't worry. I don't feel anything for him now. I've been married for twenty years, and César and I have a good life together. What Benedettu and I had was a sort of madness. I was overcome with loneliness, and I admit it was a mistake. But I do have my son to show for it, and I'll never regret him."

"I'm sorry, there's nothing I can tell you. I've never heard any more of Colonna since you left Corsica."

Valeria looked down. Against her will, the tears stung her eyes. She wondered if Benedettu was still alive, and, if so, where he was. At one time, she had hated him for abandoning her, and could still taste the bitterness of it, but the years had eased the pain and she now had another life. He wasn't a bad man, just proud, like all Corsicans.

"When my son grew up I told him the full story. Before that, he believed I left Corsica because of a family dispute and his father was dead. César and I discussed for a long time whether I should tell Antone everything, and we decided in the end it was fair that he should know who his father was. Was it wrong of us to keep it from him up till then?"

Her brother shrugged. "How can I tell? Given everything that happened, perhaps you did the right thing. I don't know."

"We wanted to protect Antone, so he could grow up without any shame hanging over him. César has always been like a father to him. They're very close. When Antone found out, he was very angry at first – not so much with me, but with his real father and with the Rossis and the tribunal. He was all for storming over to Corsica to clear my name and put things right. César and I persuaded him that things are rather more complicated. At length, he came to see it that way, too."

"Don't you want to clear your name?"

"I've wanted nothing more for years, but it should happen soon."

"What have you done, Valeria?"

"You don't need to know. Leave it for a few days, and then visit the notaire in Casabianca. He will have some news for you. Whatever happens, everyone in Corsica who knew me thinks I died that day in Zaronza, except for you, of course. Undoing it all would take a great deal of time and effort."

"Why?" Antone said, his voice rising. "If things happen as you say, why shouldn't people know you didn't die in Zaronza?"

"Too much time has passed, and I'm tired. Now I have another life, a different name, and it would be hard to prove I was Valeria Santucci. Don't press me. Believe me, it's easier this way. I can't live in Corsica again, and my life is elsewhere. Promise me you'll keep this between us."

Antone was silent for a long time. He looked up at her. "It means I've lost you again."

"I wish you could come to visit us in Marseille, but I suppose it's too far."

He gave a short laugh. "I wouldn't come, anyway. It's bad enough being owned by the French. I don't have to go to their damned country as well. I can't think why you're so taken with the place."

"I told you. My life is there now. Maybe I could bring César and the children to Bastia. He's always wanted to see Corsica. You could go that far, couldn't you?"

"I'll think about it. I don't leave the village much anymore."

"There's one more thing you can do. Once my name is cleared, as I'm sure it will be, there's still the house in Zaronza. After Santucci died it was mine. As far as the authorities know, you are my closest living relative. I want you to recover the house for the family. Maybe there's some way it could become Antone's one day. It's no good to me – I'll never go there again."

Antone frowned, and then shrugged. "I can't get over all this. Of course, I'll do it, but there are Pietro's children who would have the right to inherit from me."

Valeria fixed her gaze on a spot on the wall. He was right, but maybe there were ways around it.

"Well, let's deal with that when we get there. It's a long way in the future, anyway, but it would mean a lot to me just to know that it had come back into the family. I haven't thought about Quillina in a long time. How many children did she and Pietro have?"

"After Isolda, Pietro had two sons. He named the first after himself and the second Francescu after Father. I see them from time to time. I'm glad to see young Pietro isn't turning out to be like his father. He must be about the same age as your son."

"Young Pietro is a few months older than my Antone, I think, but I didn't know about Francescu. What about you? You've obviously never married."

"There was someone." He waved a vague hand. "But after all the business with you in Zaronza, her parents wouldn't let her marry me. She married someone else."

Valeria's hands flew to her mouth. "Oh, I'm so sorry. Your life's been ruined, and it's all my fault. I don't know what to say."

He leant forward. "It's not as bad as all that. I don't think I was made for marriage, anyway, so I expect I had a lucky escape. I'm quite content here, you know. I have my

273

vegetable garden, my olive trees and my hunting. They're all I need. If the stain's removed from our name, so much the better. Mind you, not many people are left here to remember it."

The conversation petered out and they sat in silence for a while, memories of their childhood succeeding each other in Valeria's mind's eye. She got up and prepared the simple meal of bread and cheese, and asked about the village.

"Now, I must go," she said, once they had finished. "I have to get the carriage back to Bastia from Casabianca, and I'll need to walk there from here."

"I'll come with you."

"No. I'll have to walk fast, and I'm afraid it will be too much for your leg. Let me just remember you sitting here in this house. When I get back to Marseille, I'll talk to César about visiting Corsica one day, and I'll send you word when we do."

They embraced again. It seemed to be the pattern of her life to leave her brother behind, but at least he was alive and said he was satisfied with his life, although it was plain that he was short of money. She rummaged in her bag and brought out a purse full of coins, which she left on the table.

"What's this?" Antone said. "I can't take money from you."

She touched his arm. "It's the least I can do. Please take it. Don't forget, you gave me your savings when I left Corsica. I didn't have anything else. I'd be dead but for you, and so would my son."

He gave a nod and they parted. When she reached the track to Casabianca she turned and waved. He raised a hand in reply.

CHAPTER 32

Valeria went back to Bastia and re-joined Antone. He said he had spent the time walking around the town and up into the hills, and was full of questions about what she had done in her absence.

"I've taken steps to clear my name. It might take a while for it to be official, but at least I've done what I came for."

"But how…?" Antone began.

Valeria held up a hand.

"Later. For the moment, it's enough that I've done it." When they were back in Marseille she might tell him more about her visit to Antone, but she would not mention that she had asked her brother to reclaim the house in Zaronza. Too much uncertainty surrounded that.

Antone looked at her for a moment and then gave a brief nod.

"I'm rather taken with Bastia, Maman. It's nothing like Marseille, of course, but I like the atmosphere here. The scenery is every bit as beautiful as you said. I made some enquiries while you were away, and they have a good hospital. I wondered if I could come back when my medical training is finished and work there for a while. Since I speak both Corsican and French, I might be useful to them. That is, of course, if you and Sissa agree," he added.

Valeria didn't know what to think. Antone was an adult. She couldn't keep him away from Corsica if he wanted to return, but for the moment she was too weary to consider it.

"Let's talk to Sissa when we get back to Marseille."

They stayed another day in Bastia and strolled along the alleys near the cathedral of Sainte-Marie, talking of Antone's future career. The same melancholy singing as before arose from a nearby house. Ancestral voices mingled in a rising chant that pierced Valeria's soul. A pang of longing for Corsica struck her. While she and Antone stood listening, a man came out in haste from a tavern and almost collided with them.

"Excuse me," he said in Corsican, touching his rough woollen hat, and then his mouth fell open. He gaped at Antone, who stared back. His gaze switched to Valeria and he pressed a hand against his chest.

"Madonna," he breathed. "But…" He pointed at Valeria and struggled for breath, his lips blue.

Her heart pounded. The hair and beard were threaded with grey, and he was thin and stooped, but she would know those eyes anywhere. The same eyes as Antone's.

They stood for what seemed like an eternity, while the man fought for breath. Frowning, Antone looked from one to the other.

"Benedettu?"

He nodded, closed his eyes and then reopened them. "Valeria. I thought you were dead. This is a shock. I don't understand." He pointed to Antone. "And this…"

"Is your son, whom you abandoned." The resentment welled up.

Benedettu put his face in his hands and shook his head.

"But you died. In Zaronza. They told me you were dead."

"As you can see, I didn't."

"You're my father?" Antone broke in, the frown deepening.

The two men were almost mirror images of each other, except that one was much older.

"You went off and left my mother alone." Antone raised his voice and passers-by looked at them.

Benedettu's eyes flared with the old pride. "You're quick to judge, but you know nothing, boy."

Antone opened his mouth, but Valeria put a hand on his arm.

"We can't stand in the street like this." She looked around. The cathedral was close by. They wouldn't be disturbed in there.

Once they were inside, Benedettu sank with difficulty on to a chair and removed his hat. Antone continued to stare at him. No one spoke for a while.

Valeria breathed out. "You left me and went off to the militia. I couldn't bring myself to get rid of our baby, but you didn't know about that. I thought you didn't care."

He gazed at her for a long moment. "I did care, but I didn't know what to do. You infuriated me when you said I'd taken advantage of you. And then I was called up. I wanted to punish you, but I admit I was wrong and I let my pride rule me. I couldn't stop thinking about you while I was away, so later I decided to come back for you. But I was too late. One of the other shepherds told me you'd been tried and were dead. I still don't understand how you escaped." He shook his head. "I can't believe it's you in front of me and not a ghost. What are you doing here, anyway?"

She looked into Benedettu's eyes, still a startling blue.

"I'm real enough. My brother helped me, and I got away to Marseille, where I've lived ever since. In Corsica, only he

277

and you know that I'm still alive, but I've taken steps to clear my name." The anger swelled. "You must have known that I didn't poison Santucci, and yet you obviously did nothing to prove my innocence."

He looked up and his eyes flashed. "What could I have done, a poor shepherd, against a sentence like that? Who would have taken my word? Instead, they might have hanged me as your accomplice. In any case, you were dead, or so I believed, and I was eaten up with sorrow and guilt. I couldn't bear to be with people, so I went up into the mountains and lived alone there. I have done ever since. I've never been anywhere near Zaronza again."

Antone's mouth was tight with anger. "If it hadn't been for you, my mother would have been able to stay in Corsica."

"If it hadn't been for me, you wouldn't be here now," Benedettu shot back.

Antone reddened and looked down.

"I'm sorry," Benedettu said after a moment. "You're my son. We mustn't quarrel. I've gone all these years without knowing you were alive, and now it's almost too late."

The resentment started to drain away from Valeria. Life had been as harsh to Benedettu as it had to her. He hadn't abandoned her in the end. He had come back for her. The bitterness of the years shrank and disappeared like the snows on the mountains in the spring. They had both been proud, and each of them paid a price for their love: he in the coin of solitude, she in exile. Things turned out better for her in the end.

She frowned when his words sank in. "What do you mean, it's almost too late?"

"My life's taken its toll. I have a weak heart, and I know I don't have much longer to live."

A pang of sorrow pierced her. She put her hand over his.

"But you could see a physician, be treated," Antone said. "I'm studying to be one myself, like my father... I mean, my stepfather." A tide of red crept up his cheeks again.

Benedettu's eyes crinkled. "I'm pleased to hear you've done well, boy. What's your name?"

"Antone."

"My brother's name," Valeria explained. "I felt very bitter against you for a while, when things were so hard for me in Marseille. Of course, I had no idea that you had come back for me."

"I can't blame you for thinking that. As for a physician, there's no point. I've lived most of my life up on the mountain. I'd rather die there than in some bed in a backstreet or in a hospital surrounded by other ailing people." He shuddered.

Valeria swallowed. It was useless to insist. Benedettu had made up his mind.

Benedettu looked at Antone. "You mentioned a stepfather." He switched his gaze to Valeria. "Does that mean you married again?"

She nodded. "He's a doctor. We've been married twenty years, and I have a daughter as well. We have a good life together."

"I'm glad. You deserve it after everything that happened. If only I'd known you were still alive." He shook his head. "My life has been spent up on the mountain with the flocks. I didn't even consider marrying, not after I'd lost you."

Valeria's heart turned over as she took in the implications. What a lonely life Benedettu had led compared with her.

"What are you doing in Bastia?"

"I still have a few sheep, and I come down for the market sometimes. It gives me an excuse for the other things I do." He gave Antone a guarded look.

279

"You can speak in front of Antone."

"When Paoli was driven out back in '69, some of us didn't give up hope. He's living in exile now, in England, but he still has a lot of support here. No one takes much notice of an ageing shepherd, so I can come and go as I please and make myself useful by reporting back what's going on. Like I did when Santucci was alive. I may not live to see it, but things won't stay the same for ever."

Valeria gave a small smile, and her eyes held Benedettu's. Even after so many years in France, she had never stopped being Corsican.

The bell chimed. Her stomach shrank. Just when they had found each other and had so much to say.

"We can't stay much longer. We must take the boat back to Marseille this evening."

Benedettu nodded. "It's been a shock seeing you like this, but it will cheer my last days knowing that you didn't die in Zaronza. And I'm proud to know I have a son who's making something of himself." He looked at Valeria. "I wonder what would have happened to us if I'd come back in time."

Valeria wondered too. Would they have had a chance, or would the inevitable exile from Corsica have driven a wedge between them? Hard as it had been at the time, they were never meant to be together. She shook her head and blinked to dispel the veil of tears.

"I don't know, but we can't live in the past. That would be too painful. Antone and I must go." She took Benedettu's hand and squeezed it.

His eyes shone. He turned to Antone and gripped his hand. "My son. Make your mother proud of you."

Without a backward glance, he walked to the church door, which clanged shut behind him. Valeria and Antone stood and looked at each other for a moment, and then she folded him in her arms. He shook a little. She released him and dabbed at her eyes.

"It's time to go home," she said.

***

When the ship weighed anchor, Valeria thought she spied a tall, dark-haired figure on the quayside, but her eyesight was no longer sharp. She looked again and he had gone.

The vessel sailed along the eastern coast of Cap Corse, rounded the cape and steered away from the island. Valeria stood in the stern, Antone beside her, watching the peaks recede into the haze. The scent of the *machja* grew fainter. A wave of relief, tinged with sadness, flowed over her. She had done what she came for. More than that, the chance meeting with Benedettu had washed away the rancour of years, but he belonged to her other life, the one she had left behind. The price of escaping a terrible fate like Delfina's, and the destiny of the bone, was exile from Corsica and a life of secrets. Not even César knew about the angel-making. That would rest between her and the women she had helped; one secret she would never tell.

"I suppose I might not see my father again," Antone said and sighed. "I would have liked to get to know him, but Sissa has always been my father really, hasn't he?"

Valeria smiled at him, but was too full to speak. Taking his arm, she looked back towards Corsica. The first time, she had been forced to leave. This time it was her choice, but the island would dwell within her wherever she went, and Benedettu was locked in the deepest recesses of her soul. That would have to be enough.

The End

281

Ocelot Press

Thank you for reading this Ocelot Press book. If you enjoyed it, we'd greatly appreciate it if you could take a moment to write a short review on the website where you bought the book, and/or on Goodreads, or recommend it to a friend. Sharing your thoughts helps other readers to choose good books and authors to keep writing.

You might like to try books by other Ocelot Press authors. We cover a range of genres, with a focus on historical fiction (including historical mystery and paranormal), romance and fantasy. To find out more, please don't hesitate to connect with us on:

Email: ocelotpress@gmail.com
Twitter: @OcelotPress
Facebook: https://www.facebook.com/OcelotPress

Author's note

Like my first novel, *The House at Zaronza*, *The Corsican Widow* is loosely based on a true story.

Corsica has always been a land apart. The island was invaded and conquered but never quite vanquished by successive occupiers. Today Corsica is part of France, but was owned by the city state of Genoa until 1768, when it sold the island to France behind the Corsicans' backs. The people have retained their distinctive cultural and social traditions, even if modern values and French administrative structures have overlaid them.

In the mid to late 18th century, when The Corsican Widow is set, Corsica was still a Genoese possession, but was riven by uprisings and vendettas that amounted to mini civil wars. For much of the century, the Corsican people had tried various forms of government designed to win independence and drive out their Genoese masters. They even backed an eccentric German adventurer, Theodor von Neuhof, who styled himself King of Corsica. He was unable to live up to his extravagant promises, and lasted a few months before his subjects turned against him and he fled from the island.

A far more serious statesman was Pasquale Paoli, an intellectual who was invited to head the Corsican republic from 1755 and drew up its constitution, an early experiment in democracy. This short-lived venture ended at the battle of Ponte-Novo in 1769, when the French routed the Corsican forces. Paoli was ahead of his time in many ways, and made great efforts to get his people to abandon some of their more bloodthirsty practices. He legislated against vendetta, and even sentenced one of his own kinsmen to execution for breaking that law. Even so, it took more than a 15-year republic to stamp out the customs and rituals of centuries. Those traditions concerning family honour and the place of women were the hardest to change.

In her book about female criminality in 18th-century Corsica, Marie-Josée Cesarini-Dasso explains how Corsican women were expected to lead blameless lives and to be above any suspicion of immoral conduct. Those who committed "crimes" of morality were harshly judged. Acting against parental and family authority and Corsican tradition could incur severe penalties. Marrying a man outside the same social class or milieu was a dishonour, and punishable on occasions by death. A family might kill a daughter who erred and fell pregnant if she would not divulge the name of her lover. If she did, the lover became the object of the family's wrath. The alternative was to submit to execution by the authorities as the "just" punishment for their crime. To us today in Western society this seems inconceivable, although we still hear of such "honour killings" in other cultures. To 18th-century Corsicans this was the logical consequence of tainting the family reputation, and they accepted it as the way things were.

I came across a few lines from the Abbé de Germanes' chronicle, *Histoire de la Corse et de ses Révolutions*, quoted by Marie-Josée Cesarini-Dasso. The translation is mine:

A young widow, who was rich and beautiful, suffered from her solitude. She employed a shepherd, who brought her the products from the flock. During one of these visits, he had the audacity to seduce her. The widow submitted and became pregnant. A local tribunal was convened and decided that, since she could not marry the shepherd without dishonouring herself, she must die. Condemned to drink poison, she requested a delay of three days to prepare herself, during which her mother and brothers did not leave her side. On the morning of the third day, she drank with Socratic bravery the poison prepared by her mother and fell dead an hour later.

What a stark destiny. This fragment intrigued me, and I have used it as the foundation for The Corsican Widow. To make it more plausible to a modern audience, I have modified some aspects of the account and added further accusations to those of the original story.

I have been unable to find further details of this episode, which is now lost in the mists of time. Shocking as the treatment of the real-life widow was, it is unlikely to have been an isolated incident. Even so, women in Corsica were not the downtrodden victims you might expect them to be. They were often heroic, fearless and independent-minded, and I have tried to recreate these qualities in the character of Valeria.

Corsican people have always held strong beliefs in magic and the supernatural. Some references in the novel may need explanation:

The Evil Eye, known as *mal d'ochju* in Corsican, is a malevolent force that is held responsible for various illnesses, especially in children, but also in adults. The Eye constantly looks for ways to enter a person and wreak harm.

Signadore are female soothsayers and healers, who practice a precise and curious ritual to exorcise the Evil Eye (described in the scene when Santucci is on his sick-bed). They can only transmit their knowledge orally to another woman on Christmas Eve while the church bell rings.

Mazzeri (*mazzere* in the feminine plural), or dream-hunters, can be male or female. They roam at night, armed with a heavy staff known as a *mazza*. Curiously, they are

285

often seen asleep in bed at the same time. During their nocturnal wanderings they kill an animal, and in its face they see that of a person known to them, who will invariably die within a short time. They may be shunned by their neighbours, but live alongside them.

This is a work of fiction. I have checked the historical facts, but I have had to make educated guesses at times and I will be happy to correct any errors, all of which are mine, at the earliest opportunity.

Select bibliography

As with all historical fiction, the challenge has been to put myself in my characters' shoes and to try to understand their preoccupations and the background against which they lived their lives. For readers who might be interested, here is a list of sources, in French and English, which I have consulted and found useful. It includes other novels offering a flavour of life in Corsica in the past.

D'Angelis, Gaston, Don Giorgi and Georges Grelou, *Guide de la Corse Mystérieuse* (Editions Tchou, 1995).

Arrighi, Jean-Marie and Olivier Jehasse, *Histoire des Corses et de la Corse* (Tempus Perrin, 2013).

Arrighi, Paul, *La Vie Quotidienne en Corse au XVIIIe Siècle* (Hachette, 1970).

Balzac, Honoré de, *La Vendetta* (Librio, 1999, first published 1832).

Black, C.B., *Itinerary through Corsica by its Rail, Carriage & Forest Roads* (A & C Black, 1888).

Boswell, James, *An Account of Corsica, The Journal of a Tour to that Island, and Memoirs of Pascal Paoli*, (Dilly, 1768).

Castellani, Laetizia, 'Maison et Habitat dans la Balagne Rurale Littorale du Début du xviiie à la Fin du xixe Siècle', *Histoire & Sociétés Rurales* 2010/2 (Vol. 34), pp. 79-108.

Carrington, Dorothy, *Granite Island: A Portrait of Corsica* (Penguin, 2008 edition).

Carrington, Dorothy, *The Dream Hunters of Corsica* (Phoenix, 2000 edition).

Carrington, Dorothy, 'The Corsican Constitution of

Pasquale Paoli (1755-1769)' *The English Historical Review* Vol. 88, No. 348 (Jul., 1973), pp. 481-503.

Cesarini-Dasso, Marie-Josée, *L'Univers Criminel Féminin en Corse à la Fin du XVIIIe Siècle* (Les Éditions Albiana, 1996).

Dumas, Alexandre, *Les Frères Corses* (Société Belge de Librairie, 1844).

Flaubert, Gustave, *La Corse par les Champs et par les Grèves* (first published 1840).

Gherardi, Eugène F.-X., *Précis d'Histoire de l'Éducation en Corse* (CNDP-CRDP de Corse, 2011).

Gregorovius, Ferdinand, trans. A. Muir, *Wanderings in Corsica: Its History and Its Heroes*, 2 vols (English edition 2008), first published in 1852.

Mercurey, François-Noël, *Le Pastoralisme en Méditerrannée. Un Exemple: Le Pastoralisme Corse* (2013).

Mérimée, Prosper, *Colomba* (first published 1841).

Mérimeé, Prosper, *Matteo Falcone* (Flammarion, 2000; first published 1829).

Seton Merriman, Henry, *The Isle of Unrest* (first published 1900).

Multedo, Rocco, *Le Folklore Magique de la Corse* (Nice, Belisane, 1982).

Wernick, Robert, 'Corsica - Isle of Beauty, Isle of Bandits', *Smithsonian Magazine* (2002).

Wilson, Stephen, 'Infanticide, Child Abandonment and Female Honour in Nineteenth-Century Corsica', *Comparative Studies in Society and History* 30(4), (October 1988), pp. 762-83.

www.corsicatheque.com—website containing articles on Corsican history and culture.

The author

Vanessa Couchman lives in Southwest France and is fascinated by French and Corsican history and culture, which provide inspiration for her writing. Her first novel *The House at Zaronza* was based on an intriguing true story she stumbled upon when on holiday in the Cap Corse region of Corsica. She also writes short stories.

Vanessa has a degree in history from Oxford University and works as a freelance writer. She is a member of the Society of Authors, the Historical Novel Society, ex-pat writing community Writers Abroad and the Parisot Writing Group in Southwest France. She was a founder of the Parisot Literary Festival in 2013, now a well-established landmark in the literary calendar.

You can connect with Vanessa on:

Her website: http://vanessacouchmanwriter.com
Facebook: www.facebook.com/vanessacouchman.author
Twitter: @Vanessainfrance
Sign up for Vanessa's newsletter: read exclusive content and find out about new releases and special offers. http://eepurl.com/comA9v.

Also by Vanessa Couchman

"Vanessa Couchman has a huge potential talent and will be an author to watch." - *Discovering Diamonds*

"Emotionally powerful...Vanessa Couchman writes with intelligence and skill." - *Historical Novels Review*

"Beautifully written, evocative of this small island. A lovely book." - *Tripfiction*

"...hooked me right to the end... I would highly recommend this book." - *BookMuse*

Set in early 20th-century Corsica and on the Western Front during World War I, *The House at Zaronza* is loosely inspired by a true tale. Maria Orsini is the daughter of a bourgeois family in a Corsican village. A new schoolmaster comes to the village and they carry on a secret romance, but Maria's family has other ideas for her future. She becomes a volunteer nurse during World War I and the novel follows her fortunes through the war and beyond.

The House at Zaronza was a close runner-up in the Flash 500 Novel Opening Competition in 2013 and is available in paperback and e-book editions from Amazon.

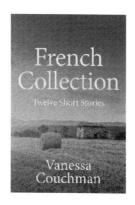

"Thoroughly enjoyable snippets of life in France." *The French Village Diaries*

"The characters are so well-drawn that the reader comes to know and care about them in a matter of a few short pages." *BookMuse*

A collection of short stories inspired by France's fascinating history and vivid landscapes. Available in paperback and e-book editions from all branches of Amazon. http://mybook.to/FrenchCollection.

52484600R00168

Made in the USA
Middletown, DE
10 July 2019